From his earliest years, Bill Corfield wanted to be an airline pilot and a writer. He was a licensed pilot and part-time newspaper reporter when he was in high school, and has continued those careers ever since. Corfield has over twenty titles of fiction, history and biographies to his credit and created hundreds of speeches for politicians and businessmen. He lives in London, Canada.

THE PILGRIM FILE

Ben and Danielle Courier could not resist the sad-eyed pleadings of the widow even though it disrupted their pilgrimage to France with Canadian veterans to celebrate the twenty-fifth anniversary of Victory in Europe. The only clue to the November 1943 disappearance of bomber navigator Joe Pilgrim was in a military cemetery record that eventually led them to an empty grave on a hillside in a remote valley — and one of the strangest shrines in the religious turmoil of wartime France . . .

BILL CORFIELD

◆

THE
PILGRIM FILE

Complete and Unabridged

ULVERSCROFT
Leicester

First published in Great Britain in 2007 by
Robert Hale Limited
London

First Large Print Edition
published 2009
by arrangement with
Robert Hale Limited
London

British Library CIP Data

Corfield, William E. (William Elwyn), 1920 –
The Pilgrim file.
1. World War, 1939 – 1945- -Missing in action- -France- -
Fiction. 2. World War, 1939 – 1945- -Veterans- -Great
Britain- -Fiction. 3. Canadians- -France- -Fiction.
4. Large type books.
I. Title
813.6–dc22

ISBN 978–1–84782–931–3

Published by
F. A. Thorpe (Publishing)
Anstey, Leicestershire

Set by Words & Graphics Ltd.
Anstey, Leicestershire
Printed and bound in Great Britain by
T. J. International Ltd., Padstow, Cornwall

This book is printed on acid-free paper

PART ONE

1

The letter arrived as I was starting my breakfast.

Danny heard the box's lid slam as she poured my coffee at the kitchen counter. She shook her head and frowned. 'He'll never learn, that postman!' Getting tired of chasing after my newspapers, or rescuing soggy masses from the doorstep, I built a sturdy box at the front door large enough to handle both our papers — one French for me and one English for Danielle. The delivery boys now co-operated, after generous tipping. The postman found it easier than the slot in the door, and seemed to enjoy slamming the lid as a signal he'd arrived. 'I'll get it,' she offered, as she put down my mug and pushed the sugar closer.

She tightened her housecoat belt and disappeared down the hall, her figure something I had always admired. Sister LaFlamme had been the most beautiful vision in the world to my war-weary eyes as she nursed me on the hospital ship coming back to Canada. After three years behind German wire, I guess any friendly female would have looked good. However, her calm efficiency and quiet patience stuck with me after I left veterans' hospital in Montreal and I kept in touch with her. Now, twenty-four years on and two sons later, she was still the smooth, trim manager of our home. She returned, reading from a large envelope:

'Corporal and Mrs Benoit Courier. From Veterans Affairs Canada. Probably want to increase your pension.'

'More likely another questionnaires for me to prove my back pains are from German rifle butts and not reckless living.' I used my table knife to slip the flap and drag out the package of papers. A government letter was on the top.

'Well, well, well, Danny, listen to this. Dear Corporal Courier. Congratulations on having been chosen to represent your Regiment, Fusiliers Mont-Royal, as part of the overseas delegation which will travel to Normandy, France to mark the 25th anniversary of Victory in Europe. You and your Caregiver, Danielle Courier, will travel to Ottawa to join the delegation on Sunday, 3 May, 1970, for departure by Department of National Defence aircraft the next day. Return to Canada is scheduled for Wednesday, 13 May.'

I sat back, stared at the rest of the details, and then put the message on the table. 'I guess it's for real,' I puzzled. 'It's signed by a fellow named James Lynn, Conducting Officer, and on official paper, but I wonder how they got my name? And who did the choosing? And who decided you were my caregiver?' Danielle didn't respond but went on silently getting her cereal. I finished my eggs and bacon and sat back with an air of indifference. 'Anyway, I'm not interested, so Mr James Lynn can choose somebody else to go in my place.'

Danielle ignored me while she slowly ate and studied in silence, a silence that grew longer and longer. Finally she said softly, 'Maybe you should read these documents and give the opportunity a little more thought.'

'I don't need to give it any more thought. I don't want to go back and remember those horrible years. I've tried to forget them for twenty-five years.' I could sense that she was disappointed by my reaction.

'OK Ben, I understand, but let me explain. The local legion branch recommended that the President, Dr Gil Vanderberg, go on this pilgrimage because he was a medical officer in the Air Force and they seldom get much recognition. He can't go, so he suggested that I go in his place, because nurses also don't get much recognition. Then he asked me if my husband was a veteran, since you aren't a member of the legion. When I told him your war record, he said perhaps it would be less embarrassing for you if you were the official veteran and I was the Caregiver.' She reached across the table and picked up the envelope. 'You will notice that it's addressed to Corporal and Mrs Courier.' She gave me a soft little challenge with her eyes over her coffee mug. 'I suppose I could feel hurt that Veterans Affairs Canada didn't address it to Corporal and Lieutenant Nursing Sister Courier.' This time her look was mischievous. 'Or perhaps Lieutenant Nursing Sister and Corporal Courier. But then, I've been proud to be your caregiver for a quarter of a century so I really don't mind how it's addressed. But I do mind how you reacted without even reading the material. I know you feel that war prisoners are the forgotten veterans, and maybe you're right, so maybe this will help to make amends.'

I got up to gather my dishes and carry them to the sink, and then stood staring out the window. Although a March rain had washed away most of the winter's snow, patches remained under the trees and amongst the bushes. I could see ice cakes floating down the Richelieu River and the flags on the Saint Johns Yacht Club were whipping in a strong westerly. This was not a new discussion, my bitterness about the war. We'd been over it several times in the past when somebody wanted me to join the legion or parade to the cenotaph or decorate the war graves. I did my tour. Three bloody years behind wire, months in shackles, beatings that almost broke my back, lousy food, cruel treatment, no promotion, no medals, no nothing, just a few bucks a month to keep us quiet, while these guys go parading around as if they won the war and making out that the guys who bought it were the lucky ones. 'We will remember them. They will not grow old.' What nonsense! They're dead, blasted to bits, drowned in the oceans, shot out of the sky, gone forever. I felt myself getting worked up, so turned and smiled at my wonderful wife who was always the calming influence in my life.

'Well, Danny, if you know how I feel, then there's really not much sense in hashing it all over again.' I retrieved my mug, poured more coffee, and sat. 'Honestly, I don't want to go back, to remember all those guys who died screaming on the beach at Dieppe. What sort of a person enjoys that?'

Her lips were a thin red line as she pushed back her hair. It had been a lustrous shining black in 1945, which was an attractive contrast to the white clinical coats, but now it was a lustrous grey, which I found just as appealing. Her voice, however, retained the firmness of a medical order. 'You might put aside your prejudices for a little while and learn more about the invitation, before you decide. The letter says: 'there are important requirements which you must meet before your departure and we request that you deal with them without delay'. Perhaps you won't qualify, then you won't have to make a decision.'

I knew she didn't want to hurt me. That wasn't her nature, but she did have the knack of going right to the nub of any discussion. Maybe I wasn't a real veteran. Maybe I wouldn't qualify. I reached for the documents. 'Where does it give the requirements?' I scanned rapidly and a paragraph stopped me. 'Listen to this: 'thirteen young Canadians, who will be representing the youth of Canada, will be an integral part of the delegation. One has been selected from each province and territory. They will learn about your great accomplishments and sacrifices during this opportunity to hear your stories and experiences. To assist with the youth learning, it would be appreciated if you could take the time to answer the enclosed questionnaire. Once completed, I would ask that you return it to VAC in the enclosed prepaid and addressed envelope'. Yeah, I bet those dear little boys and girls will be thrilled to hear how the Germans shot my buddy because he was searching the garbage for food. Not dead of course. A corpse is easy to get rid of. They shot him in the knees so he'd be a cripple and we had to look after him. I can show them the scars that the rifle butts made. They'll jump for joy when I show them how skinny I was.' I shook my head in disgust. 'That's what's wrong with the whole scheme, Danny. They make the war look like a great adventure, fun and games, pomp and ceremony, medals and bands, everybody happy and . . . ' I stopped. Danielle had her elbows on the table, supporting her head in her hands and there were tears in her eyes. She shrugged with just a hint of resignation.

'Don't be bitter, Ben,' she said, and shook her head as if dismissing my outburst. 'You're too nice a guy to carry resentment all these years. I'll make a deal with you, Ben. There's an information session at the Legion on Thursday night. I think we should go and learn more. Then you can make up your mind. There are five other vets selected from this part of Quebec, and they'll all be there, so you can talk to them and see how they feel.' She paused and gave her professional, throaty chuckle. 'With their caregivers!'

'How do you know that?'

'The Legion called.'

'When?'

'Middle of last week. You were at work.'

'And you didn't tell me.'

Now she was really upset. 'No, I didn't tell you. I didn't want to go through this hassle twice, because I figured you'd react just as you have. They said more information was in the mail from Ottawa, so I thought it better to wait and have the discussion only once. Now, all the information is here on our table, we are discussing it and I have told you.' She marched to the counter and began putting the dishes in the dishwasher. 'So, if you don't want to go, I'll go by myself.'

I slumped and forced myself to control my emotions. There was no reason for me to get irritable with her. Most of the time I never thought about the hatred that was imbedded in me against the Germans, and the bitterness I still felt against the brainless Brits who sent us into that death trap. I forced myself to forget and try to forgive, but it all comes back when these people push the remembering jingo and expect me to join in. I guess if I was honest with myself, I'm afraid, afraid of what I might say or what I might do if I join in, so I just avoid them. I couldn't avoid Danny's questioning eyes.

'Sorry, love. I was a bit abrupt, but I really don't want to go back to all the horror and pain that I've been trying to forget all these years. What's the point? So it's twenty-five years since I had to fight every day to stay alive. It's long past. I'm happy, so, as I said, what's the point?'

Danielle came back and sat, organizing the papers on the table very slowly and stared at me. Her voice was emphatic with its softness. 'And as I said, Ben, I understand your reaction. I know how you suffered. I was Nurse LaFlamme who nursed dozens of guys who were wounded and broken and burned and dejected. And it's also almost twenty-five years since I said I would marry one of those broken, emotionally unstable, handsome young veterans. And I've always been proud. Together we've succeeded. Not without a lot of sacrifices, your long hours to build the business, my long hours to raise the kids and keep the home going. But do you realize during all those years we've never had one vacation out of this province? Never been on a big plane or seen the rest of Canada?' Her eyes were wet with tears. She flicked a hand toward the invitation. 'Here is an opportunity for us to get away, fly the ocean, see new things, together Ben, together. And it's all paid for, because you fought for Canada. And you toss it away without even considering. You don't have to wear your medals. You don't have to wear a legion uniform. You don't even have to go in the parades or attend the ceremonies. You can sneak away and do whatever you please; they'll never miss you. There'll be crowds all over the place.' She reached across and squeezed my hand. 'And I'll be with you. I'm your caregiver. It says so right here.' She squeezed again. 'Oh, Ben, please. Let's go on Thursday, at least, and hear what they have to say. Please?'

As soon as I agreed, we started down the list. Danielle picked up passport applications at the Post Office and I made an appointment at the photographers to have our pictures taken. We'd never had passports and it was all new and interesting. I filled in the questionnaire on the state of my health and telephoned our doctor about an examination. Danielle completed her documents as my caregiver, to which I couldn't help remarking, 'What a hell of a name. Wouldn't friend or companion be just as good?' I wrote my military career as concisely as I could, trying not to sound bitter, and attached pictures of us, which, I read somewhere, would be used in the pocket guide.

'And, if you do decide to go, may I suggest

you get your medals out of their mailing boxes and have them hung. You'll be conspicuous without them. There's a fellow at the legion who will do them properly. And, while you're there, may I suggest you order trousers, jacket and beret. I can't do that for you.' She went on with her housework in silence.

The weather was simply rotten all day on Thursday, with a cold wind and driving rain. We could hear the rigging slapping against the aluminium masts on the sailing boats, and the waves pounding on the riverbank. It was dark before we finished dinner and left for the meeting. The rain was so heavy at times that Danielle stuck her head out of the car window to read the signs as she directed me toward the Richelieu Branch, Canadian Legion, on Rue Carrieres. The parking lot looked like a skating rink with piles of dirty snow around the edge.

'Let me out at the door, please, I don't want our documents to get soaked.'

I had to park at the far end and ran back. Soggy shoes and damp trousers didn't improve my attitude as I hurried inside. She was sitting at a table that had our names on a little card. Already she was stirring a cup of coffee. A buxom lady was chatting as if they were old friends and she turned to me with a blossoming smile. 'Mr Courier, I presume.' She wiped her hand on her apron and we shook. 'I'm Janette Voiseau.' She turned to Danielle. 'So you talked him into coming, eh, Danielle. Good for you. Welcome to our Legion, Ben. What will you have to drink? Coffee? Tea? Beer? Hot Chocolate?'

I sat and straightened my damp pants. 'Say, a hot chocolate might be just the thing, take the chill off my bones.'

'How about an Irish Crème?' She smirked. 'The drinks are on the branch tonight, so enjoy them.' She skipped away with a flutter of her hand. I looked around. It was rather an attractive clubhouse: maroon curtains on the windows; a collection of shiny trophies in a glass case; pictures of military aeroplanes, tanks and warships on the wall and no drunken legionnaires staggering around exercising their voices. The tables were in a half circle at one end, each with a name card and couples sitting and chatting over drinks. As my gaze passed over them, I received a friendly nod of greeting or a flick of a salute. The whole atmosphere was warm and friendly and I saw no one parading around loaded with medals for being secretary or president. I was trying to figure out who might be the government representative so I could tell him my reaction to the pilgrimage, but Janette returned with my hot drink and I stayed at our table. The drink was good! I could feel the warmth spreading through my chilled body. I relaxed and smiled at Danielle, but she had swivelled in her chair and was chatting with another woman who had come out of the kitchen. I smiled at the fellow at the next table and when Danielle turned back, I said cheerfully: 'You seem to have a lot of friends here.'

'Yes, Ben, I do. In fact, I'm a member. I am a veteran, remember? However, I don't come in here very often because this clubhouse is mostly for couples and I don't like having to explain where my husband is.' That made me think, too, but before I could respond she touched her lips for silence as someone started to speak. A giant of a man with a trimmed, grey beard, a huge smile and a bouncing step as if coaching basketball, was pulling the cord of a microphone into the centre of the room and waving greetings as he moved. His voice rolled across the room like an announcer at a boxing match.

'Evening folks, I'm Malcolm Boyle, your pilgrimage co-ordinator and I'm Scottish and I speak French with a Scottish accent and that's why the folks in Veterans Affairs Canada put me in charge of the Quebec delegation.' He laughed and scratched his beard. 'I just got in from Ottawa and I have to do another briefing in Montreal in two hours so we'll move along. Skip the applause until after I have gone. I'll talk to the vets who are going with me. I'm not ignoring the caregivers but everything I say to the vets applies to the caregivers. In addition, the caregivers have to make sure that the vets understand and remember to follow instructions. Do I make myself clear?' He laughed and slapped his knees like a vaudeville comedian. 'I understand everyone is here. Good! In no particular order, we have Captain Maurice Narcoix of the Sherbrooke Hussars.' He nodded as Narcoix gave a little wave. 'And Flying Officer Sydney Fox of the Royal Canadian Air Force from Chambly. John Simundson from St Luc. Grenadier Guards. Sergeant Simundson, there will be reps from the War Amps to look after you, and don't hesitate to ask for help.' I looked around and realized for the first time that the jolly fellow at the next table was in a wheelchair. 'And Leading Seaman Roy Munro of the Royal Canadian Navy. You're from D'Iberville across the Richelieu? Is that right? Sergeant Major Joseph Paquette, Royal Montreal Regiment, Farnham. And Corporal Benoit Courier of the Fusiliers Mont-Royal, who lives right here in St Jean-sur-Richelieu. Corporal, you are the only POW in the whole delegation, so we are particularly pleased that you have agreed to come.' He gave me a snappy salute and quite a few people clapped.

While he was talking a brisk young man in a tight blue suit was placing papers on our tables. Malcolm Boyle pointed. 'That's Deno Pineiro, man of many talents. He distributes paper. The government has a lot of papers for you, a lot of instructions, and I insist that you read them carefully and act accordingly because it is a gigantic task to gather people from all over Canada, get them to one spot at the same time with all their documents.' He rolled his eyes to the ceiling. 'Somebody always forgets something. You must have a Canadian passport. If you don't have one ten days before departure, telephone the number we have given you and we will speed it up. You must have your medical documents. You must have all your medications clearly identified with your doctor's supporting directive. You must adhere to the luggage weight. We are on a military aircraft, not a luxury airliner. There are media relations officers with us. And journalists. We want you to talk to them, but we want you to use discretion. There are tips for speaking to the news media. There are special instructions for the caregivers. Doctors and nurses will be with us. Use them if necessary. We don't want any preventable incidents. Now, I'm rushing. You'll wonder why we came all the way from Ottawa to hand out papers when we could have saved money and mailed them. However we have another chore. Deno is also a photographer and will take your portraits so they will all be the same for the tour guide with no blank spaces. I know we asked you to send photographs. Some will be OK. Some will be awful. And some will never arrive. So Deno has set up his screen and camera, over there, and I ask you to come quickly, in the order on the list, and smile for Deno. Captain Narcoix, then your caregiver, Flying Officer Fox, and so on.'

The quiet clubroom erupted into noisy chaos of many voices. Danielle was circulating with the ease of a professional who was used to meeting strangers, leaving me to agree with Sergeant Major Paquette on whatever point he was trying to make. Finally he was called to the camera, and I followed with Danielle sliding her arm in mine while Deno finished his artistry. I was very impressed with the organized way the team went about their tasks. They had brought a plain background on a roller that fitted on a tripod. Boyle deftly positioned each person in front of the screen, Deno took the picture and Boyle moved in the next one. He seemed to know who was who even though he had been here such a short time. Their departure was just as efficient, and I figured they'd done this before to avoid having to answer a multitude of questions that were all answered in the literature. Boyle had his raincoat on and waved farewell. 'Good luck and see you in Ottawa. Remember the name. Mac Boyle. I'm your den mother to France and back.' Our leader departed with the same jovial energy that he displayed as he arrived, a flick of a salute with a white-tooth smile. Deno followed, carrying his camera and tripod. I could hear the rain lashing against the windows and wondered how the blue suit would survive. I silently wished them a safe race to Montreal.

I returned to our table, a little disappointed that I had no opportunity to explain my feelings about the trip. 'No chance to talk,' I muttered, but Danielle was already chatting with Sydney Fox at the next table. John Simundson was wheeling his chair across the room with a florid grin and a pumping shake of my hand. 'Glad to meet you, Mr Courier. I see from the biog you were at Dieppe.' He shook his head, 'Better you than me.' He tapped his knee, where there was no leg. 'I lost that in Holland. Stepped on a mine. Silly of me. Always was clumsy. I'm resting up for the march, Ben. I'm OK when I'm walking, but I can't stand for long. So I'll take the old chair, just in case.' I nodded, smiled my understanding and felt a little uncomfortable. The ladies were bustling around with plates of sandwiches and cakes. Others were bringing trays of coffee and drinks. Janette Voiseau came sailing through with a steaming hot toddy. 'For our special guy.' She winked, and hurried away. I was beginning to get the feeling that I was part of the pilgrimage and would appear a real stinker if I backed out now. I was going to talk about this with Danielle when a tall fellow walked over and stood beside our table.

'Hello, there,' Danielle smiled up at him, 'I'd like you to meet my husband, Ben. Ben, this is the President of the Branch, Gil Vanderberg.' I stood while we shook hands and then he pulled over a chair and sat.

'Glad to have you with us tonight, Ben.' He spoke very quietly so that no one else could hear. 'I hope you and Mrs Courier decide to go on the trip. I understand all the others are going. The briefing was a bit rushed, perhaps, but they seem to have done a very complete job with the paperwork.' He looked around nervously. 'While you're here, I wonder if you would mind coming into the lounge with me. I have a lady who wants to talk to someone

20

who is going to France, about contacting her son.'

I looked at Danielle with a little show of exasperation, and said to Vanderberg, 'But we haven't even had a chance to look at the itinerary or discuss our plans.'

He nodded. 'I know. This is a bit awkward for me, as I'll explain later, but if you and Danielle would come and listen, I would be very grateful. And if you agree to help us, I would be even more grateful.' He sat back wearily so that he could see my reaction and I realized he was wound up very, very tightly. I could see the sweat on his forehead and the unease in his eyes.

Danielle nodded and stood. 'Well, Ben, I don't see any reason why we can't go and meet Dr Vanderberg's friend.' She moved from behind our table. He stood, picked up his chair and carried it to the far wall, then turned and looked back. She slid her arm around my waist as we followed.

The lounge was a pleasant room with soft lighting, gaily-covered easy chairs, a gas fireplace that was flickering cheerfully and several low tables. There was nothing to recall the war, which I thought was a nice touch. An elderly lady was sitting with her hands in her lap, staring into the distance. She could have been seventy. She could have been ninety.

21

Her face was parchment white with lines of worry or sorrow making deep shadows. No hair escaped from the black kerchief that covered her head. She was wearing a dark grey dress, which was full and belted, like a nun's habit, a gloomy cape sagged from her shoulders. She looked as if she'd been out in the rain.

'Madame Mary Pilgrim,' Vanderberg introduced. 'And these are Danielle and Benoit Courier who are going to France on the pilgrimage.' Her head rose slightly and her eyes came up to acknowledge us with just the hint of a nod. 'Thank you for coming.' Her voice was a deep contralto. Very refined. A cultured accent. Her sad eyes touched mine and I felt the vibes of gentleness that I remembered from nurses as I struggled away from prison nightmares. Her eyes were pale blue, so pale and washed out that the pupils looked huge and there was a lifetime of sorrow in their depths. 'Thank you,' she repeated and a hand fluttered toward the chairs on each side. Vanderberg pulled his chair closer so he faced us and we formed a sort of a circle.

'Madame Pilgrim has asked whether you would contact her son in France.'

I was feeling a bit of irritation creeping into my voice. I hadn't even agreed that I was going and here I was being dragged in to something else. I asked. 'Why us, Mrs Pilgrim? We don't know France. We've never been there to visit.'

She nodded without any change of expression. 'I saw that you were a prisoner. You have suffered. I saw your wife was an army nurse. She also knows suffering and compassion. I knew you would understand my suffering because my son has not come home like he should. That's why I asked if I might meet you. I hope you understand.'

Vanderberg jumped in: 'And also, Mr Courier, because you live in Saint Jean. Madame Pilgrim lives at the Ursuline School, which is affiliated with Saint Athanase Parish Church across the river in Iberville where she teaches religion and psychology. So you are close, which we thought would be an advantage.' He was leaning forward. I could see he was anxious for us to agree but I wanted more information. I was about to ask when Danielle spoke, kindly and comfortingly, as if to a patient,

'Of course we understand, Mrs Pilgrim. Yes, I was a nurse and I'm also a mother. But we are going to a very small area in France, in Normandy, and perhaps into Provence. Where was your son when you heard from him last?'

The hands were folded again in her lap; her eyes flickered across our group. 'I'm not sure. Dr Vanderberg has the details. He's been most kind and helpful.'

'Yes,' he injected. 'I'll tell you all I know.'

'When did you hear from him last?' Danielle persisted.

'9 September, 1943.'

There was a long silence. I felt a chill go down my spine and curl around inside me. I kept smiling because I was too embarrassed not to. Her voice was stronger, compelling,

'But he's alive. I know he's alive. He was hurt. He was badly hurt. I heard him scream. But he got better. I can't understand why he doesn't come home.' Those washed blue eyes were pleading at me. 'You'll find him. I know you will. Just tell him I love him and miss him and his room is all ready for him.' She smiled, as if from the memory of his boyhood, and for a brief, brilliant second her features glowed like one of the saints in the cathedral. 'It would make me very happy.'

Danielle was frowning with her clinical stare. She patted the thin, clasped hands and said warmly. 'I understand, Mrs Pilgrim. You must be very worried. Of course we'll try to find your son. Dr Vanderberg can give us all the details and we'll do our best.' She leaned forward and kissed her on the cheek. 'Now we know where you are, we'll come and visit you when we get back and tell you all our news. What is your son's name?' Smart, smart Danielle, using the present tense.

That deep, musical voice responded: 'Joseph, after the father of Jesus. Adam after the first man whom God created. Joseph Adam Pilgrim.' For a second the sadness waned and pride warmed her face. 'Thank you, dear friends. You will find him. I will pray for you every morning when I pray for Joseph.' The room was silent for a long time as three people stared at the crumpled form, head bent, eyes closed. Then she straightened as if she had finished praying and received her message. 'Yes. You will find him. God will guide you to him.'

★　★　★

The rain was still pounding down and the wind was much colder. I let the engine of my Chrysler warm up so the heater could clear the fog off my windshield. I felt a whole lot better about the legion and its pilgrimage than I did when I arrived, but I sure wasn't anxious to go looking for a person who had been missing for a quarter of a century. However, I was so busy driving I had no time to discuss anything with Danielle. I waited

25

until we were snug at home and I was warm and dry.

'You know, Danny,' I began softly. 'I have the feeling I've been manipulated. A well-planned scenario. No time to discuss with the jolly leader. Then the weepy widow bit. How can I say I'm not going without looking like a real shit.' I hoped my voice reflected a bit of the humour that I intended, but Danielle didn't react. With the quiet calm that was so much a part of her character, she held out one of the briefing papers we had received. 'You agreed to go and listen. You went and listened. Now you can make up your mind. There's the number. Telephone right now if you really won't go. You'll probably get an answering machine so you won't be embarrassed. Give them your decision and that's that.' She slid the paper toward me. 'I can assure you, Ben, that there was no special arrangement. I didn't know that guy Boyle was going to take off like that. In fact, I didn't know what was going to happen.'

'What about Mary Pilgrim? You agreed pretty fast to see her.'

'A total surprise to me.'

'You acted as if you knew her, patting her hand and soothing her fears.'

Now her voice rose and she was just a little bit angry. 'I thought we could hardly refuse.

26

After all, we wouldn't be on the invitation list at all if it wasn't for Dr Vanderberg. And as far as the way I treated that poor woman, I could see she was a very distraught, nervous person, maybe not mentally unstable in a medical sense, but certainly under a great deal of emotional turmoil, so I simply acted as a trained nurse. There was no sense in even attempting to change her mind. She's believed her son is alive for twenty seven years and she'll continue to believe her son is alive, and anything we would have said wouldn't have made the slightest difference. So I got us out of there as fast and easily as possible. You should be grateful.' She pounded her fist on the papers. 'Now, what's your decision?'

I really wanted to go, but after my rather impulsive performance, I thought I better waffle a little so I said: 'Well, you know, I kinda liked that fellow Boyle. I think he'd be fun to travel with. And the other guys were sure enthusiastic. The fellow with one leg, Simundson, very friendly, and intends to parade. So I guess if he can, maybe I could go along with the crowd.' Danielle was grinning. 'And maybe we could sneak away for a few days, look around a bit, sort of a holiday, a second honeymoon . . . ' I let my voice trail off. She got up, put her arms around my neck and kissed me repeatedly. 'Thank you, Ben. I was hoping, really hoping, that you'd say yes, but, I knew you had to make up your own mind, so I didn't try to convince, but I will confess, I suggested to Janette Voiseau that she give you a hot toddy.'

'I'll forgive you for that!'

★ ★ ★

Dr Vanderberg telephoned the next afternoon. Danielle told him we were definitely going and invited him to come to our house that evening which suited me fine. I wanted to get that matter out of the way as soon as possible. Although the rain had gone, the cold made me quite glad I didn't have to go out. He arrived early, muffled in a car coat and wool toque. I hung his damp coat in the closet and we settled in the living room. Danielle had opened a card table and he dropped his briefcase on it before sitting. Coffee was ready on a castered trolley.

'I'm a bit early,' he began 'and I can't stay long. I have a patient in hospital that I must see before I go to bed.' He took his cup from Danielle and settled back. He was tall, over six feet, but very thin. His shoulders were already showing the weary hump of old age. He wore loose corduroy trousers, that were

28

bagging even more with the damp, and a Harris Tweed jacket that sagged at the pockets. His hair was full and crinkly but turning grey. He looked tired and harassed and welcomed the chance to sit for a few minutes.

'First, dear lady, I must thank you for being very professional last night. Mrs Pilgrim can be a little wearisome when she gets onto this fixation about her son. There's no sense in arguing with her. You diagnosed that pretty rapidly. I was praying there wouldn't be any abrasive reaction.' He turned to me. 'Be proud, Ben, she's a very smart lady.'

'I've known that for years, doctor, but thanks for reminding me.' She bobbed daintily as she served my coffee and passed the biscuits to our visitor. 'I gather you've known Mrs Pilgrim for some time.'

He sighed. 'Yes, Ben, for many years, and she's never wavered in her belief that her son is alive. I've never seen anything like it. I've experienced a lot of reactions to death — sorrow, anger, depression, weeping and accusations against the doctors and nurses. I've seen the added anguish of flickering optimism and fading hope when there is no body. 'Missing, presumed dead' is a terrible message. Mrs Pilgrim received that message and nothing more. Her form of mental release was never to admit that he was dead, therefore, he must be alive. When she learned that five veterans from this area were going to France, she pestered me to ask someone to help. You see, I'm also the medical officer for the Ursuline School so I can't avoid her. I sat in my office this morning and looked at the file with Joe Pilgrim's name on it and felt uncomfortable about the way I'd manoeuvred you into helping. I hope you folks will understand and hopefully, together, we can concoct some explanation that will satisfy her.'

Gil Vanderberg dropped a sugar lump into his cup and stirred slowly. 'You must understand that she is a deeply religious person. Totally religious. I understand she was a novitiate in a convent in France during the first war. A wounded Canadian soldier named Pilgrim was carried in and sheltered by the nuns in the basement. She accepted the name as an omen from God and devoted herself to him. She left the Order, married him and followed him to Canada, believing it to be divine guidance. Shortly after the boy was born, Pilgrim took off and left her destitute. Rather than shattering her belief in divine destiny, it made her almost a fanatic. The Ursulines took her in and she remained as a sister of the Order, bringing up her son in this totally religious world.'

I really didn't want to know about Mary Pilgrim or her problem. I burst out, 'That's all very well, doctor, but twenty seven years . . . Jesus wept, man . . . twenty seven years . . . She must be crazy!'

Gil Vanderberg shook his head patiently. 'No, Ben, she's not crazy. She's not even mentally unbalanced. She's normal other than when she's pleading for her son. She's an excellent, patient teacher at the school. And she sings in the choir, a memorable contralto — beautiful. No, she just hopes for a miracle. You must remember that she's saturated in a religion that believes in miracles, indeed, teaches and promotes miracles. What will happen if there is some sign that Joseph is alive, for sure, or Joseph is positively dead, I don't know. I asked a psychiatrist friend and he said that evidence either way might bring about her complete mental destruction, the death of the normal side of her personality. Or it may have little or no impact. He couldn't really say. So you see our challenge is very delicate. If we can devise some response which would not destroy her faith but satisfy her yearning for closure and if we can make it appear that you brought this knowledge back with you from France . . . '

He dropped his hands in resignation, and the

lines on his face were deep. 'So we must get together when you return and discuss it, make very sure about the story we develop, before she even knows you're back.'

Danielle and I sat in silence while we thought about his proposal. My reaction was still to throw up my arms and shout 'No. Leave us alone. This is our first real holiday. No. Let her go on dreaming that he's alive. What do I care! Some day she'll die, and that will be the end.' But I stayed quiet and looked at Danielle. She was frowning, rocking slightly, eyes intent on Gil Vanderberg. 'We can at least try, but I think you should give us all the facts before we start thinking about what we'll tell her when we get back.'

He opened his file. 'Yes, I'll tell you everything I know, then I'll leave and you can discuss on your own and let me know.' He put on reading glasses and began, 'Joseph Pilgrim joined the air force as soon as the war started. He was almost twenty one. He went to Lachine for initial training and earned his aircrew wing at the navigation training school at Ancienne Lorette north of Quebec City. He was, or perhaps I should say, is, fluently bilingual and I suppose that may have played a part in making him an instructor. The British Commonwealth Air Training Plan was English and a lot of French kids had language problems, therefore I've done a lot of research to pacify her.' He referred to the great bundle of working papers. 'In August 1943, there was apparently a critical shortage of navigators in the Royal Air Force. He was rushed overseas, sent to the Royal Air Force base at Waddington and placed with an experienced crew that needed a navigator. He went on his first mission to bomb railway traffic at Le Mans in France on 21 November, 1943. That was considered a rather easy operation and all the bombers returned except Pilgrim's.' He leaned back a little and finished his cold coffee. 'As far as I could find out, no trace was ever found of the Lancaster bomber or any of its crew. Not unusual.' He paused and settled back. 'Apparently there was a huge blizzard that night with no really big raids. Waddington sent only eight Lancs to Le Mans and seven returned. There's nothing in German records of any Luftwaffe crew claiming a kill that night. So, the whole thing's a mystery.' He leaned forward and pointed to the file. 'There's one clue, however, and I've listed the details. The pilot was an American who had joined the RCAF. His name was Lloyd Hogan. A Hogan, with initials B.L. appears on the roster of the US military cemetery at Colleville St. Laurent, which, I have researched, is on top of the cliff overlooking Omaha beach and has almost 10,000 graves. The Hogan entry has a notation that the remains were moved from a burial plot near a village called Ste Agathe. There's one chance in a thousand it's the same, but . . . ' He ended with a weary sigh.

'Does Mary Pilgrim know that?' Danielle asked.

'No. Raising hope, then dashing it is worse than nothing; I didn't take the chance.' Vanderberg began putting away his records.

'If that was the pilot's body, wouldn't the rest of the crew and the wreckage be in the vicinity?' I countered.

'I don't know, Ben. That's all I've been able to discover. And that's taken me a lot more time and worry than I can spare.' He closed the last file. 'I just want you to make some inquiries so you can truthfully tell her that you tried.' He hurried away into a rather unpleasant night, very grateful, and, I thought, rather relieved.

I tried to watch a little television while Danielle cleared up and gave her hair its nightly brushing, but my mind was having trouble settling down. There was just too much churning around in my head. I was still having trouble getting to sleep when we were both snuggled down and the lights had been out for over an hour. I could tell Danielle was still awake by the way she was restless. Maybe talking would help.

'Y'know, Danny,' I began cautiously. 'I think I'm getting a bit excited about this trip, the more I think about it.'

She seemed to relax as I spoke. She wriggled closer, hugged me and nibbled my ear. 'I always was. I thought it was a wonderful opportunity and a sort of national gratitude for what you and I did during the war. Not much, maybe, but every little bit helps.' She kissed me warmly. 'We're gonna have fun.'

'You bet we will,' I yawned, suddenly feeling very sleepy, 'and we won't spoil it by worrying about this guy Pilgrim.'

Danielle was silent for a long time, breathing warmly down my neck. Then she whispered. 'Nothing will spoil it, Ben, but I can't help wondering what happened that November night in '43?'

'We'll never know, but I can tell you one thing for sure.'

'What's that?'

'It was bloody cold.'

PART TWO

21 NOVEMBER, 1943

1

Sergeant Navigator Joe Pilgrim was sweating inside his flight suit even though his fingers were so numb from cold that they could hardly work his calculator. He twisted the knob again onto their magnetic heading and squirmed.

'Please God, let it be right!'

He tried again and moaned at the same result. Here he was on his first flight and he was questioning the weather forecast that the meteorology officer had presented . . . He was so thrilled that he'd been chosen as a navigator on this famous British squadron. He deserved it. He'd worked hard, ever since he escaped from that girls' school. He'd been a good instructor and his classes had always had above average results. With another little prayer he checked his dead reckoning on his chart and knew he was right. He switched on the microphone in his oxygen mask and called the pilot, a huge, rollicking American who was almost tour complete.

'Alter course 15 degrees port on to 158,

skipper. Looks like a stronger north-east wind than forecast.'

'Done already.' Hogan's American lingo was a nasal rasp over the throb of the engines. He had doodled on his flight sheet throughout the briefing as if he was ignoring the officers who were preparing them for the raid on Le Mans. When it was over, he'd slapped Joe on the shoulder, grunted 'piecacake' and stomped out into the cold night. Joseph didn't see him again until he climbed into the cockpit and said, 'Let's get the show on the road'. The rest of the crew ignored him and were busy doing their own chores and checks. Pilgrim had a load of navigation equipment to carry out and was grateful that the little tail gunner had carried his map case out to the loading truck. This tiring, confusing routine was old stuff to them, apparently. Pilgrim wondered what had happened to their regular navigator but in the stress of pre-operation checks there wasn't the time to ask. And why all the rush? His posting had been stamped, 'accelerated departure' and he was sure cleared off RCAF Station Chatham, New Brunswick in a rush. No time for the usual 'go ops' drink. He'd been flown to Dorval Airport outside Montreal in a Douglas Dakota of Transport Command. He'd been crammed into an

American B-17 bomber with a bunch of aircrew and flown across the Atlantic. His papers had moved ahead of him, and he'd barely unpacked on Royal Air Force Station Waddingtion when he was called for briefing and assigned to this crew. All vets, obviously, in the 'slam damn' way they got airborne in a rush. They were off to bomb some trains in France, was about all he understood.

Hogan's snarl squealed in his headset. 'Hello, Joe boy. Always check the bloody wind soonest airborne. OK? Never trust those weather wogs. They hardly look out of the window.' He hawked and coughed. 'Anyway, Pilgrim, you can forget the courses. I'll get us there. Work out some alternate routes home, in case we meet the odd bandit.'

Pilgrim went back to his dead reckoning navigation chart and started applying the stronger winds. He had to blow on his hands to hold the dividers. It was one thing to plot aerial courses in the classroom, but this was difffent. He was in an aircraft that was bouncing and twisting and seated at a desk that was vibrating with the wind whistling through the cracks; it was dark except for a little light that was jumping about on the end of its positioning arm. Please God, let the courses be right. He wasn't afraid of flying into enemy skies. His mother had blessed him and promised that God would protect him. But already he was terrified of this vulgar, hulking pilot who flew as if he didn't care what happened and would probably chew him up if he goofed. He re-calculated all the compass courses for the trip from the target using a new dead reckoning plot because he didn't expect to be able to take any star shots, not with almost solid cloud cover. He started swallowing. The aircraft was going up to the right, then banking over and dropping down and it rolled to the left. Then it stopped going down and rolled to the right with the nose coming up. He was getting sick. Dear God. Don't let me be sick; they'd laugh at me. I'm supposed to be an experienced navigator, ready for combat. That's what my documents said. A few minutes ago he was shivering and wiggling his toes in his flight boots to keep the circulation going. Now he was sweating. He looked around. The wireless operator was tapping a pencil and jigging up and down as if listening to dance music. Surely he wouldn't —

'Enemy coast ahead!' the nose gunner shouted over the intercom.

'Bang on!' Hogan gloated, giving the aircraft a more violent twist in his 'cork screw' evasive action. They roared on through the night.

'Look at those bloody clouds,' one voice crackled.

'Great Christly blizzard,' somebody else chirped.

'No frigging Krauts tonight!' This sounded like the tail gunner.

Hogan laughed and yanked the Lancaster into another corkscrew. 'Piecacake, but stay alert. Britain needs more lerts.' He laughed and started singing.

'Twenty minutes to target,' Pilgrim made his announcement.

'Roger!' the skipper responded.

Pilgrim felt as if he was part of the crew.

2

Willi Hutt was angry and scared: he was angry because he'd volunteered to be a Luftwaffe test pilot. Sounded great! Exciting. A change from teaching kids how to fly so the British could shoot them down. A nice, safe posting far from the wicked war. So he had volunteered and was posted to a crummy Messerschmitt factory in Hungary and spent his time trying to turn that widow-maker Me210 into a fighter-bomber. It was an impossible task! What a reputation for an aircraft! Tailplanes break off; no stability;

43

no control on single engine; flicks into inverted spins; vicious ground loop on landing. Those were the remarks of experienced test pilots. Even Goering said it was a failure and had stopped production in 1942. What the hell was he doing testing one in combat in November 1943?

This experimental model had two new 1,475 horsepower Daimler-Benz engines that made the kite climb like a rocket and he had some civilian wizard technician sitting at a screen that made his face look green. He was told that this was the latest in electronic detection methods and it was supposed to render enemy kites visible in the dark. He had been equipped with a great cannon with its snout pointing upwards that was hooked to the gadget and was supposed to shoot the boffins in the belly where there was no gunner when everything was just right for a certain kill. Willi Hutt hoped this guy knew what he was doing because there was one hell of a blizzard damn close. And that's why he was scared!

He took off from Abbeville without lights and green face gave him directions to fly back and forth across the lanes that the Brits used. So they patrolled back and forth while the fuel gauges went down as if there were holes in the tanks. Nothing showed on the green scope. Even the Brits were not stupid enough to fly on a night like this. After Willi's hands had begun to sweat with the tension of keeping this brick in the air, green face finally gave a shout,

'Lancaster!'

Willi Hutt looked up from his instruments. Black as a coal mine! Great white snowflakes streamed at him out of the big black sky, swooping over his head as the slipstream tore them away. He searched for the target, eyes going out of focus. A good way to get vertigo. He'd told his students that dozens of times. He looked back to the instruments. The brute's already dropped one wing he thought and could be a hundred feet away by now. Haul 'er back.

'Chop speed to 200.'

Green face started chanting vectors. Willi felt the sweat down his back. This was work! This was stalking the enemy, curving around low behind him, sneaking up where they couldn't see . . . he hoped.

'Starboard 10. Starboard 10. Steady, steady. Speed to 220. Hold it. Hold it. Hold it. Speed 230. Starboard 5. Hold it. 1,000 yards. Dead ahead. Down 100. Hold it. Speed 225. That's it. Hold it. Ten seconds.'

Willi gave up thinking about the Brit gunners, all waiting to kill him and locked on his flight instruments. The cannon fired. He jerked. The aircraft reared. Another short burst.

'Circle right. Max speed.'

He was having trouble flying this beast straight and level in a blizzard with some helldammer turbulence. He jammed the throttles forward and rolled her over. Round she came, chattering on the edge of a high speed stall. Green face started chanting again.

'Coming on target. Level flight. Speed 220. Left 10. Steady. Steady. Up 100. Steady. Right 5. Steady. Steady. Steady.'

The cannon snarled again. One long burst.

'Left 5. Stay on target.' One short squirt.

'Let's go home.'

Willi breathed gratefully. His eyes flicked across the glowing panel and ice hit him in the stomach! Christ! Red, red warning lights . . . flickering . . . both engines . . . fuel low.

'What course?' he shouted.

Green face was gone. The scope was shut down. The voice came over the intercom out of the dark, 'That's your problem.'

Willi broke radio silence and requested homing. Fast response. Course 347 . . . distance sixty-four. Jesus wept! He was miles from the base. He throttled back . . . power glide . . . lean mixture . . . save fuel . . . gas gauges . . . emergency red . . . request new course 045 degrees . . . seventeen minutes to base . . . five minutes . . . panicking . . . check again . . . head wind sixty eight knots . . . a gale . . . three minutes . . . forty miles . . . going down . . . emergency . . . emergency. The big engine on the starboard wing coughed, caught, coughed, and quit.

'No control on single engine.' That's what one pilot wrote on his test report on single engine performance at low altitude.

Willi Hutt felt the rudder pedals judder under his feet as his directional control surfaces reached the stall. Cut back power on the port engine to prevent a power-on spin. Now the bloody goony-bird was dropping like a rock. He stopped the plunge and levelled at 1,000 feet. His speed was way too high to get onto the runway, and there was no 'going around' for a second try. He chopped the power, dropped the wheels and put on full flap. The port engine was dead. All tanks dry. He could see the lights of the runway. With luck he'd make it! He sighed with relief. The blizzard hit. Wind over 100! He suddenly wondered what happened to the Brit plane as he rode the Messerschmitt down on instruments.

But Willi Hutt didn't make it!

The fire glowed through the snow squalls for almost an hour, four hundred yards short of the runway!

3

The first splatter of cannon shells tore through the floor of the Lancaster just behind the main wing spar and shredded a section of the upper fuselage. The tail guns chattered, barking.

'Where the hell he come from?' The tail gunner cursed as he swivelled his turret.

'Keep your goddam eyes open,' Hogan screamed, 'Where's the bastard?'

'Can't see nothing in this friggin' snow.'

Wind blasted through the tear in the skin, whipping up the dirt from the walkway.

The bomber shuddered and wallowed.

Hogan fought for control, jamming his feet on the rudders and rocking the wheel. The machine came back under control and the huge Rolls-Royce engines kept running. Number three went out of synchronization and Hogan wrestled with the pitch controls until it was back in harmony and they continued their throaty roar. The bomber bored into the blizzard, as if determined to hit the target, thirty-two miles ahead.

The wind whipped Pilgrim's charts off his plotting table. He released his seat belt so he could turn and grab them back. He missed and leaned down, reaching.

The upper turret was swivelling, searching.

'Nothing here!' the gunner screamed. The Lancaster vibrated but Hogan kept control, 'Come on baby!' he roared, 'We can beat those bastards!'

There were almost two minutes without any attack and the crew started breathing again. Hogan had the engines delivering full cruise power and all the controls were working.

The second attack cracked somewhere in the starboard wing and through the floor beneath the navigator's station. The inboard engine raced, spluttered and squirted orange fingers that lit up the crumbling wing spar.

Joseph Pilgrim was scrabbling for hand-holds to pull him up off the floor, prayers dribbling from his chattering lips, when a third burst tore into his left leg. He screamed 'Mother!' as the metal frame of his instrument panel collapsed on him and a tangle of wires held him down. The freezing tornado tore at his flesh. He sobbed, looking desperately for help. Part of the fuselage seemed to have disappeared and his eyes stared into black nothing! Empty sky! His world was tumbling, tearing, screeching! A sheet of metal flapped, vibrated, was gone. He squirmed, fought, prayed, 'Dear God. Mother. Save Me!' Hope shrivelled. 'No! Not yet! You promised!'

'Get out!' Hogan was clipping on his parachute with one hand, holding the wheel steady with the other. Blood was dripping off his chin. He staggered back with his hand extended to help Pilgrim. The oxygen line had yanked Pilgrim's mask and helmet off so that he was gasping for air and struggling with frozen fingers to retrieve his parachute. Hogan yanked it from the restraining cords and clipped it on, handed him the release ring and shoved him toward the escape hatch. Pilgrim felt as if his leg was on fire as he crawled past the guy in the upper turret who was screaming, his body slithering out of his harness, legs dangling, blood spurting into the ammunition rack. His clawed fingers were clutching his spilling guts.

In one horrible, wrenching, searing flash of revelation, Pilgrim's soul shrivelled. God was not protecting him! His mother was wrong! He was going to die! He was going to die! He sobbed, puked. Slime dribbled off his chin. He struggled toward the escape hatch. The bomber twisted and fell. He was thrown against the bulkhead, then driven onto his one good knee, clawing at the freezing metal as the aircraft gave another wrenching flick, then one gigantic quiver of dying agony and plunged upside down.

The blackness of pain and cold and horror

poured into Joe Pilgrim's brain and drove away everything except one last little prayer!

Please God!

And suddenly it was quiet.

The stillness of an empty cathedral.

The peace of the faithful.

Floating . . . gliding.. drifting . . .

Home . . .

On a cloud.

Softly . . . softly . . . his mother was singing.

All's right with the world.

His brain sent one flickering message before it shut down.

He was going home!

4

Ste Agathe huddled in a tight little valley surrounded by the plains of Normandy. Argentan to the south was the closest market town but in 1943 was a remote memory for the villagers because the Germans had banned all travel. Rouen was the Diocese Cathedral but contact with the bishopric ceased when the jackboots arrived. The stone and wood parish church of Ste Agathe on the hill had survived because Captain Bruno, garrison commandant, used the priest to keep the natives docile.

The Vesle rose sluggishly in the ridge of low hills to the north and entered the valley in a twenty metre high falls. The river divided the valley plain until it pooled near the old gristmill, now desolately empty. It plunged through the millrace and left the Agathe branch between hills to join the Sarthe River ten kilometres to the south.

The two main roads in the valley followed each riverbank. To the east the way was little more than a dirt track, once secluded by trees, but now chewed and battered by army vehicles from The Seigneury, occupied as German barracks. It was part of the patrol road up Church Hill, it ran past the church and on to Falaise, a major rail terminal. The main road followed the west bank, lined with cottages and peasants' huts, which clustered into a hamlet of narrow streets. The valley widened to surround the square that contained the Hotel de Ville, firehall, and a clutch of shops around the ancient bistro boasting the name Café D'Or.

The eastern slopes of the valley were steep, wooded, and pocked by hewn caves where stone had been cut for buildings and the humped bridges. Beyond, the country was flat, pleasant grassland where generations of sheep had fattened until war demanded their slaughter to extinction. To the west, the valley sloped gently and merged with woodlands and the large Forêt du Nord.

The people of Agathe had been isolated and independent in their tiny world since medieval times. The leaders of the Neapolitan revolution took this independence to be insurrection and sent a company of soldiers to subdue them and burn their church. The villagers conformed and re-built their church, cunningly including a look-out station in the spire so that no army would surprise them again.

Father Bree huddled in the saggy old chair in the tiny vestry of L'Église de Ste Agathe and stared at the candle as he paused in his devotions to listen to the aircraft droning overhead. He shivered and dragged the heavy wool cape tighter around his shoulders. The room was small and cluttered with the registers of hundreds of births, marriages and deaths, plus the memorabilia of countless priests and vergers. It smelled of old age, damp and neglect, but Father Bree found comfort in its familiar disorder and lack of draughts. The slit door that once led to a secluded garden had been closed and curtained since the occupation, giving the impression of warmth. He prayed that no bombs would fall on his village. The number of bombers that droned in from the coast had increased as the nights grew longer and he often heard the crump of bombs in the distance. He heard only a few that night as an early blizzard swept across France.

He had given up wondering whether God heard his prayers, but thought that the insignificance of Ste Agathe as a military target was probably the reason for their survival — if you could call it that. The few parishioners who were left were dying fast enough from starvation and loss of the spirit to live. Two funerals this week already and the ground frozen so that the graves remained open, ready for the next wasted corpse with less effort for the few men who could dig. His heart was sick for he could no longer draw strength from chanting vespers in a draughty, empty church. It was late. The precious candle, sheltered in the miner's helmet lamp, was his comforting companion as he tried to read his Compline to end another day. It was hard to respect the rigid timings of the canonical days when guns and hunger and fear were ruling your life. For months after the Germans came, he arose every morning and held Matins for the devoted few who struggled up the hill past the guards. Now his congregation was gone and his leg was so weak he sat for prayers. He prayed that the Lord and the good Bishop would understand his physical limitations. The chair embraced him like an old friend and, while he wasn't warm, he was no longer shivering, and his mind slid to happier times.

The soft, serene days of his youth, when he could run and play games, were so far, far away. The terrible pain of losing his left leg in a motorcycle accident only strengthened his faith. Those beautiful years in the seminary, when the revelations of Christ's teachings warmed his soul and moulded his character. The memory of his great joy when appointed the parish priest of Ste Agathe, rekindled a smile beneath his beard and the warming cowl. All gone with those marching feet, those grinding wheels, those shiny helmets. Would France ever smile again? Would his church survive? It was hard to convince others that their God was a kindly God when all around was sorrow and hunger and death. He stirred as another airplane throbbed over. He was twenty-nine years old and felt like an old man. His black hair and beard were wild and unkempt since the village's only barber had been taken away. Although his shoulders and arms seemed to be keeping some strength, his leg was wasting away. This handicap probably saved his life when they rounded up the workmen of the valley. What good was a one-legged man in this war? What could a crippled priest do against the German Army? So they let him stay, the youngest man in the village. His zeal to preach the Gospels dwindled into a fluttering determination to survive, and to save as many of his flock physically as he could. Some rejected him for co-operating with the Germans, but he saw no sense in arousing their fury and seeing his parishioners tumble to earth as the guns chattered: survival was worth humble obedience.

There was vigorous hammering at the south porch.

Reluctantly he threw aside the ancient cape and put on the miner's helmet to light his way. A cripple had to adapt and this relic from the days of the stonecutters lit his path and left his hands free. He fitted his crutches and struggled from the chair, tightening his habit with the frayed cord and missing tassels. He pulled on black gloves before grasping the crutches and moving into the church. He shuddered at the thought of confessional in the freezing church, the only remnant of catholic service that Captain Bruno permitted. The knocking was repeated. Few came and seldom on a wild winter night like this. He unlatched the door and was nearly hurled to the ground as the wind blasted it open.

A figure lunged in and around the door,

forcing it closed with his shoulder. Bree could see that the man was not in uniform, not a guard making a surprise check, nor someone wanting shelter from the weather for a few minutes.

'Damn cold.'

Father Bree recognized the voice and the squat, agile movement. He tutted. Pierre Bernay, woodchopper in Le Forêt du Nord, was beyond redemption, but they were good friends anyway. Without his fuel, French and Germans would freeze. The Germans gave him a special permit to move through the woods and not conform to the curfew, which forced villagers indoors at night. Bernay was a creature of the night and was seldom seen in the village during the daytime.

'Confessional, Father.' He hissed, his eyes bright in the candle glow. His hand felt for the pews as he moved down the aisle in the shadows. A flicker of long-lost humour tried to return to Father Bree as he thought, 'Pierre's confessions would take all night'. The request sounded urgent. He opened the portal a crack to see if the lights of patrol vehicles glistened through the snow. The roads were dark. He slammed the heavy bolts into their sockets and followed. Bernay was already in one stall and Bree sat on the step, saving his leg. This was the only way messages could be passed with any degree of safety.

'Flier . . . near my hut.' The woodman grunted almost before Bree got settled. There was sharpness to his tone that made the priest turn his head to see his expression.

'Hurt?'

'Dead!'

'Why come here? You must tell Bruno.'

'No!' Bernay's voice hardened without getting louder. 'I need his boots.' He stuck a leg to show his tattered, soaking shoes. Bree didn't look. He knew Bernay needed better boots. Every villager did.

'You know what will happen.'

'I know. I'll die. I'll die anyway if I don't get boots. And you'll die because you'll get no wood.' The young priest grimaced his agreement in the darkness and tugged his cloak around his throat. No Bernay meant no wood and no rabbit stew.

'What's your plan, Pierre?'

'I'll take his boots and bury the body. Nobody'll know.'

'They'll see the dirt in the snow.'

'I'll put him in Goineau's grave.'

The priest wiped his nose slowly and smiled at his wily friend. Bernard Goineau had been one of the oldest men in Ste Agathe until he failed to arise last week. Bruno detailed two soldiers to dig his grave.

Goineau had been lowered to rest in a snowstorm, but the soil was too hard to fill the grave. A few token spades of dirt were scraped over him, some snow, and that was all. The grave was still open.

'Where is he?'

'Outside!'

The priest jerked and his crutches clattered to the stone floor. 'The patrol!'

'Relax, *mon ami*. I'm no fool, you know. He sleeps . . . on my sled . . . wood for a cover . . . a fine rabbit for his pillow.' The old man chuckled. 'The bomber crashes, part of it goes 'plunk' in the swamp and disappears, part chops down trees by my hut which will help with firewood, and a hunk kills a rabbit. God is good.' He clambered out of the confessional closet. 'I saluted the guard at the bridge, he checked my papers and I passed, so we don't have to worry about him. Anyway, it's too cold for patrols.'

The priest hopped to a pew and settled back, a tired smile for his smart friend. 'We best get busy,' he said. 'You shall have the boots and I will have his warm socks, underwear, and maybe his gloves.' He fitted his crutches and hauled himself up. Bernay held his arm. They felt along the cold stone wall toward the portal, the candle lantern lighting the way. They had managed to get

59

half way when they both heard it.

They froze!

The ancient structure was full of creaks and groans as the storm battered Church Hill.

But this was a strange sound . . . an unnatural sound . . . a menacing sound . . . at the front.

They listened, their breath making tiny clouds in the flickering shadows.

A knocking . . . faint . . . repeated and persistent.

The priest breathed his thoughts, 'From the tower.'

The sound came again, this time a kind of thump, then scratching.

'Rats!' Bernay spoke aloud, throwing off the fear that had gripped him. 'Good. I'll trap and stew them. Rats are better than nothing.'

'Not rats.' Bree grunted. 'All were caught last winter.'

The woodman held on to the priest's surplice as they moved along the centre aisle toward the south porch. The sound seemed closer, more distinct. Bernay motioned the priest to stay while he kept on slowly, listening, until he was in the base of the tower, under the bellchamber. Now it was distinct, as if the wind was thrashing a branch against the side of the building. Impossible!

The church trees had been cut down and burned the first winter when there was a congregation.

'Outside, mebbe,' the woodchopper whispered as he joined the priest at the door. He pulled up his black hood and yanked back the bolts. 'I'll see.' The priest closed the door and leaned against it while he waited.

Bernay sheltered against a stone buttress until his eyes got accustomed to the eerie light of the snowstorm. He followed the gravel path, buffeted by the gale that swirled between the church and the rectory, until he came to the front of the building and was able to look up. The snow wet his cheeks and matted his beard. He squinted.

'*Mon Dieu!*' he breathed.

A white halo glowed from the spire. It spread down one side, undulating, like the wings of an angel fighting against the storm. No heavenly visitor, Bernay realized, as he made out the figure hanging beneath it, legs dangling, arms spread. It swayed and banged and scraped against the ancient siding. The old man crossed himself. He didn't believe in miracles, but here was someone from heaven, hanging on the cross, knocking to enter. He must be saved. Bernay hurried back to tell the priest.

'A flier, Father. His parachute caught on

the cross. We must save him.'

Father Bree knew he should tell the Germans immediately. That was the order. But he suddenly felt an inner glow of defiance, spiritual warmth he hadn't had in years. Perhaps it was a sign. And Bernay was a trusted ally.

'We can try.'

Bernay turned to go out again. 'Ladder, in the woodshed?'

'No, Pierre, better from inside.' Bree bolted the door, then squeezed the old man's gnarled hand, saying earnestly, 'These are evil days, *mon ami*, but I must do what I must do, even if I have to break my oaths to God and the Germans. Come.' He moved back into the vestry with more vigour than he had felt for months. 'Light the oil lamp, Pierre, there, on the shelf.' He was leaning against the wall, strapping pads onto his knee and stump. 'Another gift from the stone miners.' They went back into the tower and Bree placed the lamp on the baptismal font that was built into the original stonework of the foundation. The light shone on the plaque and the list of the parish priests over the centuries.

'See that cleft, Pierre, beneath the foot of the carved seraph. Put your fingers in there and pull the release.' Bernay did and there was a faint click, 'Secret passage?' he breathed.

'To the belfry. Not used since the bells were taken.' He leaned one crutch against the wall and grasped the edge of the plaque. The door creaked open to reveal a flight of narrow stone steps that disappeared into darkness.

'I'll go first,' Bree said. 'You follow with the lantern and light my way.' He left his crutches leaning against the baptismal font and went up on hands and pads. The dust swirled from their scuffling. The woodchopper followed. They reached a tiny stone landing in the tower corner and the steps turned to the left. Another flight and they emerged into a timbered room where the ropes from the three-bell peal were still looped over their pegs, their padded grips striped spirally in red and white cotton like a barber's poles. The walls were the stone parapets of the original tower on which the timber spire had been added. A plank bunk and low table was at the back. In the far corner, an open-treaded stairway, solid and safe, slanted upward into a narrow, dark trap.

Bree sat, panting and dirty, and pointed to the stairs. 'They go to a look-out room. Go up, Pierre. There are observation ports. They open in. See if you can reach him. I'll go get Nicole as soon as I get my breath; we'll need her strong arms.' He watched the woodman climb, the flickering light making dancing shadows on the rough timbers.

Bree slid rapidly down the worn steps, retrieved his crutches, and hurried to the narrow door that led to the covered rectory walk. The wind whipped his robes and almost made him lose his balance. The shelter kept the snow from drifting across the walk so that he made the kitchen door rather easily, although gasping for breath and feeling the tightness in his chest.

In the scullery, where a log still glowed on the cooking hearth, Nicole Joyal slept in the chimney alcove, her back against the warm stone. She woke at the priest's urgent whisper and opened her eye. She was the slow, lumbering daughter of the village tailor, strong, more like a boy, a familiar figure making deliveries for her father. When the Germans came to take away her mother and father to make uniforms, Nicole fought them, ran after the truck until the butt of a Mauser shattered the right side of her face. She fell, screaming and bleeding and lay in the street. A villager risked his life to cart her in his wheelbarrow up the hill to the church so that the priest could give her the last rites. Instead, Father Bree nursed her back to health, although she still had a terribly mutilated face and only one eye.

'Come, Nikki, we need you, hurry.' She pulled on her baggy trousers, loose sweater and German boots salvaged from the garbage behind the barracks. The priest stoked the fire into a blaze and added wood. He filled the kettle with water and put it close to the heat. He swung the soup pot over the blaze, all the time telling her what they were trying to do. Although she knew she could be shot for helping the 'enemy', she simply nodded and followed.

They found Bernay peering down through the trap, waiting. 'Have to go higher, Father. Gotta get above to release the harness. I need Nikki to help.' Without question, she left the priest squatting on the floor and climbed the steps confidently, grabbing Bernay's guiding hand. They were in a low room, not high enough to stand, with a stout, boarded floor, roughly finished. The room smelled of old lumber with a hint of smoke, as if a fire had burned there long ago. In the far corner, a round-runged ladder led to another level where the bells once hung.

'Up here,' Nikki followed as Bernay climbed. They moved carefully along a narrow walk to where a slatted frame had been removed. Snow was swirling in great gusts and the shrouds of the parachute were swaying and twisting outside. Above their heads, the spire narrowed and disappeared into darkness. 'Hold the lamp, Nikki.' Bernay slipped his skinning knife from its sheath, leaned over against the headstock where the bell once hung and slashed the rope. He pulled it up through the guide and coiled it around his arm. He clambered onto the sill and balanced with one hand holding the frame. He stretched down and looped the rope through the airman's harness. The muscles of his arms and legs were jumping they were so tired from chopping, lugging the body of the dead airman; loading the logs over him and pulling the sleigh through the forest down the road beside the falls and then into the churchyard. Ice was forming in his nostrils and on his beard from breathing so hard. He tossed the rope ends down to Nikki.

'Put down the lamp. Pull the rope when I lift.'

Balancing on the narrow sill, the wood-chopper grasped the silk cords with both hands. Then he stopped and fear swept over him and he almost fell out.

A car was roaring up Church Hill, slithering and skidding, headlights weaving through the snow. The alarm was on! Nikki heard it too and covered the light. Bernay gritted his teeth, closed his eyes and held on.

The lights flashed over the church. He waited for the squeal of the brakes, the slamming of doors, the guttural command that would send them to oblivion.

The vehicle slowed by the church gate, straightened and sped on. Bernay's breath whistled out in relief. The lights raced on and disappeared, 'Great German officer rushing someplace,' he muttered as he flexed his freezing fingers and grabbed the cords again.

'All clear, Nikki, heave!'

The flier's lolling head and shoulders came level.

'Heave!'

Bernay was able to grab the parachute harness and wrestle the body over the sill.

'Once more.'

He rested and blew on his fingers.

'Ready Nikki, ease him down.'

Together they worked on the airman's body inside, swung his legs over and lowered him to the walkway. Bernay sat, legs straddling the airman, and released the parachute harness. He pulled him along by the shoulder straps on his flight jacket while the girl guided the legs and brought the lantern. They reached the trap.

'Go down, Nikki. You guide. I'll lower.'

As gently as possible, Bernay swivelled the body until the legs slid down the opening. He straddled the trap and used the rope to slide it down the ladder on to the floor.

'*Bien!*' he grunted as he descended. 'Now down again.' Together they slid the airman to the steps where the priest waited. Finally, on hands and knees, the three manoeuvred their patient across the floor of the bellringers' room until he was beside the bunk.

'Now, slide your hands underneath.'

The priest was at the shoulders, Bernay under the buttocks, and Nicole at the legs.

'One, two, three, together,' Bernay grunted and they lifted the airman onto the plank bunk. The girl got the lantern from the floor and hung it from a peg on the wall at the head of the bunk.

'*Mon père!*' she gasped, 'look at his feet!' The toe of the right boot was pointing up, but the left foot was limp and level on the plank. 'His leg.'

Father Bree heaved himself up to sit on the edge beside the boy and unzipped the flight jacket. The skin was cold. His face was white like frozen stone. The hair was black and wavy. So young, the priest thought as he unbuttoned the blue battle tunic and slid his hand over the heart. He could feel a faint flutter and some warmth.

'He lives!' The priest whispered, 'A miracle!' and prayed that he might be saved.

He crossed himself and raised his head to look at Pierre. 'We better help the good Lord with this miracle.'

Nicole Joyal started to cut the flight suit from the left, then gave a sobbing gasp of despair when she saw his wound. The left leg was shredded below the knee, a hardened, frozen mash of bone and blood and flesh. Strands of wire garrotted the upper part of his leg, embedded deep into the padded pants of the flight suit. A bundle of ripped ends hung loosely, one still connected to a tiny contact. She was no stranger to smashed bodies and broken bones and motioned Bernay to come.

He took down the lantern and held it closer and shuddered. 'Nikki, we need bandages, needle and thread and hot water. We must be quick.' The girl put on the priest's helmet with the miner's candle still burning. She scuttled away on hands and knees and went slithering down the steps on her bottom. She hurried into the tiny sacristy and pulled out the sacramental cloths, stored away by the altar guild when the Germans were approaching; they were damp and musty, but they were clean. A pair of scissors, needles and thread was wrapped in oilpaper, waiting for the ladies to resume their religious embroidering, she grabbed this and stuffed sacramental candles into her pocket. Finally the little bottle of communion wine was shoved down the front of her sweater. She hurried them up the tower steps and, with only a meaningful grunt, passed them into the woodchopper's arms. Back down into the church she ran, through the narrow door, along the path into her scullery. She ripped the blankets and pillow from her grass-filled pallet and rushed them back to the tower room. The next trip took her longer. She raked up the ashes and fed more wood. She stirred the rabbit and potato stew and put a metal beaker to warm. She moved the kettle closer to the fire and put a tin pan beside the beaker. When all were hotter than she could touch, she pulled on her leather mitts, placed the kettle in the pan, filled the beaker with soup and slid it into the kettle, and carefully carried it back into the church and up the belfry steps. Then she sat on the floor, crossed her legs and watched as Bernay unsheathed his skinning knife to cut the wire. He stopped when he saw how tightly they were holding the flying suit to the wound. He slit open the trouser leg further.

'Mother of God!'

The leg was a mass of flesh and bone and blood and cloth, frozen solid. The foot was flat on the plank. He'd gutted rabbits and deer for food. He'd slaughtered calves in the field. He'd even dug bullets out of his buddies when France was still fighting. But this? What could he do? Save the leg. No! He honed his knife briefly on his trousers.

'Better get started,' he said to himself, 'Or I'll never get done.'

He saw the bottle of wine, yanked out the glass stopper and drank. The wine was bitter, like vinegar, and made him swallow rapidly. Then he poured some on the blade of his knife. The amputation was easy. No bones to saw. He cut through tendons and muscle with a few deft strokes, but left as much of the skin as he could. He pulled the padded material of the flying suit and folded it over the bloody end of the amputated leg. He lifted up the amputation and held it out without turning his head.

Nikki was beside him. She took it without a sound, removed the boot, and slithered away down the steps. She left by the south porch this time, crouching against the wind and snow and struggled into the churchyard. Bernard Goineau's open grave was only a shallow depression in the snow. She shoved the limb down out of sight. No need to smooth the surface. The wind would do that in seconds. She went back to the kitchen, filled another pot with snow and hung it over the fire to boil. On her way through the church she detoured into the small choir loft and stripped it of cushions and kneeling pads. Then she collapsed on the wooden floor and watched.

Pierre Bernay continued his surgery.

'Help me, Nikki.'

The girl came to his side and looked at the mangled limb. 'Take off your mitts. See the artery there?' He pointed with his bloody knife. 'Use your fingers and stretch it out for me.' She grasped the edge of the bunk and swayed.

'Don't be afraid, little girl. He can feel nothing.'

She grasped the dangling artery and pulled it away from the flesh and bone.

'*Bien*! Now I tie a little knot with the good ladies' embroidery thread, like that. Now that other artery there, like that. Tie again, then we snip off the ends with the ladies' little scissors, like that, and that's done.' He tucked the arteries into the flesh.

'The knee is OK so we'll bend it back as far as it will go and hide those nasty, jagged bones back there.' He delicately folded the flaps of skin over the jagged parts of the knee and sewed, one after another until the raw wound was covered.

'Maybe not such neat stitches as the ladies

sew, but they will do. Now, my good nurse, hold up the stump.'

The great wound was bandaged with layers of altar cloth and bound with towels until it was well padded. He wound thread around many times while Nikki held it up. The priest was sponging the boy's face and hands with towels warmed in the pan of water. A faint sigh and rapid breathing were encouraging signs of life, and there seemed to be a little colour in the lips. Bernay finished padding and bandaging the stump. She helped him fit the cushions along the wall, then slid the pillow under the patient's head and spread her blankets over him.

The three slid to the floor, exhausted.

'Thank you,' Bernay said, grateful that the girl had remained so calm and efficient, knowing that they would be shot if the Germans caught them helping the enemy. 'He felt no pain, but when it thaws . . . ' He slumped against the wall and closed his eyes. 'I must go. Soon as he wakes, hot soup, hot water and lots to drink.' The trio rested.

Nikki looked at the boy under her blankets. She knew he would live. Father Bree would save him. He had saved her life. She gave him love in return. It was all she had. She loved him like a sister. She loved him like a daughter. In the fantasy of her dreams she loved him like a lover. And she loved him like a mother when he was sick and weak and in pain. Father Bree was a man of God and God was in him, even now.

The woodman returned to his patient. 'Now I'll finish.' He tackled the wire. His knife loosened tie strands that were imbedded in the cloth. He worked several coils over the stump and dropped them to the floor. He sheathed his skinning knife and reached into a pocket for his clasp knife. With its jagged edge he sawed through the rest of the wires. Using his sharp knife again, he cut back the clothing until the bandages settled easily.

'He will live?' Nikki asked, and her eye showed tired concern.

'He will live,' the old man repeated. 'Dr Bernay said so. Now I will go.' He slumped once again to recover some strength and almost fell asleep.

A blast of wind shook the tower and they heard the knocking again. His head snapped up and he was wide-awake.

'The parachute!'

He groaned with fatigue as he struggled to his knees.

'They'll see it when it gets light!'

He crawled toward the ladder and regained the belfry. The shrouds and buckles were thrashing against the spire. He climbed, grabbed and yanked. He held on and raised both feet off the sill. He collapsed inside, gasping and wild-eyed. They could see his dejection when he returned to slump at the bottom of the steps.

'I can't pull it down. I can do nothing.' He leaned back against the ladder and the flickering lantern made his face into a shadowy black mask. 'What shall we do?'

Father Bree closed his eyes and felt the cold tentacles of defeat twine inside him. They would fail. They had tried to do God's bidding, be kind, save a life, and they had failed. His faith deserted him and he felt like a hollow shell, nothing remained. For some reason the warm face of an old teacher swam across his mind's eye; a glimmer from the seminary, the kindly wise man who taught theology, who believed so totally in the resurrection, life after death, the promise that it was not over that . . . the dead . . . the dead may help the living. In one brilliant flash that lit his mind and jolted through his senses like an electric shock, he saw it.

'The other one!' he exclaimed.

Bernay's mouth was sagging open, showing his brown, chipped teeth and he made no response.

'The one on your sleigh!'

The woodchopper stared at the priest with

dull eyes. Slowly the bearded face curled into a crafty smile and the look brightened. He scrambled to his feet. 'You are one smart priest!' He shook the girl by the shoulder. 'Come, Nikki.'

Together they hurried down the steps, through the church and out into the night. The snow was easing, but the cold winds persisted, sculpting forms around every obstruction. They scampered around behind the rectory where Bernay's sleigh was half buried in a drift. Snow and logs fell aside under their frantic efforts until the corpse was bare.

'Who's this?' She stared at the frozen corpse.

'Later.' Pierre lifted it by the shoulders and it sagged across his shoulder.

'Lift the feet.'

Nikki hoisted the feet onto her shoulder and together they carried the corpse toward the church. Twice they slipped and fell under their load and silently recovered. Inside, they moved rapidly through the nave and up into the belfry. The parachute harness was still on the catwalk, with snow sprinkling over it from the open louvers. Bernay fastened it on to the corpse, then reached for the discarded rope. He threaded it through the back strap and tossed it over a timber beam.

'You pull while I heave him up.' The corpse came upright, bobbing and turning, making grotesque shadows inside the steeple.

'Hold him. He's a heavy bugger.'

The woodman climbed on the sill, grabbed the flailing shrouds and pulled them in.

'Now, Nikki, one last hoist and . . . ' He snapped the metal loops onto the harness. 'And out he goes.' He looked longingly at the boots, almost new, and with one mighty shove, they teetered the airman over the sill and left him dangling in the coming dawn. They closed the open ports and slid down to join the priest.

Father Bree was trying to spoon soup between the boy's lips but it bubbled up and dribbled down his chin.

'What's his name?' Nikki asked as she slid to the floor and massaged her arms.

Bree opened his eyes with sudden realization and nodded. He searched around the neck for a chain. The identity discs were at the back and he had to lift the head to get them free. Bernay held the lantern close.

'Pilgrim, Joseph Adam. Canadian. RCAF. R.C. — R202260.' His face reflected wonderment. 'Pilgrim! And a Catholic.' He was silent in meditation. His racing mind wondered if this was a divine sign, a miracle, a wounded Christian from above, cloaked in a storm, saved by the cross of Ste Agathe.

'Hooking the spire saved his life,' Bernay supposed, as if reading the cleric's mind and bringing him back to reality. 'So did the wire around his leg, if he'd hit the ground he would have been helpless and would have frozen to death.' He shrugged. 'The freezing weather probably stopped the bleeding, too.' He moved towards the steps. 'Someone up there must like Joseph Adam Pilgrim.' They went down to the church. Nikki and Pierre collapsed on a pew while the priest closed the ancient door. When it clicked closed, he turned and pointed a crutch at the girl.

'Nikki, off to bed. Fast. You have been in bed all night and know nothing. Pierre, you had better sling the wood into the shed. Then go in and sleep on the couch. You brought the church's quota of wood and decided to stay the night because of the storm.'

'And you, Father?'

'The sound of the storm kept me awake. I came to my church to see if all was well. I saw an enemy hanging from a parachute, hooked on the steeple. My orders are to report such things to Captain Bruno. That's what you will tell the Germans if they come before I get back.' He went into the vestry and put on the heavy cloak and a wool toque. 'I'll go and report.'

78

He was so tired that his leg was throbbing and would barely hold his weight. He managed a nod and a cross for the altar before he left the shelter of the sanctuary and set off down the steep, winding road from Church Hill. He slipped frequently. He fell several times and sobbed his anguish into the snow as he rested his head on his arm. The padding on his knee and stump cushioned the impact, but an elbow cracked on a rock and he cried with pain. A crutch slipped away from his feeble grip and slid down the slope. He followed on his knees and belly until he had it firmly in place again and stood erect. His shoulders ached. His hands were stiff with the cold. His shoes and garments were soaked. He couldn't stop his teeth from chattering. The stabbing pain in his chest worried him the most. The sky was clearing but the gusting wind continued to drive the snow in blinding squalls when his squinting eyes finally saw the guard shelter behind the parapet of the humpback bridge, which carried villagers and conquerors over the Vesle River.

He straightened and held his head as high as he could. 'Guard!' he croaked. The wind blew his voice away. He staggered on. 'Guard!' After three shouts the young German heard and came running, rifle at his side.

'Paratrooper!' Bree gasped, 'At the church.'

The soldier whirled and raced across the village square, shooting his rifle in the air and shouting. A light went on in the town hall that was now garrison headquarters and a second voice took up the cry 'They've landed! They've landed!'

The priest heard it faintly and knew he could do no more. He shuffled into the shelter of the bridge parapet, sank to his buttocks, slowly rolled on his side and pulled the great cloak about him. Mental and bodily exhaustion rolled over him like a black, comforting blanket. He felt no guilt about his deception. He was comforted by the increasing roar of engines as the entire garrison awakened to invasion alert. The warmth of his faith spread through him and he dreamed of paradise.

★ ★ ★

Captain Bruno slid bare feet into combat boots, hauled his greatcoat over his pyjamas, slapped on his helmet and shouted orders in the quarters that were already full of confusion. He gained the compound as a Porsche armoured personnel carrier loaded with troops ground its gears to commence rolling. He ejected the gunner beside the driver and climbed in, waving action. They roared out of the barbed wire fencing, across the bridge and started skidding up the steep curves of Church Hill. The entire squadron of armoured vehicles was fanning out across the valley, with the main force using the south exit to reach the flat fields that were their action stations. In the communications centre signallers were transmitting coded messages for enemy alert.

Bruno's carrier skidded onto the flat yard in front of the church where other vehicles were blasting clouds of exhaust gases into the frigid air and gunners were hunched over their swivel-mounted Schmeissers. He jumped out and stared up at the body swaying and bumping against the church spire. A sergeant marched up, saluted, 'British, sir, presumed dead. The French woodchopper says an aircraft crashed in the forest.' Bruno ordered his troops to form a defensive perimeter, protecting the guards on the upper bridge. He turned and marched back to the woodshed where a shabby Frenchman was slumped on a pile of firewood in front of a shed, circled by soldiers who pointed their weapons at him. Bruno recognized Bernay and ordered the guards away with an angry sweep of his arm.

'What are you doing here?' he demanded in

his limited French.

'I brought the quota of wood for the priest,' was the dispirited reply. 'The big storm,' Pierre gestured behind him, 'slowed me down and I'm still unloading the damn stuff.' Then as if to gain German pity, he added, 'It's damn cold, eh?'

'Where are the paratroops?' Bruno demanded.

The old Frenchman shrugged. 'A big plane crashed in the Forêt du Nord.' His hands waved expressively. 'Most of it went in the swamp and some in the bush.'

Bruno swivelled away toward his troops and rapped out orders that sent most of his force racing to the bridge above the falls and north to the forest. A tank recovery crane ground slowly up the hill toward the church, its mighty treads chewing up ancient flagstones and memorial plots. It stopped and flopped down supportive pods, then the hydraulic arm reached up and out, hooked the shrouds of the parachute and yanked. The silken fabric stretched but did not give. The arm raised slowly, lifting the silken lines higher, and jerked. The cross of Ste Agathe cracked, splintered and dove into the ground near the tower base. The body came down feet first, hit the porch roof, bounced, and thumped into the snow. It rolled once, threw one arm over, and lay still. Bruno wheeled and marched to where a corporal and his platoon were gathering up the remnants of the parachute and corpse. He saw immediately that this was no armed paratrooper, but an enemy airman. He relaxed. This was not the invasion. There were no great fleets of attacking aircraft, as he had been briefed to expect. Perhaps a diversion, by the maquis. Perhaps . . .

Bernay stumbled to his feet and staggered over, plucking at the German's sleeve. 'Where's Father Bree?' He pulled a crumpled paper from his parka pocket. 'He has to sign for my wood so I can get past your guard by the bridge.' Bruno knew all about that. He issued the forms to make make sure this Frenchman didn't smuggle wood to the villagers.

'Haven't you seen him?' the German snapped.

Bernay spread his arms and shrugged, shaking his head.

Bruno was thinking furiously. Headquarters would demand a complete report of why he deployed his full complement in battle formation because one airman came down in a parachute and hooked on the church spire. He needed a good story. How did the invasion alert originate? Was this a false alarm triggered by the French resistance? Was there any indication of military activity amongst the locals? Where was the damn priest? He gave orders to his two lieutenants to start finding some answers. Then he was driven back to his office where he hoped the orderly had a good fire and warm drinks.

Father Bree was unconscious when they found him almost buried in the drifts beside the bridge wall. They carried him into the little infirmary that was once the mayor's office. After a quick examination, the doctor said, with a terminal shrug, 'pneumonia' and went to leave. Bruno stopped him. The guard from the bridge had testified that the priest had shouted, 'paratrooper'. He needed the priest to support that story, and provide somewhere to shift the blame. 'Save him,' he ordered the medic. 'Move him to your medical wing and save him!'

He turned to his orderly officer. 'Have the airman buried in the plot on the hill. He is a dead warrior and we will give him his due.' That will show that the German army respects the dead and will help to keep the villagers in line if the priest does not live. If he was going to keep this cosy posting, headquarters must be satisfied that he believed the invasion had started and simply followed orders. So, if Father Bree continued to cooperate, he'd survive the inquiry that he knew would come.

While the soldiers were clambering back onto their carriers and the vehicles were churning up gravel and snow in the courtyard, Pierre Bernay carried wood from his sleigh into the shed. When it was unloaded, he tipped it up against the wall and cleaned packed snow and ice from the runners. As soon as the last half-track disappeared down the hill, he dragged the rabbit from under the logs, and dug a little deeper for several frozen potatoes and carrots. He carried them into the kitchen where Nikki Joyal was sitting cross-legged on her straw mattress and leaning against the chimney.

She sagged with relief when she saw him.

'I thought they were coming for me.' Her battered face was weary and desperate, but her eye was eager for news. 'What was all the noise?'

'They came to get the parachutist. I think they thought it was the invasion.' He gave a guttural laugh and stirred the fire.

'Where's Father Bree?'

'Still down in the village.'

'Are they keeping him?'

'I wouldn't think so. He's exhausted. Probably resting someplace.' He split some wood. 'Get the pot boiling, Nikki. We're gonna eat.'

With his skinning knife he rapidly chopped the vegetables ready for the stew. The frozen rabbit took a little longer to prepare, because he wanted to save the hide. As the wind blew itself out and dawn crept over Vesle Valley, the old man and the girl ate their best meal in days. 'Save some for Father,' he cajoled, 'and a little hot broth for the boy in the tower.'

When they were finished they crept back to the tower to see their patient. Joseph Pilgrim lay in his plank bunk, padded with choir cushions and bandaged with communion cloths, his body struggling to survive the battering, his mind successfully pushing away receding waves of coma. His mother's worried face floated up and down in the mists, as if she was drifting toward him gently. The dreamy feeling was washing away as jagged jolts destroyed the peace. My leg, Mother, it hurts. And I'm cold. Why am I so cold? It's right inside me. And I'm hungry. Hungry and cold and hurting. Suddenly the scene became lighter.

'Is he alive?' Nikki ventured as the woodsman pulled back the blankets that covered his face. The boy's skin showed a hint of colour. The stump was a mass of crusted blood as the flesh thawed. It was barely warm.

'He lives. My doctoring looks good. But

. . . fever . . . pneumonia.' He wrapped a folded altar cloth over the bloodied bandages and used more thread. 'We must keep him warm. And lots of hot drink, when he is awake.'

Faintly, as if in an empty hall, Joseph heard voices. He knew not what they said, but it was comforting to know others were with him in this strange world. His fingers were tingling and he moved them. Coldness grasped his hand.

'He's moving his fingers,' Nikki whispered, and she clasped his hand.

They were talking like his mother, and his priest, not like the officers who had ordered him about so often in the air force. He felt the warmth of home seeping inside him, but his leg still throbbed and pained. They shot my leg mother, but I'll be OK. Then he heard the friendly voice again.

'Try a little broth.'

The girl slid her hand under his head and tried to spoon hot liquid between the colourless lips. There was no response, except a little bubbling from his rapid breathing.

'Too soon.' Bernay piled the blankets over him and shoved the cushions closer to keep him from rolling off. 'I must go, Nikki. I'll come back during the night. Tell Father Bree.'

The French girl lingered with the battered

boy for several minutes after the woodsman had left, watching for a flicker of an eye or the twitch of a muscle. Finally she returned to the rectory and busied herself with the domestic routine. She cleaned the priest's room and prepared his bed for his return, praying that he was safe. When it was light, she went frequently to the study window where she could see down Church Hill. She watched two soldiers climb the hill behind the barracks. Close to the spot where two German soldiers had been buried last summer, they used picks and shovels to dig a grave. Two hours later she watched a small contingent stumble through the drifts, four of them carrying a shrouded body on a canvas stretcher. For a few minutes they clustered, a small, black grouping against the grey horizon. The brief ceremony over, they returned, leaving the shovellers to finish. Warrant Officer Second Class Lloyd Hogan, American citizen, Royal Canadian Air Force pilot attached to the Royal Air Force, had landed for the last time, and nothing marked his ending.

Captain Bruno brought Father Bree back to his rectory just after dark that night. Two medical orderlies lifted him from the back seat of the staff car and carried him in between them. One returned for his crutches and cape, the other helped him to his bed.

'He's very ill,' Bruno told Nikki in his schoolboy French. 'He has pneumonia, but if you keep him warm and give him these pills, he should get better. I have also brought some high energy rations which are issued to our soldiers.' She cringed inside as he patted her on the head and placed a package on the table. 'We Germans are not all bad,' he said, and Nikki wondered what he was after. The orderly inspected the priest's stump and re-bandaged it. 'Father Bree injured himself while he came to report.' Bruno continued. 'He must have fallen while bringing the message. He was very brave.'

Nikki spat on their footprints in the snow after they had gone and then moved from room-to-room waving a tiny wooden cross as her effort at purification. She checked her priest regularly until he awoke and then fed him his portion of the rabbit stew, as hot as he could stand. She made him swallow his medication and let him sleep while darkness covered the valley and one precious candle lighted his room.

When dawn arrived, he stirred, raised his head, and called Nicole. 'Bring me my Bible, my precious helper, and sit close.' When she had done as she was asked, he placed his pale, cold hand on the Scriptures: 'I must confess. I have no priest to absolve me. I will confess to God on His Book with you as my witness. I have made a pact with the devil.' He settled back and closed his eyes. 'I will explain, so you will understand, and you must tell Pierre, but nobody else, nobody else.' She moved close because his voice faded at times until only a whisper. 'I reached the bridge at the bottom of the hill and told the guard there was a paratrooper at our church. That was a lie, which I must confess but I did it on purpose so there would be a lot of confusion and they wouldn't search the church. The guard thought the invasion had started and fired his rifle into the air. Bruno turned out his whole garrison as he is supposed to do when the invasion comes. Now he must explain to headquarters why he ordered a false alert because one dead airman was hooked on the spire. He wanted to report that I reported that paratroopers had landed and the assault had commenced. I knew if Bruno was sent away and there was an inquiry, the boy in the tower would be found and Pierre, you and I would be sent away, or shot. So to save us all, I agreed. I also had to admit, for his report, that I had heard confessions that the villagers had received arms and were ready to revolt and kill the soldiers. I suggested that my people would feel better if

90

he gave the dead airman a decent burial.'

'He did,' Nikki confirmed. 'I saw them, on the hill, behind the barracks.'

Bree opened his eyes. 'Good. And how is Pilgrim?'

'Still unconscious. Pierre said he was afraid of his developing pneumonia.'

'Ah, yes, the doctor was very unkind but Bruno made him send pills for me. We can share them with the boy. Now I must sleep.'

For four days, while Father Bree tossed in his fever bed and Joseph Pilgrim groaned and cried with the pain of his wound, Nicole Joyal nursed and fed her patients, ever anxious that a watchful German guard would ask why she was visiting the church at night. Although she talked and crooned to him, the airman did not speak.

The second day, Pierre Bernay arrived just before dark, pulling an empty sleigh. 'I unloaded the wood for the Germans.' He reached under his great parka coat. 'But I kept this big, fat muskrat for our pot.' He laughed and hacked it into stewing meat with his favourite knife. When he had finished, he washed in the bucket and padded into the bedroom to check on the priest. 'Better,' he reported with the wisdom of a veteran physician 'The fever is going. In two days, we must give him a good bath. How is the boy?'

he asked, jerking his head in the direction of the church.

'Still not awake. I feed him hot soup. Some he swallows.'

'Good!' Bernay tightened up his jacket and pulled his hood close. 'I'm going out for a little time. Save me some stew.' He was gone almost an hour, and Nikki began to worry, until finally he came stamping and wheezing through the scullery, red-nosed, watery-eyed, but happy. He was grinning like a youngster and pointing to his feet.

'My boots!' He raised one foot in triumph. 'They buried the airman with his boots on. I gave him mine. No matter to him if they got big holes.' He sat and took them off, wiping them lovingly. Then he ate while Hogan's socks dried by the fire. When they had eaten, he dressed, and was gone again into the cold, winter night.

Two nights later he was back with wood to build a great fire and heat all the buckets and pans. Nikki hauled the big tin tub from the outhouse and poured in water until the kitchen was full of steam. Pierre went into the little bedroom. 'Come, Father, a bath to kill the fever.' Bree was very weak getting out of bed but with the woodsman and the girl supporting him, he hopped into the warm room and stood wheezing for breath as they stripped off his nightshirt. Nikki brought his crutches so he could straddle the tub and use them as guides while they lowered him slowly into the water. At first his eyes went wide with the warmth, then he lay back with a sigh of enjoyment and worked the knots out of his leg muscles. Nikki poured more water into the washtub and boiled his clothes, like her mother had taught her, to kill the germs. They wrapped him in a flannel blanket, fed him more of the German pills and supported him as he hopped back to bed where he slept for twelve hours. When he awoke, the fever was gone. He called for his crutches with surprising vitality and Nikki smiled that her priest was mobile again.

The other patient lying on the wooden bunk in the church steeple was making slower progress. The throbbing pain was easing slightly so that Pilgrim's tortured brain drifted more and more out of the paralysing blackness and toward the light of consciousness. The hazy world of dreams, in which his mother was so dominant and yet so ethereal, gradually changed to a pattern of wooden braces that didn't look like a person at all. He could hear creaking of timbers far above him and the moan of the wind all around him, bringing back the searing horror of his disintegrating bomber. He could hear the screech of metal tearing apart, the overpowering turmoil of wind, and then a strange silence that seemed like another world, a place of quiet and peace and sleep. The vision blurred and faded as a cold hand caressed his neck and raised his head. Hot fluid warmed his lips and he swallowed. He seemed to see a white fuzzy shape bobbing in the blackness as the sounds of his anguish came back into his tortured brain.

Some days Nikki wept in frustration and doubt. Others she was grateful for the flicker of an eyelid and prayed her gratitude to the saints of healing and mercy. On 6 December, 1943, two weeks after he had left RAF Station Waddington on his first operation, although he had no idea of time, Sergeant Navigator Joseph Pilgrim came out of his coma and looked around at total darkness. He felt someone holding his hand and crooning softly as his mother used to do. Nikki closed her eye and whispered another prayer of thanksgiving.

'Mother?' His throat barely formed the word.

'Joseph!' a strange voice replied in the blackness, 'You have come back to us at last.'

He felt the hardness of his bed, the coarseness of his blanket, the coldness of his room. 'Where am I?'

'You speak French?'

Pilgrim croaked a 'yes' and she gave him a sip of water.

'Good! That makes it easier. You're safe,' Nikki answered softly. 'You've been badly hurt.' Quietly, as if reciting a dream, Nicole Joyal told him what had happened since he was suspended on the Cross of Ste Agathe. She spoke French with an unusual accent and he strained to hear every word. 'You're still in great danger, Joseph Pilgrim. If the Germans find you, we will be executed and you will go to prison camp. We can come safely only at night and when the patrols have passed. We have little food. We are always hungry, but we will share with you. Be quiet and rest during the day. We will come again tonight.'

'Is this a church?'

'Yes. A small room in the tower.'

'Who else is here?'

'Father Bree sleeps in the rectory. Pierre Bernay saved you. He lives in the Forêt du Nord. Nobody else knows you're here. We'll tell nobody, because we can trust nobody. The Germans control everyone. If you have pain, you must be silent.'

The young airman from St Jean-sur-Richelieu in Canada thought about his survival. Was it a miracle, his parachute catching on the cross? Was it his mother's blessing that had guided him here? Was this the divine destiny that his mother taught and believed? He clenched his fists with the throbbing of the great wound and the pain was so intense that his brain took pity and he slipped back into restful sleep.

The next night Father Bree was able to crawl up the stone steps on his padded knees, with a bottle of hot soup inside his habit. While he sat on the bunk and fed the boy the hot fluid in great gulps, he listened silently while Pilgrim babbled disjointedly about his mother, her belief in divine protection, about her singing in the chapel, the games played on the frozen river, and on and on until he finally was silent from exhaustion. Nothing about his air force days, the priest noted, no questions about the destruction of his aircraft, or what happened to his friends in the crew. Strange, Father Bree thought, and although he admired the boy's sincerity and his devotion to his mother, felt he must also make him aware of reality.

'You have been saved, my son, by the blessed kindness of God, but also by three friends, Pierre, Nicole and me. We are risking our lives to hide you, but we will die if you are discovered. Never forget that the Germans are outside. So do as you are told, you understand.' The sallow face, now showing thick whiskers, mouthed faint agreement. 'Now do you feel strong enough to sit?'

In answer, Pilgrim swung his leg from under the covers and wiggled his toes.

Two nights later, when the clouds were low and the darkness deep, Pierre Bernay slipped into the rectory again. 'We must get the boy here for a bath. The bandages must be changed. Father, you look after the hot water. Nikki and I will make a sling.' He wrapped a pillow in a blanket from the priest's bed and led the way to the tower room. In darkness they lowered Pilgrim onto the padded sling. Bernay gathered one end of the blanket and Nikki lifted the other. 'This will hurt but you must not make a sound,' the woodman ordered as they wrestled him down the stone steps. They rested at the tiny landing and moved the pillow under Pilgrim's buttocks. Pierre went first down the straight descent to the church, taking most of the load over his back and shoulders. Across the cold, stone floor they slid him, over the snow of the path, and in through the scullery door to the warmth of the kitchen.

As they came into the light, Nicole pulled a black patch over her right eye socket and tightened the scarf to hide her face. Pilgrim stank of urine, excrement and stale sweat. He sat wearily on a chair beside the tub while they removed his tunic, shirt, and underwear. Bernay supported him while they pulled loose his faeces-encrusted trousers and pants. Nicole gathered the filthy uniform and took them to the scullery where the laundry tub was bubbling over the fire. She tipped them in and hurried back. Pilgrim sat on the low stool beside the bath, swung his leg over the side and they lowered him slowly. He cried out for the first time when the warm water hit his stump. Carefully he settled back and relaxed as his body warmed. The water slowly became red in little strings and swirls. Bernay made no attempt to loosen the bandages but instead scrubbed him until the water was brown.

'Now, out you come and we'll dump this dirty water,' and Pilgrim was lifted back onto the chair. Nikki dragged the tub to the floor drain, emptied it and brought it back. She was just reaching for the kettle to re-fill it when there was a banging on the front door.

They all froze.

'Germans,' Bernay whispered, then acted swiftly.

'Off with your clothes, Father, and into the tub.'

He grabbed the airman under his shoulders. 'Come, up, lean on me.' He almost carried the one-legged airman into the bedroom, lowered him onto the bed and covered him with blankets. 'Lie still or you're dead,' he hissed as he left and closed the door.

He motioned Nikki away, 'Go, out of sight, anywhere, fast.'

The commanding knock was repeated.

The priest was naked and climbed into the empty tub, laying his crutches on each side. Bernay poured in water, lathered his back and went to the door with dripping hands,

He opened it carefully.

A German soldier barged in, bringing with him wind and cold air.

'Come in, sir,' Bernay said, pointing to the kitchen. 'Father is bathing.' He hurried back and began pouring more warm water. 'Father's been very sick. Pneumonia. Captain Bruno gave him pills and saved his life. He is getting better. But weak, weak.' Bernay kept talking as he continued to wash Bree's back. 'He cannot bathe alone.'

The German edged in, looking slightly uncomfortable after the imperious entrance.

'I know he has been sick,' the soldier said in halting French. 'I'm the medical orderly.' He moved closer to the bath and squatted. 'You're better, Father? No fever?'

Bree managed a croaking response and nodded while splashing water over his torso.

'Captain Bruno sent me to see how you were, and ask you to sign this statement.' He pulled a folded document from an envelope and a pen from his tunic pocket. He held it out.

'It's in German,' Bree said as Bernay helped him to stand and wrapped a towel around him.

'The same statement that you made to Captain Bruno.'

'Then I will sign.' The priest dried his hand, took the pen and added his name.

'And I will witness.' The orderly scribbled, put the pen in his pocket, the document in the envelope, clicked his heels, turned and marched out.

The priest stared at the door for a long time, then looked at his friend. 'I had no choice, Pierre. Bruno is in trouble with headquarters. If he goes, Spaegle will take over and he's the devil.'

'You don't know what you signed.'

'It puts the blame on the guard for panicking and firing his rifle and shouting that the invasion had started. It praises me for reporting the parachute, even though I made a mistake and thought it was a paratrooper.' He looked at his friend for understanding. 'We have come through this better than I expected.'

Bernay nodded. 'Finish your bath, Father, he may return.' When the priest was done and in his nightclothes, Bernay went outside and made a quiet circuit of the buildings. He gave the 'all clear' and went directly to Bree's bedroom.

'Come, airman Pilgrim, we must fix that leg.' He helped him back into the tub. 'Now we must soak off those cloths.' Carefully he loosened the crusted towels as they softened until the red and lumpy stump was bare. 'Good. No infection.' He massaged the tissue with goose grease, re-padded the bone and wrapped clean altar cloths around it. Nikki came with a warm drink, made from their tiny ration of powdered milk and water. 'Your clothes are washing.' She offered priestly habits, which Pilgrim put on.

'You're Nikki?'

She nodded and shrugged. She had discarded the patch and headscarf in the terror of the German intruder, and now stood humbly beside him.

'What happened to your face?'

She stared defiantly at him. 'The Germans.' She made a spitting sound and went into the scullery to pound the washing as it boiled.

They fell into a schedule. The priest resumed his routine as much as he could as his strength was slowly returning. A visit to the village left him weak and gasping and he worried about the chest pains after he'd climbed the hill. 'Nikki, I'll have to wait for spring, I think, to tackle that hill again.'

Nikki returned Pilgrim's uniform and told him to put it on. 'Father said you must wear it or you may be shot as a spy.' She brought hot food and drink every night and they talked in the darkness to save precious candles. She told him about her happy days in the village when her parents were successful tailors. 'There are a lot of caves in the hills where they cut stone for the buildings. We used to play in them and pretend we lived there. My favourite was in the gully just behind the church. I still go there, sometimes, when the weather is good, and pretend the Germans are not here and my mother and father are waiting for me at home. I'll show you some day.'

'Do you think I'll walk again?'

'Sure. Like Father Bree. He was young like you when his motorcycle skidded and shattered his leg. You will walk again.'

Joseph Pilgrim told her about Canada and the Richelieu River where he trapped eels and the great forests where they made maple syrup, and the church school where his mother taught about God and sang in the choir. They shared their hopes and their fears and Father Bree realized that his adopted ward was happier than she had been for a long, long, time.

Pierre Bernay brought a rope, with a cross handle at one end. He tied it to the rafter above the bunk so that Joseph could grasp it with both hands. 'You must exercise to strengthen your arms and shoulders. Soon I'll bring crutches and you can practice.'

The sixteenth day of December was so cold that the Vesle Falls froze solid and no water went under the humped bridges. Nikki took the last blanket from her bed and spread it over her sleeping patient. She slumped on the floor and shivered as the tiny candle made sparkles on the frost along the stone wall. She snuffed the light, pulled her coat around her and nodded in sleep until the cold awakened her. She climbed under the pile of blankets beside him and immediately went to sleep. When she awoke, her hand was across his chest and her fingers could feel the softness of his beard.

'Are you awake?' she whispered close to his ear. He grunted. 'I was cold so I got in with you to get warm.'

'Isn't your bed warm?'

She giggled. 'All my blankets are here.'

He swivelled to look at her. 'Why?'

'There are no more, except Father Bree's.'

He put him arms around her and pulled her close. 'I'm a bit of a burden, aren't I, eating your rations and stealing your blankets.' She snuggled. 'It's nice to share.' And they talked of many things until dawn and she had to leave.

And so another pattern developed in the little household on Church Hill in Ste Agathe. Two days later Nikki found him hopping around the tiny tower room, using the bunk and walls to steady himself. 'It's time you tried crutches.' But when she asked the priest about his spare pair, he shook his head sadly, 'They're in the vestry, Nicole, but one is broken. The handle's split.'

'Then I'll get it fixed.'

'How?'

'I'll take it to Jonquierre.'

'A long walk and it's very cold.'

She tossed her head in confidence, put on many clothes, got the crutch from the vestry, slung it over her shoulder and started down hill with a jaunty pace.

'I see happiness,' Father Bree mused as he watched her from his office window, and he was glad.

When she reached the bridge she saw Jacques, the waggoner coming along with his sleigh and the only horse left in the village.

The plodding of those weary hooves and the harness bells reminded her of happier times and she blinked away the tears. Jacques gave her a ride almost to the blacksmith's shanty.

'What happened?' Jonquierre asked, looking at the broken crutch. 'Father Bree fall?'

'Yes, but he's all right. Can you fix it, fast?'

Nikki sat by the little fire and soaked up the warmth while the blacksmith put a new iron pin in the handgrip. 'As good as new, little girl.' She thanked him with three of Bernay's carrots, taken from the secret storage in the woodshed and the blacksmith hid them fast.

The next night Joseph Pilgrim slid down the steps into the church all on his own. Father Bree was there to greet him while Nikki, jumping with excitement, watched for the patrol. Joseph needed no instruction. 'Used them before,' he grinned and struck off along the aisle beside the pews and around in front of the altar. First he was very cautious and moved slowly but after several turns around the church he walked faster. His left crutch slipped on the flagstone and down he went. He gave a gasp of pain as his tender stump hit the floor. He rolled over and clambered onto a front pew, holding his stump and rocking back and forth. The priest went into his vestry and returned with a set of kneepads. He sat beside his student and placed them on his lap. 'The stone cutters used these in the quarry caves when the ceilings were low. They'll save you a lot of pain.' Pilgrim fitted them on and practised up and down the church aisles until he was exhausted but happy.

He and the priest rested on the front pew. Joseph pointed to the crude drawing of a girl on the door above the list of rectors. 'Who's that, Father?'

'That's a crude, medieval painting of Ste Agathe. She's supposed to be the patron saint of bellringers, so I guess it's logical that it is on the door to the belfry.'

'She's carrying something on a platter.'

Father Bree gave a bit of a humorous snort. 'The old vicar who was here when I came told me the story, which I have difficulty believing. Let's call it mythology, then we don't have to believe it. Agathe was a Christian virgin, all saints have to be virgins, a Christian virgin, in Sicily in the early centuries. She was pursued by Quintian, the son of a noble family. She rejected him, so he tortured her but she fought to retain her virginity. He cut off her breasts and sent her wandering. She was portrayed carrying her breasts on a tray. The shapes evolved into bells and so she became the patron of bellringers.' Bree arose. 'A silly legend, Joseph. Now we must go.'

'One moment longer, Father.'

Joseph Pilgrim got painfully onto his one leg and went to the front of the church. He lowered himself onto his padded right knee before the altar and the faded statue of Mother Mary and prayed his gratitude for being alive, with a special message to his mother.

Pierre Bernay came by daylight on Christmas afternoon with more wood. Nicole made a great pot of stew with fresh beef that a villager had stolen from the barracks kitchen while collecting garbage. There were carrots and potatoes from the dwindling cache in the shed, and a precious onion that Mother Maas had grown in her garden and saved as a gift for her priest. Father Bree decorated the table with cones and leaves to give a touch of the season. Joseph Pilgrim put on the heavy cloak and cowl from the rectory and arrived rosy-cheeked and smiling, 'I made it!' he exclaimed, hugging each in turn. 'Thank you for my life. A wonderful Christmas present.' And so the four ate in the tiny rectory on the hill and prayed to the Prince of Peace although they knew that war and death were still their masters.

Joseph Pilgrim lay in his bunk that

Christmas night and thought of his home. What was his mother doing? Did she miss him? Was she crying? Praying for him? Was she singing in the candlelight Christmas mass? Would she know that he was sleeping with a girl? Was it bad when they kept their clothes on and warmed each other? Did her blessings really save him? Did she still believe he was alive? All the rest of his crew were dead so he'd be reported dead too. Maybe a miracle did wind that wire around his leg to stop him bleeding. Maybe a miracle did guide his parachute to the church steeple. But the rest was no miracle. Three courageous people saved him. He began to wonder about his mother's total faith in divine protection and decided that he should help a bit.

He reached up and grabbed the stick Bernay had suspended above his head. The stronger he was the more he could do. He exercised while he thought. Another miracle might get him out of here, but he figured the chances were mighty slim. He'd have to do it himself, and do it without endangering his friends in the rectory. They had enough problems of their own. A crippled priest trying to keep his church alive. A terribly disfigured girl living in fear. An old forester surviving on hunting. By the time he fell asleep, Joseph Pilgrim had made up his mind what he was going to do.

The next morning he climbed on hands and knees up the ladder into the lookout. He moved around from louver to louver studying the village, the road above the falls, the German barracks and vehicle pool, and the village square. It was cold and he crept back to the warmth of his bed after closing the trap.

That afternoon when Bernay visited on his way to the barracks with wood, he asked him to come to the steeple.

'Tell me directions, Pierre,' he asked, staring out an aperture. 'Is that west? Over the forest?'

Bernay corrected. 'No, no, *mon ami*, that is north and a little bit east.'

'And where is the coast?'

'North and west, that way.' He swept his arm in an arc.

'The British will come from that direction?'

'And Americans. Yes from that general direction, but we don't know where. It is a long coast. It could be anywhere.'

'Any idea when?'

Bernay looked at the airman for a long time. 'Not in a blizzard, that's f'sure.'

'Why not?'

'They will come by sea, most of them, we know that for sure. So do the Germans. They will come with soldiers from the air, paratroopers. The Germans know that too. So they will have to have many aircraft protecting the soldiers landing on the coast and the soldiers dropping from the sky. So I think for sure they will need good weather. But the Germans don't know when, and that's the big secret.' He shrugged and smiled. 'Donquierre at Café D'Or says this spring. He's guessing. Nobody knows.'

Pilgrim followed him down into the church and when he had gone, walked up and down the church aisle practising turning corners without slipping. His arms started to ache so he went into the vestry to rest in the big padded chair that was so comfortable . . . There he found a dusty wooden trunk of clerical robes, vestments and habits for priests to wear during masses and ceremonies and also outside. He selected several of the warmest and put them on. He rested in the sagging chair and thought about the dozens of priests who had used this vestry and had their names preserved on the door. He reached over and pulled back the curtain and saw the narrow door. He put on his kneepads to get closer. After a lot of shoving and hammering, it opened out and he saw a level, snow-covered plot surrounded by a low stone wall. To the right were gravestones and several tombs with large slab covers, some of them cracked and crumbling. The great stone sepulchral monument of the medieval Grenadine family loomed like a blunt-bowed ship with heraldic carvings and religious figures. A large angel spread white wings and arms in everlasting supplication for peace and goodwill on earth, which reminded Joseph of the Christmas cards his mother used to send to her friends. To the left was the road that passed in front of the church and headed north until it forked at the bridge and joined the main road to Sees. Having got the scene firmly in his mind by daylight, he returned that night and ventured out for a brief walk along the stone divider. He slipped only once and was pleased how rapidly his leg was getting stronger. He was able to move through the snow on his crutches without difficulty. Here was his exercise yard, he decided.

Again at dawn he climbed the ladder and watched the barracks at the far end of the valley. The kitchen at the rear showed a lot of activity and caught his attention. The borrowed habits proved remarkably warm and he was able to follow the action of the kitchen staff for over an hour. Another idea slid into his plan.

That night, when Nikki brought his food

and climbed under the blankets beside him, he talked about the village. 'Tell me everything you know about the streets and the buildings.'

She closed her eye and let the happy scenes of her youth roam across her mind and named the families who used to live in the cottages and the few old folk who remained. She described the few shops that clustered around the village hall with the shed for the fire wagon. The little schoolhouse came to life in her description with friends and teachers long gone. She talked about the mill at the bottom of the valley and the grand family that lived in The Seigneury.

'Is that the big place the Germans are using as barracks?'

'Yes, and the courtyard's full of trucks and tanks.'

'Is there a path from here down to it?'

'Yes, but you have to slide down the hill behind the priest's house and then there is a stretch of level ground. It goes past my cave . . . '

'Your cave? What's that?'

'I told you before, my sanctuary, my 'all alone' place. It's one of the larger caves which the stone masons cut to build the church and rectory. There're quite a few along the eastern cliffs and the youngsters turned them into play homes. I fixed mine up with chairs and a table and a little rug for the floor. I still go there when I want to cry for my mother and father and pray that we will live.' She was silent for a long time. 'I also go down to the big house and steal food from the garbage. The Germans are very wasteful,' she giggled. 'You've been eating some of it.'

He was silent.

'Are you angry?' she asked. 'Eating garbage?'

'No, Nikki. I'm ashamed that you have to risk your life to steal garbage to feed me.'

'It's fairly safe. Brush and trees except close to the house hide the path. You can't see my cave at all. It's covered with brambles and vines. I'll show you, if you can get over the wall.'

'Which wall?'

'The cemetery. It's about as high as my waist. I get over easy, but you . . . '

'I'll get over,' he promised. Every night that week he exercised in the vestry garden and practised getting over the wall. It wasn't easy. With two legs, he would have jumped and thought nothing about it. On crutches, he had to experiment. Several methods hurt and he dropped a crutch. Finally he perfected a combination of run, hop, swing the good leg, jam one crutch solidly on the other side, then his body and the other crutch over and stand. After two or three failures, he was able to do it in one motion without his stump hitting the ground at all. He went back to bed and rested with the exhilaration of his accomplishment flowing through his young body.

One starlit night there was a lot of noise in the valley, voices from the barracks and headquarters, engines of personnel carriers gunning and gears changing. A convoy of staff cars zoomed up Church Hill and took the road to Sees. He watched a bit fearfully until he suddenly realised: 'It's New Year's Eve! Tomorrow will be 1944.' A feeling of excitement swept over him and he felt daring. He put on the huge black cassock, which came down to his ankles and covered his crutches, with the deep hood that hid his face except straight in front. He clambered over the west wall of the vestry garden and headed along the north side of the church. He leaned in the shelter of the corner buttress and looked into the valley. There was a lot of activity so he figured the garrison was having a party. He rested on his crutches, the great cloak and hood flapping around him, his breath making moisture that froze on his beard. He pondered the scene and dreamed of St Jean, those happy days back home, the huge Christmas tree, his mother's beautiful voice singing those Christmas carols . . .

Suddenly he realised he heard voices!

At first he couldn't be sure where they came from in the stillness of the night.

There was the snatch of a song, the giggle of a girl, the hammer of a boot on a stone, a slurred remark . . .

He looked down the hill toward the village but all was clear.

He looked to his right and saw them.

Two German soldiers staggering toward him, supporting a girl between them.

He turned to escape back into the vestry.

One spotted him and shouted something in German.

Pilgrim froze and all the joy drained out of him. He was captured. They'd take the priest and the girl. Terror made the sweat burst out all over his body. His hands clenched the spools of his crutches.

The girl was singing. A companion shook her arm and she stopped. Then she saw Joseph and straightened. 'Sorry, Father,' she said in French. 'I didn't see you.' She nodded and hurried past. The German on the far side lowered his head and looked at the road as he tried to walk straight. The youngster on this side smiled, touched his cap in a clumsy salute and knocked it off. He bent unsteadily to pick it up while the girl giggled, made some remark that made them laugh and they weaved down Church Hill.

Pilgrim's whole body was trembling. His fear had turned to excitement. Strength flowed through his veins like adrenalin in a soccer game. His thoughts were racing at the possibilities that their mistake had opened up for him. This was an opportunity that he'd never thought about. And all because of a drunken German. He scratched his beard and smiled after them as he heard their happy cries sliding down the hill.

The next morning, the first day of the New Year, he decided to test his impersonation. He put on his warm priest's clothing, went out the vestry door and started up the north road, walking slowly but with no appearance of deception. The weather was clear and there were a lot of aircraft to the north. Periodically he could hear gunfire. The crutches settled comfortably under his arms and he started striding with more strength at a pace that seemed to cover the most distance with the least effort. He came to the fork in the road. One branch, the most heavily used, went right to Sees, where the Germans partied when on leave. The left led across the Vesle and into Forêt du Nord, the route that Bernay followed with his sleigh loads of firewood. The bombers were moving closer and the rumble of engines came on the wind. He paused for a few seconds when one black spot blossomed into a red sphere, arced earthward trailing smoke, then burst into a mottled cloud that slowly disappeared. He drove himself to maintain a pace that his breathing could handle without appearing to hurry. He was pleased that his heart was steady with no sharp pains in the chest.

As he approached the humped stone bridge over the river, the guard left the shelter of his hut and swivelled his rifle on the sling across his shoulders so that he could fire from the hip. Pilgrim kept the same pace, brushed past the snout of the gun, and collapsed on the low parapet of the bridge. He grinned at the guard through his tangle of beard and expressively mopped his brow.

'Been sick,' he said and the guard nodded, although he probably didn't understand French. 'Need exercise.' The guard offered his canteen, he took a drink, wiped his mouth and nodded toward the road back. He thumped away with a surge of excitement that carried him smoothly to the church vestry. He cried: 'I did it. I did it!' as he flung off the cloak and collapsed in the chair while the strength of youthful excitement swept over him.

The next evening Nikki brought his food as

soon as it was dark. She looked worried and blurted out: 'Father Bree is sick. I think he's really sick. Maybe the pneumonia has not all gone. He sits and sleeps and doesn't eat. He doesn't go out like he used to, down to the village to see the people. He was so good at cheering them up. They loved him because they knew it was hard for him to get around.'

'What did he do in the village?'

'Sit on the bench in the village square so the Germans could watch him. He never went in the homes, unless someone was very sick or dying. Then he would get permission and a soldier would go with him. He just listened and talked.'

Joseph ate in silence for several minutes, then decided it was the only way. Hesitatingly he told her his secret. 'Nikki . . . I've been exercising . . . outside . . . on my crutches . . . wearing the big cassock from the vestry. The other night I went to the front road. Two soldiers and a girl passed me. They thought I was Father Bree.' He heard her gasp in the darkness. 'Yesterday morning I went to the bridge above the falls. I spoke to the guard and he gave me a drink from his canteen. He thought I was Father Bree. D'you see what this means?' Now he was plunging ahead with enthusiasm. 'As long as Father Bree stays out of sight, I can go out. As soon as it gets a bit warmer, you and I will go down and sit on the bench in the square.'

She didn't answer.

'What do you think?' he persisted.

'I think you will be caught, we will be shot and that will be the end of Father Bree.'

'How will the Germans know? They've never met him, except for Bruno and a couple others. He's just a figure in vestments.'

'The villagers will know and someone will inform.'

'Tell them I've been ill, all winter, pneumonia.'

It was Nikki's turn to quietly think about this unexpected news. 'Well, it might work, but I think he should teach you some of his blessings and expressions. Your French is different, somehow.'

'No. I don't want him to know. If I'm caught, he can truthfully say he didn't know. It's safer for him that way. And maybe I shouldn't have told you, except I can't go into the village without you knowing, because people will tell you when you are shopping that they have seen Father Bree. Anyway, let's think about it. But I can get over walls now so you can show me your secret cave.'

The January night was crisp and clear when Joseph and Nikki met on the south walk beside the church. The stars gave enough light for them to move over the snow while the throb of allied bombers to the north disturbed the silence. He was wearing his warm priest's habits while she was muffled in a greatcoat with deep hood. She wore the black patch over her empty eye socket.

'I'll lead,' she whispered and set off along the low wall that was built at the lip of the gully and joined the cemetery border behind the church. She stopped and pointed.

'There's a flat patch on the other side and then it slopes down to the path. Take your crutches over and put them against the wall. I will take them down for you this time. Then you follow, slide down on the snow.' She went over, waited for him, sat down on the edge and slowly slid into the darkness of the ravine. He followed and was surprised how gently he arrived. He fitted his crutches and leaned forward eagerly.

'Now follow the path for ten metres.' The snow was fluffy and beneath it the ground seemed hard and level. He moved quite rapidly behind her. 'The stone-cutters levelled this corridor centuries ago to move the quarried pieces down to build The Seigneury.' She stopped and pointed up the slope into the thick growth. 'We'll crawl up through these bushes.' Carefully he lowered himself to his padded knee and stump and they moved through the undergrowth, sometimes wiggling on their stomachs, using their elbows to inch ahead, dislodging cascades of snow from the overhanging vines and shrubs. The ground became steeper and clear for a few feet and then total blackness ahead. Her hand guided him until they were sitting on cold rock, facing the village. The moon was rising and painted the Valley of Vesle with silvery light. The church and its spire was a black, comforting bulk to their right. The village square was a picture postcard. To the left and below, the ancient gabled architecture of the barracks was highlighted by the backdrop of the southern hills.

'Isn't it beautiful? This is my 'all alone' place,' Nikki said, hugging Joseph's arm. 'Shall we go in?' She laughed softly, rolled over and crawled into the darkness. He heard the scratch of a match and a tiny candle fluttered in the far corner of the cave, throwing flickering shadows over the rough ceiling. There were two low chairs and a table to match in height. A mattress was on the floor along the far wall. 'Isn't it cosy? Cool in the summer and no wind in the winter.' She propped a rag doll up on one chair. 'And that's my best friend, Gigi.'

Joseph looked around and smiled his understanding. He saw a playhouse for a

121

lonely little girl — and also another unexpected addition to his plan.

★ ★ ★

A great storm came sweeping across the North Sea out of the Norwegian Peninsular at the end of that week and blizzards raged across France. The garrison was placed on alert. Columns of troop-laden trucks roared through Ste Agathe and across the plains to the north and west. Joseph Pilgrim was forced into hiding, but spent many hours on the look-out level becoming familiar with the uniforms and vehicles. He was alarmed when he watched a smoke-puffing diesel tractor haul several large guns into position around the bridge above Vesle Falls. Ammunition carriers came the next day, followed by their crews. The strongpoint was camouflaged under netting.

When the weather showed signs of improving, Allain Boulanger came knocking on the rectory door, pleading with Father Bree to come to his wife, Fleury. They lived in a little cottage across the river from The Seigneury and were lifelong residents of Ste Agathe. 'She's very low, Father,' he pleaded. 'Just a few prayers would let her soul rest.' Father Bree was weak and sucking in breath as if drowning, but he nodded and gathered his sacraments. Nikki helped him into his warmest clothes, draped his cloak over his shoulders and the crutches, and fastened the cowl over his black toque. They left in mid-afternoon when a shadow of sun was lighting the clouds. Nikki watched them go down Church Hill, an old man supporting a sick, and one-legged, priest; she prayed for their safety.

She kept busy heating water and washing clothes in the scullery, but every few minutes went to the window in the tiny study and looked anxiously down the hill. After the flurry of the invasion report during the storm, military activity had dropped to a minimum as the troops returned to readiness bases. The garrison of Ste Agathe was snug in quarters and few villagers ventured out in the snow and cold. Nikki's anxiety turned to concern as the valley became darker and darker and she could no longer see the bridge or the village. She became worried when the priest's dinnertime passed and he had not returned. By seven o'clock she was frantic as she saw the wind picking up and swirls of snow obscure the road. She pulled the food vessels away from the cooking fire, put on her greatcoat and toque and ventured out of the rectory door into the gale.

She fell twice on the walk before she left the shelter of the church and struggled across the forecourt and onto the road. The wind lessened as she slithered down Church Hill into the protection of the valley. She kept to the near side where there was less snow and crept around the first turn. From here she could see several metres ahead until the next curve. She was looking frantically around when she made out a dark hump in the snow piled up against the slope. As she tramped nearer she could see Allain Boulanger on his knees, head down, humped over the body of Father Bree, arms trying to shield him from the wind. Nikki rushed to his side, crouched low and shouted: 'What happened?'

The old man could barely speak as he gasped for air. 'He had pains, in his chest. He fell. His crutch slid down the hill.' He motioned back. 'I couldn't find it.'

Nikki lay down and put her mouth close to the priest's ear. 'Father, can you hear me?' He moved his head and tried to rise. 'We'll get you up.' They managed to slide Bree away from the slope so that Boulanger could support him on one side. Nikki scuffled in the snow and found the lost crutch. She clambered back and wrapped his left arm around her neck and struggled to her knees. With great difficulty they were able to stand.

Father Bree fitted his crutches and managed to move in small hops with the two supporting him on each side. The climb to the rectory was pure torture and all three were shaking with exhaustion and cold when they finally reached the shelter of the rectory. They dragged the priest directly into the bedroom where he fell face down on the mattress and passed out.

Boulanger collapsed in a chair and groaned. Nikki shed her coat as she staggered into the kitchen. She ladled two cups of warm soup out of the pot and carried them back. She sagged to the floor and they drank before she managed to ask: 'How is your wife?'

Boulanger just shook his head and sobbed. 'Bad. Very bad. I must get back.'

'Rest a few minutes. I'll stir up the fire and make a hot drink.'

When she got back, he was asleep. She woke him, watched him gulp the steaming milk-mixture, and helped him to the door. He was shaking, unsteady on his feet, and in no condition to walk home, but she knew he could not stay.

She dragged the damp cloak off Bree's body, removed his wet boots and socks, put on dry socks and managed to roll him under the covers. His breathing was fast and shallow. His skin was cold and clammy, but he was alive. Nikki kept repeating the prayer of gratitude as she poured boiling water into a bed crock and shoved it under the covers beside the priest's body. Then she sank to the floor for her vigil.

The dark, cold night hours passed with agonizing slowness for Nicole, even though she kept busy by coddling the fire and keeping the waterbottle hot. Just before dawn, she returned to the priest's bedside and listened for his fluttered breathing.

She crawled, sobbing and shaking, up the stone steps into the belfry in the grey shadows of the morning. Without removing her boots or jacket, she crawled under the blankets beside Pilgrim and shook him. He jerked awake, felt her trembling body and cried in alarm: 'What's the matter, Nikki?'

'Father Bree. He's dead!' Her crying developed into a sobbing wail that started her coughing.

'Dead! What happened?'

Between snuffles and gasping and sobs and coughs, she managed to tell him how Father Bree had gone with Boulanger to administer the rites to his wife and she had found them in the snow.

'He was so cold. He was gasping for breath. I sat by him all night. He just slept away. He just stopped breathing. His heart. I think his heart was tired. He said he had pains.' She cried again and he hugged her close, trying to stop her trembling. 'He's gone, Joseph, what shall we do?'

'He shouldn't have gone out in that blizzard.'

'He had to, Joseph! He was her priest. Fleury Boulanger was the head of the Altar Guild for years, long before he came here. She made those choir cushions that you're sleeping on. She embroidered his communion vestments. She sewed the sacramental cloths that bandaged your leg, and packed them away when the Germans came. He had to go.'

Pilgrim closed his eyes in the darkness. This could upset the timing of his plan. He was now uncertain, confused. Yesterday's surge of confidence was draining away. He needed time alone before he started offering suggestions about what they should do. If the weather stayed bad, they could stay in without anyone getting suspicious. But what about the body? That was a real problem. What would they do with the priest's body? Nikki had turned away and was blowing her nose and sobbing, which didn't help him very much.

'When will Bernay be back?' The wind was screeching around the ancient tower and somewhere above a loose board was banging.

'Not until this storm blows itself out. I don't know. He used to cut wood one day and bring a load into the village the next day, but now he comes when he thinks it's safe. He doesn't trust the Germans even with his special papers.' She gave a soft wail and started sobbing again so that her shoulders were shaking under the blankets.

'Well, I don't think we should do anything until he comes. He'll know what to do. In the meantime, you stay in the rectory, keep the fire going and carry on with the usual routine as if Father Bree was alive. If anybody comes knocking, tell them Father Bree is very ill because he fell in the snow after visiting the woman in the village. Tell them his pneumonia has come back.'

She had stopped snuffling and was wiping her eye while sitting on the edge of the bunk. Her voice was barely a croaking whisper, 'What about the body?'

'I was thinking about that, but what can we do. Just fix him in bed as if he's asleep. Close the curtains and close the door as if he really is resting. And, as I said, carry on. I'll stay here until Bernay comes.'

It was three days before Bernay came. Nikki brought Pilgrim's food only at night and didn't speak; her spiritual fortitude beaten with sorrow and fear and cold. Pilgrim exercised as best he could in the tiny room in the tower as the wind was too strong for him to venture outside. The storm ended during the third night but the snow was so deep that Bernay waited until the ploughs had opened the road. The hulking, bear-like Frenchman came plodding along in the late afternoon with the worn harness over his massive shoulders and the sleigh following, an outline so familiar it seemed as if they were created to be together. He took the news with head bowed and eyes closed when they gathered in the belfry. He squatted on the floor in a corner and stared at nothing for a long time. Pilgrim sat on the bed and Nikki squatted, back against the bunk. They could hear the creaking of the timbers in the steeple, the wind playing around the louvers in the belfry, and the distant roar of engines as the Germans cleared snow from the compound and maintained the patrol routine. The boy and girl waited for the wise old forester to guide them.

Finally he seemed to clear his thoughts. 'He was a good priest, a man of God and he did his best. We must carry on for him.' He squirmed to ease his aching shoulders and scratched the ice from his beard. 'We have two problems. Firstly his body. We can't bury it now, the ground is frozen too hard. We can ask Captain Bruno for help, but that means everybody will know the priest is dead and that will make a lot of problems and encourage a lot of questions. How will the villagers and the Germans get along without the good father? Will Bruno keep the deal he made with Bree now that he is dead? And what about Nikki? She's lost the protection of the church.' He gave Pilgrim a grizzled scowl through his beard. 'And what do we do with you?' He straightened out his leg and massaged his thigh with a grimace of pain. 'So I suggest we do not tell Bruno that Bree is dead until we are forced to. In the meantime, we must hide the body and pretend that he is still alive.'

Nikki gave a sob and covered her face with her mittened hands. 'No mass to venerate him.' She rocked back and forth in her grief. 'No funeral. No prayer of commendation. No committal service. His soul deserves its heaven.'

'Later, the good Father will get his due, maybe, but for now, we hide him. Where? Any ideas? Not in the rectory, that's f'sure. Not in the woodshed because the guard shelters there. So, it will have to be in the church. Up here with Pilgrim? Higher up above the belfry?' Nikki made a choking sound and he paused.

'The vestry,' she whispered. 'He loved the vestry. It was his place of prayer and solitude.'

'Yes,' Bernay agreed. 'The vestry. We'll block the outer door that Joseph opened, and lock the one into the nave. The sooner we do that the better, but how do we keep his death secret?'

Pilgrim was hunched on the bunk and didn't respond but Nikki straightened and pointed at him. 'He can take his place. He's been out in the Father's vestments and pretending he's the priest so he can continue. Instead of trying to escape . . . ' Pilgrim's head came up and his eyes flashed at the girl.

'Escape? What do you mean 'escape'?'

She snorted, 'Don't play innocent. We know you're planning to leave as soon as the weather improves. I saw the food you've stolen from the kitchen at the barracks and hidden in my cave. You could get us all shot for that, a great way to thank us for saving your life.' Her grief was turning to anger. 'So here's a chance to pay us back and save your neck at the same time. I can't carry on alone.' She started to cry again and her disfigured face was twisted in misery. Pierre Bernay moved over to put his arm around her shoulders and comfort her. After a few minutes she calmed and rested her head on his shoulder.

Bernay's great beard and tangled head of hair nodded at the airman. He said softly but there was no mistaking his intent: 'Pilgrim, you have no choice. You will be Father Bree.' They all were silent while they thought about the perils they were facing.

As soon as the army personnel carrier had churned up Church Hill on its last night patrol and its slit lights had disappeared along the north road, Nikki and Bernay went into the rectory and prepared the body of their priest for his move into his church. They wrapped him in a blanket, which Pierre tied at both ends. With one at each end, they eased their burden off the bed, out into the night. Their boots crunched on the hardened snow and their breath made great clouds in the still night air as they slid the corpse along the cloistered path and in through the south porch.

The snow from their feet made the flagstones slippery and Father Bree moved easily into the vestry where he had found sanctuary from a world of violence and despair. In the meantime, Pilgrim had tossed the choir cushions and bench pillows down the stone steps and stripped his bunk of bedding. He had retrieved his crutches from the vestry and was waiting by the open door when they arrived. Bernay lifted Father Bree out of his temporary shroud and placed him in his favourite, saggy chair. He replaced the barricade across the narrow door to the vestry garden and slid the curtain across. They stood in silence for a few moments, heads bowed in remembrance, then made the sign of the cross and moved into the nave. Bernay closed and locked the door. Nikki took the key and slid it amongst the remaining altar cloths in the tiny sacristy. Bernay carried the cushions and paddings to the choir loft and laid them in their traditional places. He came back and gave Nikki a squeeze on the shoulder, nodded to Pilgrim and went to his sleigh by the woodshed. He looped the harness over his shoulders and disappeared into the dark.

That night Pilgrim lay on the priest's bed, but did not sleep. He could not shake off the sensation that his mother was in the room with him, ready to guide him in the role of the priest in her quiet, persistent manner. His brain would not stop creating her face and her smile and her oh-so-oppressive dominance. He loved his mother dearly. She was the most perfect person in the world except that her constant religious guidance drove him crazy. In his head he saw her, mouthing those trite platitudes, 'God is with you all the time, be good and God will love you, God will answer your prayers, God is watching over you all the time, and never forget that God will keep you safe.' He felt the throbbing in his stump and cried out in rebellion. He'd escaped from her cocoon of righteousness into the excitement of the Air Force where he could do his own thing and succeed or fail by his own efforts. His adventure had come to a terrifying end very early and his mother was trying to take over again.

He swung his leg out from under the blankets and sat on the edge of the bed. He was not going to be dominated again. He was going to do his own thing, even if he died trying. He was going back to the Air Force and he was going to fight in this war and be proud. Joe Pilgrim on crutches was smarter than the entire German army and he would succeed! What an adventure! What a mental and physical challenge for Joe Pilgrim, the kid who was raised in a girls' school . . . All this was not ordained. God had nothing to do with his plan to impersonate the good Father. The French Canadian kid from St Jean-sur-Richelieu will do it all on his own. The ethereal presence of his mother seemed to fade as he crawled back under the covers. He fell sleep, his tears dampening Father Bree's worn pillow.

At the same time, Nicole Joyal lay on her straw palliasse with her back to the warm stones of the chimney and felt hollow at the thought of life without Father Bree. She saw only loneliness, sadness and fear ahead and that the Germans would have no reason not to send more villagers to the labour camps. Her beloved Father was there in his vestry, his spirit was waiting for the Mass of Redemption to soar into heaven. She was here, afraid, weak in body and defeated in spirit and could do nothing for him. She had lost her mother, father and two brothers to the hated Germans, and now her saviour had gone to his reward and she was beaten. She cried until there was no more sorrow and then she slept.

In the cold grey dawn her fighting spirit struggled for survival and anger replaced sorrow, anger against Pilgrim. There was no reason to be angry with him, but she had to vent her feelings on someone and he was the only one. He was going to do as he was told. He was not going to steal away as soon as spring came. He was going to be Father Bree: Pilgrim was going to disappear. He had never existed. He is Father Bree. That's the way it will be. Joseph Pilgrim does not exist so she has no feelings for him. The good Father's pledge will be kept. His parishioners will be saved until the day of liberation. That could be soon. This spring? The rumours say this spring? Please God make it soon. She fumbled for her beads and chanted while she thought about the impersonation.

Pierre Bernay was weighed down with worry. He placed his precious sleigh and harness inside the rustic shelter away from the weather and went into his cabin. He closed and barricaded the door before lighting his little grate and warming his drink. The death of his friend must not make him forget his duty. He slid aside the stack of logs beside his fireplace, brushed away the ashes and removed a loose hearth stone. Squatting like a great bear in his furs and jacket, he slipped on the earphones and listened to the latest list of poetry quotations from Britain.

Nikki Joyal woke early with a spirit of resolve and purpose that was the opposite of the trembling girl who had gone to bed. She knew what she was going to do. She was going to follow the same routine. Father Bree was still in his rectory, but now, she was making the decisions. She stirred his cup of tea, made sparingly from the hoarded supply in the caddy that was almost empty. She carried it into his bedroom and awoke him, hours after he should have recited Matins.

'Wake up, Father. You have duties to perform.'

Joe Pilgrim groaned, thrashed his right leg

to loosen a muscle cramp, and opened one eye. 'What's going on?'

'Your tea, Father. The day looks kind. At mid-morning I will help you down to the square. The good people will be pleased to see that their priest has recovered from his fall in the snow and pneumonia. God is good. I will tell them that you still have a sore throat and will speak very little. They will understand. Please get dressed and come for breakfast.'

She retreated toward the door, but turned and added. 'I will trim your beard, Father. It is longer than the good people remember.'

The airman in the priest's bed sat up after she had left and drank the tea. As Bernay had said, he had no choice, at present, anyway. The tea tasted good. He lay back in the warm bed, warmer than he'd ever been in the tower. Maybe it would be fun to play priest. Of course! He could exercise more. He could explore the village for himself. He could listen to the rumours. He would be better prepared to go, when the time was ripe. From now on, he was Father Bree! He closed his eyes and started to imagine himself as the parish priest but his mother's face invaded his reveries again.

And she was smiling! He wished she'd go away.

The weather delayed Pilgrim's first public appearance as Father Bree. Low clouds made the valley dull and grey. Brown smoke from the damp and green wood of the cooking fires mingled with the fog. The rain started during the afternoon and continued for three days, washing away most of the snow. At the end of that week the ice broke up in the river with a sudden roar that made the valley tremble. Huge chunks tumbled over the falls, crashing and smashing on the rocks and banks, piling against the hump bridges and swirling away through the millpond and out of the valley.

Nicole Joyal took advantage of their forced confinement to prepare him for the first visit to the village square. She continually gave instructions and directions until he began to get a bit irritable. Finally the clouds broke and the sun began to warm the earth, faster in the sheltered valley of Ste Agathe. On the last day of March, they ventured out. Nikki pulled on a deep grey sweater to match the French army trousers she had rescued from a smashed supply convoy. She tied a woollen scarf over her head and under her chin because the wind made her scarred face throb and ache. She carried a shapeless string bag that held needles and wool, although she could not knit. Pilgrim wedged his prayer book in the cleft of his right crutch as directed and wore the wide-brimmed black hat he had discovered in the tiny bedroom closet.

'Go ahead!' she ordered. 'I'll keep a respectful distance behind and to one side. If someone wants to stop and talk, make a greeting and let me explain about your illness and voice, but remember, I'm your house-keeper. You must keep the impression of superiority. That's the priestly way.'

'Yes ma'am,' he said, with a dip of his head, and set off with vigour. Church Hill was clear of snow but a few drifts remained along the verges and water puddled in the flat places and trickled down. He managed to miss the worst of the mud and arrived at the bridge without difficulty. The guard, who was standing at ease with his automatic pistol slung across his back, straightened slightly and mumbled something but Pilgrim swung on with only a nod. This was the closest he'd been to the enemy camp and his heart began to hammer. He headed for the bench that backed on the river and faced the row of shops, the Café d'Or and the town hall, just as he'd been briefed. He was glad to sit and relax the muscles of his leg. Going down the steeper parts of the path had been harder on his shoulders than he had anticipated. The villagers saw him, little groups clustered on the one strip of paving, and heads nodded in his direction as they talked. As if by agreement, two ladies left and approached him. He did not rise, as directed, but leaned wearily and weakly on his crutches, as directed, and smiled his greetings.

'Why here's Lisa D'Mille, whose husband used to run the garage, and Mrs Paget who taught me at school,' Nikki exclaimed as they approached. 'The good Father has been ill and still has a bad throat.'

'So glad you are better,' the old school teacher beamed, leaning close because her eyes were failing. 'Allain Belanger told me that you fell in the snow after visiting. Fleury prayed for your recovery now that she is mending.' Lisa D'Mille nodded agreement and chatted about the weather until they looked at each other and moved on. Years of German domination had taught them not to talk for long, or the guards might think they were plotting. And so the cautious meetings went on, never more than two at a time, never lingering for long, never getting too close that they may be accused of whispering. Pilgrim was pleased that they did most of the talking while he nodded and smiled. When they were alone, he opened his prayer book and pretended to read, while Nikki fussed with her knitting.

All in all, they decided, two hours later when they had regained the rectory, a very creditable performance. The weather smiled on the village of Ste Agathe during the rest of the week and they performed the ritual for a second and third time. Joseph had gained total confidence and was beginning to enjoy the excursions.

'Today I'll go alone,' he decreed the next morning, anxious to assert his manhood.

'And I'll go first,' she responded, not willing to give him total independence, 'to do some shopping, and keep an eye on you.'

He shrugged, recognizing that he had exchanged one dominating mother for one dominating servant girl. But he had no choice. Not yet!

By himself, he ignored the benches and kept moving, making a steady circuit of the square and along the river far enough to study the barracks from across the river. He was exhausted when he climbed the hill, his knee was weakening and the skin of his armpits was sore. He was well satisfied when he dragged himself to bed, and Nikki awarded him with the cheerful news: 'Special dinner tonight.'

She woke him at eight o'clock and presented a tray of meatballs, small boiled potatoes and green peas. His eyes widened when he saw the food.

'Where did you get that?'

'From my secret place. What you stole from the barracks. I was afraid some curious German soldier would explore the cliffs and find the cave. That would be the end. So, last night I went down and brought it here, took everything out of the containers and put it in our pots.' After they had eaten she announced; 'Since I risked my neck getting them here, you will take the containers back and dump them in the garbage behind the barracks.' He stared at her.

'There's an air raid on. Don't you hear them, and the guns?'

'A good time to go, Father. The Germans will be busy manning their posts.'

He agreed. This would be another test for him. He donned the outdoor habits with practiced ease. She carried the bag of cartons and cans out to the low wall above the sloping pathway. He did his leg-swinging act to get over, took the bag and slithered down the slope, it was a bit damp but he had no alternative. This was much easier than going down the Church Hill road. There was a huge bomber force streaming overhead, a mighty churning rumble that seemed to stretch from horizon to horizon. Rumours were racing through the villlage that the invasion was coming and the increased air activity seemed to support them. Most of the aircraft were very high as if the target was distant; others were low and bombs seemed to be exploding to the west along the coast. He thought about all the airmen huddled in their aircraft, praying that they would return and he shuddered at the memory of his single mission.

He moved slowly but confidently down the path. The thicket that hid Nikki's cave was a ragged shadow against the smooth rock face. From there he went to a splintered tree trunk and rested, as he had done several times. From here he knew it was a level walk to a bald knoll and a bramble hedge which hid the garbage tip from the house. The building was dark because of the raids, but a lighter square appeared as someone carelessly opened a laundry-room door, ignoring the blackout orders. He waited behind the bushes until the light appeared again and the person had entered. He moved to the pile of refuse and quietly emptied the bag, as directed, balled it up and threw it to another part of the yard. He retreated behind the wall and watched for patrols.

Over to the west there was the roaring blast of a big aircraft low and at full power, the whining snarl of a German night-fighter and the rattle of machine guns. He crouched and followed the curving path of the exhaust flames. An arcing ball of fire suddenly blossomed and trailed yellow rivers. The sound of the explosion hit him a second later and he slid flat on the ground. The cherry-red ball burnished the black trees on the hills beyond the river and rapidly grew larger. He suddenly realized the doomed bomber was diving toward him. He reached for his crutches, pried himself to his knees, then hoisted himself to his foot and fitted the crutches, all the time watching the blazing wreck become bigger and bigger and bigger until he could see the outline of the fuselage in the light of the fires in the wings. He dropped to the ground again.

The screaming fireball hit the barracks at the second level, just above the roof of the ornate veranda that surrounded three sides of the former *seigneur's* home. The main fuselage ploughed forward, ripping out walls and ceilings and spreading the fire. The two motors and parts of the wings curved downward, destroying the main, internal rafters and ending in the cellars. The burning fuel cascaded over the entire wreckage, spreading the holocaust. The Valley of Vesle trembled.

Pilgrim crouched behind the low wall and

watched in horror as the shock wave blasted over him, flattening trees and shrubs. The solid stone rear wall saved from instant destruction the more modern addition at the rear that housed the kitchens, storage rooms and laundry. The roof burst into flames. The walls collapsed. Great chunks of masonry hammered down. Doors and windows flew out. Flames flickered beyond.

Pilgrim could hear screams from the rear laundry rooms. He tightened the sash around his waist. He pulled over the hood and tied the chin-straps. He struggled erect as fast as he could and lurched toward the nearest doorway. He tumbled inside. The stone floor of the scullery was still cool as he knelt to peer under the smoke.

Someone in a white outfit was struggling to free his leg from a timber that pinned it to the floor. Pilgrim balanced against the shattered doorframe. He lowered himself to his padded knees and mittened hands. He dragged his crutches. The crackling of flames drowned the cries for help. He was beside the German. He tried to lift the timber. He could feel the heat through his mitt. The timber didn't move. The boy was screaming and clawing at his arm. Pilgrim slid the leg of his crutch under the rafter and heaved. It moved. He motioned for the boy to help. He got his shoulder under the crutch and raised. Together they lifted the timber enough for the leg to come free.

The German scrambled out, pointing deeper into the smoke-filled room. Another body lay within two feet of the burning rear wall. The apron was smouldering. Charred embers were burning into the man's flesh along his arms and shoulders. His hair was burning.

Pilgrim scrambled to his side. He looped one arm over his shoulder and hung onto the hand. On one good knee, one painful stump, and one hand, he dragged. The boy, favouring a twisted leg and sobbing piteously, pulled on the other hand. Together, tugging, scrambling, choking, yanking, coughing, levering, they slid the body across the smooth stone floor and out onto the dirt path, followed by a shower of sparks and debris as the entire section collapsed.

Pilgrim's eyes were hurting even though closed against the blinding smoke. His lungs screamed with every breath. His heart was jumping out of his body. His clothes were burning the skin off his shoulders. He could do nothing but roll on his back and let his scorched hands scrabble in the damp earth.

With a vision of his mother smiling from the shadows, he escaped into the blackness that his brain was preparing for him.

Nicole Joyal watched Father Bree disappear into the darkness down the ravine path and returned to wash the dishes and preserve the remainder of the precious food. She looked out the study window a couple of times but all was dark. She paused several times in her work to listen to the aircraft and hoped that the increased activity meant that liberation was soon. She was banking the fire for the night when she heard the explosion. This time the southern sky was bright with the fire of the barracks and the pyrotechnics of exploding ammunition.

'Mother of God!' she exclaimed, crossing herself and reaching for her Rosary. 'Save us.' She stared as the flames leapt into the sky, fragments of wood circled and glowed, portions of the ancient building collapsed in a deluge of sparks. She could see a few tiny black figures escaping and more running through the village toward the disaster. Within minutes engines were roaring in the compounds and vehicles racing along the riverside street. She felt a sudden surge of pity for the men who were dying in their barracks. They were Germans, and hated, but death for anyone was an emotional encounter. She dragged a chair to the window and watched for several hours while the fires gradually burned themselves out. She waited for Father Bree to return until she finally fell asleep, woke partially, crawled to her palliasse and drifted off again, fearful she had lost another comrade.

A weary, dejected Pierre Bernay arrived the next afternoon. He had toured the village and seen the bad news.

'A big piece of the bomber wiped out the Boulanger cottage,' he said with a shuddering sigh. 'There's nothing left, nothing. Fleury and Allain were burned up, cremated.'

'What about Father Bree?'

He raised his bushy eyebrows in question. 'What about him?'

She told him why he wasn't here and the old man thought for a long time.

'I heard nothing. There was no body of a priest and nobody said they'd seen him, that's f'sure. Forty-three Germans were burned in the building and nine bodies were on the grass, some hurt, but no talk about our priest.' He watched her hands nervously trembling as she wiped her eye with her kerchief. 'D'you think he escaped?' he ventured.

Her head went back and forth in doubt. 'I don't know. I don't think so, but tomorrow I'll go down and find out.'

148

Bernay slipped out of the rectory and around the church to fetch a spade from the shed. He slung it over his shoulder and headed for the cemetery. The partially filled grave of Bernie Goineau and Pilgrim's leg was a hump and hollow of dirty snow and soil. He finished the filling and smoothed the dirt level. He leaned on his spade to rest. That was one worry over. The body was still in the vestry, haunting him night and day, but this wasn't the time to dig a new grave. They'd just have to watch for the opportunity. He wiped the shovel on a clump of thicket and put it back in the shed and headed for his hut in the forest.

Nikki Joyal spent the day at the tiny study window watching the soldiers search the smouldering ruins of the barracks. A hydraulic crane, used for repairing military vehicles, was lifting huge pieces of debris. Squads of soldiers, carried sagging, shrouded burdens, moved up the hill to the burial ground where Pilgrim's pilot lay. A mobile shovel had arrived from somewhere during the night and had dug a trench. A pile of earth showed against the grey skyline. Nikki watched the communal burials. There were no villagers in sight and the whole valley seemed to be in shock from the horror that had struck last night.

Before she was ready to leave the next morning, an ambulance pulled into the church foreyard on one of its trips to base hospital. The medical sergeant, who spoke French, came knocking. His uniform was dirty and crumpled, his face was haggard and his eyes swollen from lack of sleep. He did not come in when she opened the door, but simply said, in a hurry: 'Father Bree's hurt. He'll be home in one, two days. Can't stop.' And he trotted back to the muddy vehicle as Nikki watched from the door, more worry and confusion racing around in her battered head.

Two days later the ambulance returned. The sergeant and another orderly slid a stretcher out of the rear door and carried Father Bree into his rectory while Nicole Joyal led the way. They lifted him on to the bed and arranged his bandaged arms and hands under the covers. His eyes were open but his hair and beard were singed and matted.

The second orderly hurried back to his vehicle while the sergeant stood awkwardly by the bed. His eyes looked everywhere except at her disfigured face as he stumbled in French accented with the guttural throat sounds of the German voice:

'Father Bree saved two German soldiers.

Very dangerous. Very brave. We are grateful. His wooden crutches were broken and burned so we carried him on the stretcher.' The second medic had returned and the sergeant took a pair of crutches from him.

'German army crutches. Captain Bruno ordered me to give them to him. Good metal and very strong.' He held them out to Joyal while pointing to a small brass plate on each. 'We put his name on.'

Nikki stared at them with her head held high, making no attempt to hide her scars. She wanted to shout at them: 'Your murderous comrades took my mother and father, killed my two brothers and did this to me. I hope they fried in the fire.' She took the shiny crutches with a simple, 'Thank you.'

'Captain Bruno is recovering from burns and a broken wrist. He tried to save his comrades. Captain Bruno said Father Bree can hold a memorial service for the French casualties. He will post a notice.' He turned to go, still staring at the floor.

'What's your name?' the French girl demanded.

He stopped but didn't turn. 'Sergeant Otto Laing,' he said haughtily and added, 'medical student.' He pointed to his companion, who had hurried out. 'Corporal Manfred Steidl, medical student.' She watched them climb into the vehicle. The ambulance driver raced his engine and churned gravel as he sped down Church Hill. She spat on the path where they had walked and shouted: 'Laing and Steidl, I'll say a prayer for your rotten souls because you saved Father Bree, but I hope you rot in hell.'

Joseph Pilgrim's burns dried rapidly with daily treatments of sulphur powder Laing had left with him. The wrenched muscles in his back and shoulders took longer. Almost two weeks passed before he felt steady enough to try his new crutches outdoors. The unsettled weather of early April had passed for warmer days. The trees were showing green and the grasses of the valley were shedding their winter brown. His youthful vitality surged through him again as his leg muscles carried him back and forth along the cloister path.

'I wonder what the villagers will think, their priest on German crutches,' Nikki mused as he passed.

'I'll keep them under my robes.' He waved one in the air. 'The shoulder supports are more comfortable and there's a sort off spring in the metal leg so that I can take longer strides. Look.' He swung his leg high and went out to the road at a pace that would have been a good trot in his two-legged days. There he met Lilli Longuedoc who ran the tiny variety store and post office in the square and had been one of the first to greet him in the village.

She smiled and nodded. 'I was coming to see you, Father. I'm happy that you have recovered. I saw the notice that the Germans are letting us have a memorial service for the Boulangers and I was wondering when you were going to have it.'

Pilgrim rested on his crutches and smiled at her. His mind was churning savagely. What was she talking about? Memorial service? He needed time.

'My dear Mrs Longuedoc.' Lucky he remembered her name, laughed to himself about what it meant in English. 'I was considering that yesterday,' he lied. 'Come on in and we can discuss it.'

'Yes. The church will need some preparation after all this time, and now, with Fleury gone, I thought . . . ' He was moving fast into the rectory.

'Miss Joyal,' he called. 'What was the date we discussed for the memorial service?' He moved through into his tiny office and sat at the desk, sliding the German crutches out of sight. She came in with Mrs Longuedoc and said: 'The Sunday after next.' She rummaged through old papers on the desk, playing her part very well, then gave up and said: 'Sunday

28 May. Now I remember. It's the last Sunday in May.' She turned to Mrs Longuedoc. 'Kind of you to offer but there is little to do. I can fix the altar cloths. It's not a Funeral Mass, because there are no bodies, just a Liturgy.'

Mrs Longuedoc insisted that those ladies who were left from the Altar Guild should be permitted to participate. 'After all, Father Bree, the church has been closed for so long and we are grateful that you negotiated with Captain Bruno for his permission.' She turned and stalked out. 'I'll tell the ladies and we'll be back.'

Joseph Pilgrim slumped and watched her go. Nikki returned, worry creasing her face. 'I thought you had heard when the Germans brought the crutches. I was waiting for Bernay to come. We've got to do something about the body. That's more of a problem than the service; I can find the ritual for you.'

'I'm not worried about the service, either. I've sat through so many, they're pounded into my memory. I'm scared of that woman. She's so persistent. She keeps asking questions, I'm afraid I'll give myself away.'

Nikki snorted, 'Not to worry. That's the way she is. Father Bree avoided her whenever he could. What are we going to do with the body with people coming for the service?'

'All we can do is keep it locked away and have a good excuse if someone asks.'

'The key's in the sacristy. She'll find it, for sure, and go nosing around.'

'Then you better get it. I'll keep it in my purse.' He looked out of the window down into the valley and noted more armour in the compounds and patrolling. 'The Germans look as if they're on some sort of alert.'

'The whole place is buzzing with whispers of the invasion which won't help us to bury our priest.'

Nikki went to bed guilt-weary about being unable to pray for the soul of her beloved benefactor in a proper Mass, but whispered in the dark the one prayer she had memorized:

Eternal rest grant unto him, O Lord, and let perpetual light shine upon him. May he rest in peace.

To which she added her own devotion:

He was a good man.

And she went to sleep as if confessed.

Joseph lay awake in the priest's bed and resented the fact that this memorial service would delay his plans. He also pondered over and over how the impending invasion and battles would assist him to join his comrades. He was on a perilous schedule and he knew there would be no divine assistance.

It was two hours after dark and the pair in the rectory slept, a lithe, black figure squirmed out of a little window in the rear dormer of Lilli Longuedoc's cottage, swung along an overhanging tree branch and dropped silently to the ground. It ran crouching through the bushes and into the woods that cover the western slope of Vesle Valley. At a steady, sure-footed trot it moved from shadow to dark patch amongst the trees, always moving north and avoiding the road across the river above the falls. After forty minutes, it crept behind a thicket and dropped to the ground. The sound of an owl quivered in the stillness. All was quiet. The owl voiced its nocturnal song again. This time another answered, briefly.

In his hut, Pierre Bernay listened, arose from his wood and thong bed and slipped outside. He gave the owl sign again and watched the figure rise from the shadows of the thicket. He moved away and they met beneath a huge oak that cast the deepest shadow.

'Lilli,' he whispered. 'What's wrong?'

She slid to the ground and massaged her legs. She was breathing fast but managed to say: 'Bruno has allowed a memorial service for Fleury and Allain. Father Bree has set the Sunday after next. Rumours about the invasion are all over. I think the Germans are nervous. I think Bruno wants the people in the church so they can round them up and stop the resistance from rising openly. We've got to warn the others not to go.'

The wind was rippling the new foliage and the forest was a dark world of peace. For Bernay there was no peace, not while one German walked on French soil. He settled with his back against the tree trunk and stared at the clouds while he grappled with this unexpected news. What could happen? Pilgrim exposed? Threat of discovery could make Pilgrim take off. He wouldn't last two days and he'd talk. Too risky. Must put a watch on him. Bree's body discovered? Must be moved soon. Must keep the patrols away from the cemetery. But was Lilli right? Would Bruno do this on his own? Sure he would. His deal with Bree means nothing when the real fighting starts.

As if reading his thoughts, she asked: 'Any signal from Britain?'

He shook his head.

'I lost my radio when the Boulanger house was burned, but at least the Germans didn't find it in the rubble.'

He nodded his understanding and made his decisions. Bree's body he'd have to handle himself because Lilli didn't know about it, but the pretender must be guarded.

'Lilli, as soon as you can, tell Nikki to watch Father Bree.'

Her head jerked up in surprise. 'Why?'

'Don't ask, just do it. And tonight, tell Jacques, Henri and the others to stay away from the church. I'll tell André and Luc now.' He scrambled to his feet. 'Our plan goes ahead, no matter what happens,' and then, almost to himself although Lilli heard, 'Time is short.'

He padded away amongst the trees, heading north, while she forced her tired muscles to carry her back to the valley.

★ ★ ★

The days before the memorial were busy. Everybody could see that something big was going on. Spotters reported main roads clogged with army traffic. Fast, low-flying aircraft were bombing and strafing from dawn until dark. There was a big storm over the channel for several days but the air intensity was the same. Squadrons of heavy tanks manoeuvred into the forest to hide under the foliage and netting camouflage. Mobile anti-aircraft guns circled the bridge above the falls and established strong points across the plain to the east. Pierre Bernay brought

158

several loads of wood, even though the warm weather reduced the need, but his eyes were open and his little radio busy at night. Lilli Longuedoc came frequently to fuss about the church and seemed interested in Father Bree's preparations. She brought Yves Jonquierre, the blacksmith, to open the west doors at the front door of the church because they hadn't been opened for a long time and were stuck. Joseph Pilgrim was surprised at how many prayers he could still recite from memory and was looking forward to his testing. His mother would be pleased if she could see him robed in cassock, surplice, tippet and hood. Nikki had retrieved them from the vestry, along with the prayer books and orders of service, and kept the key herself. She didn't understand Bernay's message but she followed his order.

Sunday, 28 May was a glorious spring day across central France. The greens of Vesle Valley were bright and crisp, already softening the ugly scars of The Seigneury fire. The sun made a diamond cascade of Vesle Falls and the breeze drifted the spray over the rocks like wedding veils. The scene would have been a peaceful reminder of pastoral France if the sky had not been laced with the trails of fighting aircraft and the sound of explosions which made the few birds in the trees restless.

Jonquierre trudged up Church Hill early and had the doors open to warm the chapel. He was wearing his working overalls because he had no others. Lilli Longuedoc followed soon after with an arrangement of grasses and spring flowers to place on the altar table. She was wearing a grey skirt and blue jacket, the sombre outfit brightened by a yellow silk scarf knotted around her neck and draped over one shoulder. Nicole Joyal, wearing her eye cover, black kerchief and woollen shawl, preceded Father Bree to see that all was ready. He came from the rectory in white surplice flowing over black vestments and carrying a small Bible and book of funeral liturgy. He entered the west porch, recognized the Virgin Mary and walked to stand beside the main west portal. Lilli came over immediately to pay her respects and remark on the splendid weather.

Nicole Joyal stood behind him in the alcove and whispered the names as the parishioners approached. There were no bells to call the faithful and they came, hesitant and uncertain about the time because only whispered messages had spread the glad tidings.

The first was a stumpy girl with straight hair cut short. She had her head down and came in walking hurriedly, carrying a prayer book. 'Jonquierre's daughter,' Nikki informed,

'I don't remember her name. She's a bit slow but looks after her father since her mother died and helps a bit in the shop.' The girl passed in with just a bob to the priest.

A light personnel carrier came up the hill, passing two ladies, and parked at the far side of the forecourt. There were no weapons visible and the two soldiers who alighted wore only sidearms. 'Lieutenant Spaegle, the bastard,' Nikki hissed. 'Watch him. The two women are Lisa D'Mille, the short one with the wide hat, and she's leading Brittany Paget who taught me in school. She's almost blind.' The teacher's face was etched with the smile and cheery wrinkles of earlier times, but was now shadowed by loss of weight and the uncertainty of a dark world. Lisa D'Mille still possessed her attitude of 'try and you will succeed'. They chatted for several minutes, mostly with Nikki, and moved in to sit in a pew near the front.

Yves Laurent and his mother slowly crested the hill and sat on the low wall to rest before climbing the steps to enter the church. He was a big, bluff fellow of about forty, dark-haired with a grizzled beard, a good candidate for the labour camps, except that he walked with a slow shuffle on a twisted, withered leg. She was a slight, short woman who had been an energetic housekeeper, but

161

was now listless and wasted from age, hunger and the worry of rearing a crippled son.

Joliat LaFleche and André Maltais were old drinking buddies from the Café D'Or and were always together. They were wild-haired but balding. 'They clean the chimneys and fireplaces of the cottages and looked after the gardens at the barracks before the fire,' Nikki whispered. 'They're also black market, but we don't tell.' They slid into a rear pew.

The last was Marceill Gomery who had a little food and meat shop in the square and lived over the business. He was the only one who had maintained his normal figure; he wore a dark suit that was old and so tight on him that the coat would not button. His black hat was battered and dusty. Nikki whispered that she hardly recognized him without his apron. Pilgrim said it was time to start.

He walked slowly down the side aisle and mounted the pulpit steps thinking 'eight parishioners. Nikki figured there'd be more. I wonder what's going on?' He reached the pulpit, turned and faced his congregation. He saw immediately that Pierre Bernay had slipped in through the cloister door and into a short side pew where he was hardly noticed but could watch the entire nave. He also waited until the two German guards had taken up positions on each side of the main entrance.

Joseph Pilgrim felt a surge of pride and accomplishment as he looked down on the expectant faces. He knew his mother was smiling.

The small congregation looked with pride upon their heroic priest who resisted German domination and nurtured hope in their tiny community. He had survived pneumonia and collapsing in the snow after visiting Fleury Boulanger. Now he was standing in his pulpit as if on two legs, his luxuriant beard and shaggy hair made him look like a Biblical prophet. His pale blue eyes held the vigour of youth and his voice made their church come alive as he intoned the Sign of the Cross:

'In the name of the Father, and of the Son, and of the Holy Spirit.'

Their responsive 'Amen' was louder and more sustained that he expected, led by a guttural chant from the blacksmith and sopranos from the ladies.

'The grace of our Lord Jesus Christ and the love of God and the fellowship of the Holy Spirit be with you all.'

'And also with you.'

There was the strength of belief and meaning in the voices. Joseph gained confidence. He and Nikki had agreed that he must not vary from the defined service so that the Germans would have no complaints. There was no holy water to sprinkle and no coffins to sprinkle it on, so he went directly to the invitation prayer:

'My brothers and sisters, we have come together to renew our trust in Christ who, by dying on the cross, has freed us from eternal death and, by rising, has opened for us the gates of heaven. Let us pray for Allain and Fleury Boulanger that they may share in Christ's victory, and let us pray for ourselves, that the Lord grant us the gift of his loving consolation.'

'Lord, let it be so.'

Because there was no choir and no music to sing any hymn, he improvised: 'We will now have one minute of silence so that we may each pray for Allain and Fleury in our own way and remember them as friends amongst us.'

He thought that was rather good and took the break to look over his congregation. All heads were bowed, except for the guards, and he decided he would read the entire liturgy. These people had been starved for religion for a long time, so he'd make the best of this opportunity. He intoned the ten prayers that constituted the memorial liturgy and the responses, 'hear our prayer, O Lord' came back strong and sincere each time. It was particularly loud and emphatic as he concluded:

'Let us join in prayer, not only for Allain and Fleury Boulanger, but also for our beloved Church of St. Agathe, for peace in the world, and for ourselves.' He continued until the final commendation:

'Now let us pray together as Christ the Lord has taught us. Our Father who art . . . ' The voices carried on with surprising vigour and when they were silent he ended with the prayer of committal:

'To you, Lord, we commend the souls of your servants Allain and Fleury Boulanger. In the sight of this world they are dead; but in your sight they will live forever. Forgive them their sins committed through human weakness and in your goodness grant them everlasting peace. We ask it through Christ our Lord.'

The final Amen would have done justice to a congregation five times the size.

The church service provided conversation throughout the valley. The blacksmith and his daughter went home in sad silence. The Boulangers had been lifelong friends and had taken a loving interest in his troubled child. LaFleche and Maltais used it as an excuse to visit the Café D'Or early and shed a tear over glasses of weak beer. Brittany Paget visualized it as one of the good Father's devoted efforts under difficulties. 'He had pneumonia, you know, and lay in the snow after confessing to Fleury,' she reminded Lisa D'Mille as they rested on a bench in the square. 'He is a French hero.'

Lieutenant Spaegle marched into Bruno's office in the tiny town hall and expressed his views in strong terms, 'Something's going on, sir, and I don't like it.' Bruno rested his aching wrist on the desk and listened. 'That priest was supposed to be at death's door. Collapsed in the snow. But there he was, healthy as I am. And he came from the rectory, already attired. He's supposed to put on his robes in the vestry, but nobody went near the vestry, and the door was locked. I tried it three times.' His fist hit the table. 'That's where they're hiding the guns. We know the British have been dropping armaments and explosives. We've got a lot of them. But they've got some and they'll start shooting as soon as they get the message. And I'll be one of the first targets. That priest, the ugly girl and that guy who brings the wood, they're in it together. I want permisson to raid that church and clean it out, cart those French shits off to camp, and neutralize them. That's what we have to do, sir, neutralize.'

Bruno was thinking of the blast he'd received from field headquarters after he'd triggered the alarm for a dead parachutist. He had no intention of repeating the blunder with an abortive mission against the marquis, just to satisfy this ambitious and unruly officer. He locked his eyes on his lieutenant and told him, in no uncertain terms, what he would do.

Although he didn't know it, Lieutenant Speagle was the subject of conversation on dedicated ground. Nikki Joyal hauled Bernay aside as soon as they left the church through the cloister door, to let Pilgrim go ahead where he couldn't hear. Then she exploded: 'Did you watch Spaegle? He was searching. He walked around the cemetery. He went right through the church, into the sacristy. He tried the vestry door three times, all before anybody but Lilli was around. She watched him.'

Bernay's eyes widened. 'What are you thinking?'

'I think he'll be back. I think he figures we're hiding guns. I think this whole affair is a ruse so we'll relax. I think we better do something fast.'

Bernay backed off the path and leaned against the woodshed, taking his time. He stared into the distance while the breeze ruffled his wild hair. 'And I think, my young warrior, that's exactly what they want us to do, make the first move. Then we're dead.' He ruffled her hair with a gnarled hand. 'A little more patience, Nikki. The day will come, soon.'

She pouted. 'You said that a year ago.'

'I know, but they have to come in June if they're going to be strong on shore before the bad weather.' He wanted to tell her about the blizzard of messages on his little radio, but he told nobody. Then he could not be betrayed.

'Lilli told me that you had told her to get me to watch Bree. Right?'

'Right.'

'Why?'

'Because I think, as soon as they land, he'll make for the coast. He'll never get there. If the British or Americans catch him, he'll be a prisoner. They won't believe a one-legged priest with German crutches is really a Canadian airman. If the Germans catch him, he's dead. Like that. A spy impersonating a priest. And if he goes, we're in trouble. So, watch him. Don't let him go, for his sake and for ours.'

And in his bedroom, Joseph Pilgrim was so pleased with his performance, he'd fooled the people who knew best, and he fooled the Germans who came to watch. The time was near for him to head for the coast, escape, like a professional soldier.

★   ★   ★

As May rolled into June, the weather turned sour. A gigantic storm moved south across all of western Europe from the cold regions of Norway and Iceland. Bernay was not able to bury the body of Father Bree. Joseph Pilgrim was not able to carry out his escape. Lieutenant Spaegle was not able to get into the church and search the vestry quietly, as he'd been ordered to. Hundreds of French people listened on tiny radios to the British Broadcasting Company for the message that would catapult them into action, but no message came.

A brief break in the wild cloud formations occurred over the English Channel and the French Coast late on Monday, 5 June and the greatest military manoeuvres in human history left the shores and skies of Britain.

Pierre Bernay heard the cultured voice of the BBC announcer include the phrase he'd been expecting. He'd heard hundreds of such snippets in the last year: 'Napoleon's Hat is still at Perros Guirec'; 'The tomatoes should be picked'; 'It is hot in Suez'; 'The crocodile is thirsty'. Some of them may have meant something to somebody, but not to his cell. Then on the first of June he heard, '*Les sanglots longs des violins d'automne*' and knew that the invasion was imminent. It was an alert. Five nights later came the action signal, the second line of Paul Verlaine's poem '*Chanson d'Automne: 'Bercent mon Coeur d'une langueur monotone'*. The invasion had started! The Resistance was to sabotage communications, roads and railways, starting at midnight that night!

Pierre Bernay strung the tiny aerial and twisted the generator to charge the transmitter. He tapped out the only message he had ever sent: 'One hundred tanks, many guns, forest camouflage, 26 dash 31' giving the map co-ordinates of the Forêt du Nord. He had made frequent night patrols as close as he dared to the German armoured regiments which seemed to be a mobile reserve for coastal defences. He re-buried the radio and set out to round up his companions. They had decided the tanks would have to go north along the main road and they would destroy the bridges at the Sees intersection to slow them down.

The sound of aircraft was constant all the next day, concentrated to the north and west. The rumble of heavy guns and the crump of explosions were heard constantly. Bernay figured the main action seemed to be beyond

Caen, perhaps somewhere along the Calvados shore. During the day he worked warily, chopping and stacking dead limbs, waiting for the night. Tuesday the spell of good weather seemed to end and the wind brought more clouds. As soon as darkness covered his forest, he put on his black toque, dark parka and headed for Ste Agathe, travelling fast with no sleigh and no load.

He left the road as soon as he saw the church spire and slanted across the fields so that he came to the low wall at the rear of the cemetery. Here he rested beneath a gnarled old oak and waited. One by one, dark, hooded figures crept out of the shadows and squatted around him. No one spoke. They waited for Bernay's quiet orders.

'Tomorrow night we'll blow the bridges at Sees. The tanks in the forest will be bombed at dawn but some will escape and go north. Luc, Jacques, and André will come with me to prepare the explosives and go to Sees. Henri, you take Lilli and Jacqueline and gather the weapons out of the tombs. Make sure they work, load them and hide them in the bushes on the far side of the wall, like we planned. Wait for us. That's where we'll fight if we have to fight.'

Henri and the two women crept away to the far side of the graveyard and heaved up the stone lid of ancient graves where the stone markers of praying hands and flying angels had long ago sagged to the ground. They handled the packaged weapons with expert care and faded into the shrubbery behind the eastern wall.

Jacques and André split up and crouched in the shadows on either side of the church to watch north and south for patrols. Bernay and Luc fetched the gravediggers' spades from the church shed. They silently rounded the rear of the church and crossed the cemetery to the massive Grenadine memorial. Shovel by careful shovel they moved a mound of earth from the rear wall. With the area cleared, they tugged on leather thongs that projected from each side of a loose stone just above the foundation. Gradually they worked it free. The hole was large enough for them to crawl in.

Bernay went first. When he felt Luc squatting inside, he draped his coat over the opening and Luc turned on his torch. On the floor, stacked against the stone caskets of early Grenadines were neat little packages sewn inside padded burlap envelopes. The two men pulled out the worn and tattered rucksacks hidden under their jackets and began loading. Ten packages of amatol explosives went into two of them, boxes of detonators, timers and wiring into the others. Luc slid outside to take them as Bernay shoved them out. By the time they had hidden them temporarily in the tomb now empty of weapons, dawn was approaching.

And so were the bombers.

★ ★ ★

Joseph Pilgrim was in Father Bree's bedroom but he wasn't asleep. He was at the window, watching the flashes of mighty explosions along the coast reflected on the cloud base. His memory of his flight from Waddington to Le Mans, which they didn't attack, gave him a fairly good idea of their location. He figured that that was the part of the French coast that the allies were attacking. He also figured that it was time for him to head toward it so that he wouldn't be caught in the battles as they moved inland. He'd changed his strategy. He no longer needed to hide, carrying his food, travelling at night. He had Father Bree's clothes, documents, prayer book and Bible. He even had a letter from the Bishop to Father Bree, dated three years ago. He'd impersonated the priest for long enough that he felt confident of his performance. He was going to walk openly across-country as Father Bree. The French farmers would help

173

a one-legged priest on a mission for the bishop. He was sure he would succeed and the time was now.

He let himself out of the cloister door and headed along the path beside the wall. With practised ease he swung over the wall, gathered his robes around him and with the crutches beside his body, made the familiar slide down onto the stone-cutters' track. From there it was easy to follow, past Nikki's 'all alone' cave, curve around the jumble of debris that had been The Seigneury and up the slope to rest until dawn came to the decaying remains of the mill. He curled on the floor and waited until it was light enough to travel rapidly, feeling excited that he was, at last, on his own, a missing Canadian airman who was going to evade capture by the Germans and return to his squadron.

Nikki Joyal was sitting with her back to the warm chimney stone, huddled under her greatcoat. Her mind wouldn't stop thinking that something was happening, that her world was changing and that tomorrow would be different. She heard the distant gunfire and hoped it meant that France's friends were coming. That gave her little hope because she was afraid of what the Germans would do before they were driven out. The little home on the hill was quiet except for the wind around the windows and she heard the sound of crutches on the plank floor. She had a feeling this was the night he would go. She knew what Bernay had told her to do but Joseph deserved his chance at freedom. She was losing the last person she loved but she had to let him go. She closed her eye and prayed that he would survive. She waited for the door to close softly and crept to the window in the priest's tiny office. She saw his shadow flit amongst the bushes and smiled sadly. She pressed her face against the cold glass and yearned for the simple life when she was young. Her eye could no longer see any movement and she knew that he was gone. She swivelled in the priest's chair, folded her arms and rested her head on his desk, resigned to whatever fate awaited her. Overcome with sorrow, despair and exhaustion, she slept.

The sound of exploding bombs awakened her and she fled, terrified.

Pilgrim stirred from his rest in a panic! Explosions seemed to be shaking the entire valley. He hopped to the sagging doorway of the miller's room. He was shocked to see high above, barely visible in the misty glow of dawn, were dozens of American B-17 bombers; they were plastering the forest to the west and north. German fighters were lacing back and forth and the faint clatter of rapid fire drifted to him off and on. He could follow the bombs as they fell, tumbling, straightening, arcing down until they disappeared and the red and black fountain spewed skyward. Smoke and then bursts of flame dotted the forest. He recognized the bombing technique — incendiaries mixed with small explosives. They were setting the woods on fire! The pattern of bombs crept closer as the bomb aimers extended their target in the billowing black clouds.

One bomber, under attack from two fighters, veered away from the stream, smoke whipping back from the starboard wing, faint at first, then blacker and blacker. A red halo spread inward and the struggling aircraft jettisoned its load of destruction. A trail of explosions and fires moved progressively across the fields, across the river and pocked the courtyard in front of the church. A bomb landed on the cloistered pathway, blowing the rectory off its foundation and spewing debris into the gully. The shock wave blasted into the solid church wall, one corner crumbled and a huge section tumbled into a pile of ancient, dusty rubble. An incendiary hit the roof, tore through into the dry timbers of the vaulted ceiling and started it on fire that roared along into the steeple.

'Nikki!' Pilgrim screamed as he watched the roof of the rectory fly into the air in a cloud of dust and rubble. He felt a sudden stab of guilt and squeezed his eyes shut with shame. She'd saved his life. She'd fed him and nursed him and risked her life to hide him and he was running out on her when the going got tough. He raised his head and squared his shoulders, tightened the sash to gird his robes, put the crutches outside so he could take longer strides and rushed down the path to the road. Putting all his strength into his stride he raced up the valley, past the derelict gates to The Seigneury, past the three cottages and up Church Hill. He scrambled over the smouldering timbers of the rectory roof, coughing and gasping in the black smoke and amongst the rubble that had once been the quaint stone home for the priest of Ste Agathe.

'Nikki! Nikki! Nikki!' he kept screaming her name. He went down on his padded knees and used his mittened hands to pull away stone and timber. He could see the shattered table where they had eaten so often. The fireplace and chimney made a solid hump in the rubble, wisps of smoke coming from the embers of the cooking fire.

'Nikki! Where are you?' And his cries mingled with the crackling of the blaze that was roaring through the blasted church windows. He stopped, lay back on his haunches in fear and exhaustion, and watched the fire roar up the wooden steeple. Within seconds it was a searing firestorm, the force of the updraft sucking in those windows that had survived the first explosion.

Like a fiery finger beckoning the morning, the steeple blazed.

One sturdy, ancient girder cracked and weakened.

The structure started to lean.

Slowly at first.

Then faster and faster.

Over the graveyard it hung for one agonizing, blistering second.

Then it crashed, a roaring inferno, on top of the massive memorial to the Grenadines.

On top of the ancient tombs.

On top of the white angel of hope, snapping her wings.

And there it burned.

Until two massive explosions blew it sky high.

And blasted that wall of the church into rubble.

A river of boiling black smoke poured over Church Hill like an embracing shroud, spread over the cemetery, rolled down the gully and across the valley.

The throbbing of bomber engines gradually faded.

PART THREE

TUESDAY, 5 MAY 1970

We were a planeload of weary pilgrims that landed at Gatwick airport at 9:05 British time, stretching and yawning and greeting a dull grey day. The young people and their escorts filled the cabin with their enthusiasm and rapidly jammed the aisle, eager to start their adventure. I figured everyone would ride on the same buses and waited patiently beside Danielle until the congestion eased. When we alighted, Mac Boyle, who had lost none of his bouncy vitality, met us. He was a good tour organizer and was first off the plane. He directed us into the armed forces waiting-room where the washrooms immediately became focal points. After everyone seemed satisfied — coffee cups were empty and Immigration Officials appeared convinced that the number in the crowd was the same as the rosters they had scrutinized, Boyle gave us directions to the buses. The shuffling towards the blue convoy commenced, again with the young pilgrims jamming into the first bus so we headed along the ramp to the third, which seemed to be waiting patiently for us older folk.

The journey to Brighton was a subdued event, at least in our bus, as jet lag dulled our minds. I glanced up and down the seats but saw no familiar faces. The others from the St Jean briefing were obviously on another bus. I had seen John Simundson in his wheelchair heading toward a special vehicle for War Amps. Driving south, we escaped the terrifying ordeal of London traffic and sped into the beautiful southern counties.

A short, overweight woman in a dark coat with fur collar was in the seat opposite. She had braided hair curled on top of her head, held in place by large plastic pins. Her face was a network of wrinkles that seemed to be arranged in a pattern of perpetual sorrow. She had moved very slowly along the aisle while we were boarding and seemed to have difficulty breathing. About half an hour after we started, she had a rather violent coughing spell. Danielle's nursing instinct was aroused and she went to the water dispenser beside the rear exit. Her companion, a pleasant, balding man, accepted the paper cup with a smile and helped the lady take a drink. She expressed no gratitude. Her eyes continued to stare vacantly ahead, and Danny slid back into her seat, slightly rebuffed.

Our arrival at the historic Bedford Hotel on Kings Road in Brighton was a pleasure for

Danielle. She gazed at the Sussex resort with its Victorian architecture that swept along the seafront in impressive grandeur. She immediately walked across the broad avenue to rest on the wrought-iron railings and enjoy her first view of the sea. I remained beside our bus in a test of patience as pilgrims, young and old, milled around to locate their luggage. By two's and groups they headed for their allotted room numbers, grasping mighty keys with a piece of wood attached which admonished guests to leave them at the registration desk. Danielle and I appeared to be fortunate. We had a corner room overlooking the sea with the toilet and washroom just across the hall. I humped our bags onto the stands, kicked off my shoes, wiggled my toes and stretched out on the bed. I didn't tell Danielle that the repaired muscles in my back were jumping painfully from sitting so long in the cramped aircraft with no chance to do my exercises before we got on the bus. She plucked her make-up kit from her carry-on and headed across the way.

I must have slept because my caregiver awakened me, waving the sheaf of papers that were our itinerary and timetable with the warning that we would be late for lunch. We scurried along the carpeted halls and down the carpeted stairs into the carpeted dining-room to find the room alive with chatter and our den mother already calling for attention. Mac Boyle didn't need a microphone, but his attempt to give announcements in both official languages created a ripple of humour. I was pleased to learn that tomorrow's departure for France had been delayed from a morning to an afternoon ferry. The second aircraft from Canada was late arriving and the Minister of Veterans Affairs wanted Canadian pilgrims to arrive together for an official welcome from the Mayor of Dieppe. Therefore, Boyle thundered, tomorrow morning would be a free time for everyone to wander around England's most famous seaside resort. Deno Piniero popped up in his blue suit to announce that newsmen would be taking photographs of the arrivals and he wanted the Canadian Legion colour party for photographs marching on the seafront promenade.

While she was eating her lunch, Danielle was busy chatting with two of the nurses who had eaten earlier. As we finished our meal, she announced that she was going shopping with them, 'They say there're some lovely boutiques on the next street, just waiting for eager buyers.' She knew how I disliked shopping jaunts. 'So, Ben, you're on your own.'

'Great!' I responded, and they scampered away in a flurry of excited chatter like a trio of teenagers. I was thinking of a slow walk to get my legs moving and a chance to smoke my pipe. I watched them go down the front steps while trying to rub the tightness out of my back. For several minutes I stayed there, enjoying the scene and my pipe.

'Back ache from air travel?' A voice behind me asked. I turned. The coughing lady's companion was smiling from the doorway, a legion beret perched jauntily over one ear.

'Yes, just going to stretch my legs.' He stopped beside me.

'I wanted to catch your wife, Mr Courier, thank her for her kindness but she left in a hurry.'

'Yes, she's gone shopping. I'll tell her. How is your wife? I didn't notice her at lunch.'

'She ate in her room.' He swept his arm toward the walk. 'May I join you?'

I waited long enough to light my pipe and then we started off.

'I must explain, Mr Courier, she's not my wife and not really my caregiver, as they have called female companions, spouses or not. Actually I am the veteran, officially, and she's the caregiver, officially, but you can see, that's not really the situation.' He stopped and held out his hand. 'I'm Herb Broden.' We shook and resumed walking. 'My real name's Hersch Broden, but everyone calls me Herb. I'm Jewish and I'm the rabbi at Holy Blossom synagogue in London, Ontario. Mrs Caudill, Jessie Caudill, is a member of my congregation. She is in deep depression and this pilgrimage is a kind of experimental therapy, which is too involved to explain here.'

We walked along the broad path until I felt I had to say something so I asked: 'What was your outfit, Mr Broden, or should I call you Reverend or something?'

'Herb will be fine and I believe you're Benoit.'

'Ben will be fine.' He laughed and I used the shelter of a promenade booth to re-light my pipe, which never seemed to burn comfortably when I was walking and talking.

'I was a corporal gunner in the First Hussars. That was an armoured regiment and we had those floating tanks to get ashore on D-Day. What were you?'

'A bloody POW for three years. At Dieppe, with the Mount Royal Fusiliers. Supposed to be the only POW on this junket.'

'So I heard. That's why I remembered your name, from the tour guide and picture.'

We strolled slowly, as countless thousands of vacationing Brits have done for countless vacations at the seaside. While I was enjoying the atmosphere and stretching my stride to work my back muscles, I was thinking about this fellow's companion. She had a strong, intelligent face and looked like a typical, middle-aged wife and mother. Why the deep depression? Why was she, a non-veteran, on a pilgrimage to battlefields with Canadian war veterans? Why did she have a rabbi for a companion?

We walked in silence for ten minutes or more. The grey sky was getting greyer, a mist was developing over the amusement piers and I was getting shivery. 'Ready to go back?' I suggested.

'Sure, let's try the lounge at the Bedford.' He waited while I relit my pipe and added: 'Let me buy you a G and T.'

'Gin and Schweppes would be great,' I answered, because I had been thinking the same and we hurried on as a few drops of rain or sea spray dampened the pavement. We settled in the sedate carpeted lounge with portraits of men and women in Victorian clothes; the waiter was at our alcove table in seconds.

'Just in time,' I observed, nodding at the leaded window that was streaking with water. 'I hope the shoppers don't get soaked.' I settled back and waited. I had the feeling that Rabbi Herb Broden had made all these moves so he could get me somewhere to talk, so I asked: 'I'm curious about your companion, Mrs . . . '

'Caudill, Jessie Caudill.'

'Right, Jessie Caudill. Why is she in deep depression and how will this tour help her?'

The waiter came with his little tray, little white towel and our drinks. Broden signed the bill. He tried his drink, nodded acceptance, lit a cigarette and settled back. I felt my assessment was right and prepared to listen, at least until Danielle returned to the hotel with her exciting purchases.

'Jessie's only son David was reported missing in action on D-Day. So were a lot of other servicemen and there were a lot of grieving mothers. The reaction to the death of a loved one, any loved one, varies in each case. There is confusion, disbelief, anger, guilt, bitterness, fear of the future, all mixed up with the grief and loneliness. Religions, all religions I believe, attempt to relieve this anguish that death causes in many ways, but they all assume that there is a body. In fact, in some religions, the body forms part of the treatment to mitigate, reduce or alleviate this sorrow. When there is no body, there is the added uncertainty of whether or not the loved one is really dead, mingled with the hope that he or she is still alive and will return. The long, lingering fading of this hope is added to the pain of grief. In addition, the mourners are denied the comfort of honouring their dead; this is very important in my religion.'

He butted his cigarette and gave a querying smile. 'Am I making sense, or am I just an over-zealous cleric?'

'Go ahead. I'm interested.' I wasn't really because he was making me recall the sad face and pleading blue eyes of Mary Pilgrim and I didn't want to think about Mary Pilgrim and her problems. However, there was nothing else to do and I hated drinking alone. I ordered another round and listened.

'Jessie Caudill was a very private person, a widow, devoted to her only son and very, very religious. When she received the telegram that David was missing in action, she didn't cry or show any of the normal reactions that I mentioned, she just became more and more private. She closed inside herself. Friends tried to buoy her spirits by kindling the hope that he was a prisoner or that the report might be wrong and so on. All this worked against the Jewish faith that meant so much to her. She was being deprived of all the comforts for the bereaved that we have treasured for twenty centuries. We consider a body to be extremely holy. From the moment of death, Jewish custom focuses entirely on honouring the deceased. During *aninut*, the period between death and burial, mourning is tightly restricted to prayer. The spirit is not released from the body until burial when it finds its place in the afterworld. Therefore any delay is considered disrespectful to the dead. *Shiva*, seven days of intense mourning after burial, are very important to the immediate family and helps to assuage grief. Since ancient times, *matzevah*, the custom to mark the burial site with a stone or monument, reminds the living about the dead. The gravestone is an individual, personal altar. All this was denied Jessie. You could say, so what, so were thousands and thousands of other mothers, and you would be right. My gosh, Ben, there are 11,200 names on Canada's Vimy Memorial alone of boys who have no grave and they all had mothers. However, I am, at the moment, just concerned about Jessie. She slipped deeper and deeper into depression. She carried on the basic needs of living but otherwise became a silent robot. So far, no treatment, no medicine, nothing, has made any difference.'

I could see he was warming to his subject and that the end was some way off yet. My pipe was gurgling in a most friendly fashion, the gin was chasing away the chill and there was no sign of Danielle, so I nodded my interest.

'About ten years ago David's remains were found. A fisherman snagged something off shore at Courseulles. A diver identified it as a Sherman tank, the model that we used on D-Day. A rich officer of the First Hussars paid to have it salvaged as a regimental monument. When it was dragged ashore, it was identified as B for Bold, part of the first wave of amphibious tanks that went ashore, but this one, apparently sank. Inside were remains identified as David Caudill. He was in signals. Why he was in the tank, nobody knows. The crew escaped but were later killed so they can't tell us. Anyway, that's secondary. We thought the news that her son's body had been found and buried with full military honours and Jewish devotions, would bring Jessie out of her depression. Unfortunately, she didn't respond, as you can tell.'

I stirred and changed position in the rather over-padded chair because my back was having spasms again. 'How is this pilgrimage going to help her?'

'David's buried in the cemetery at Beny-sur-Mer and we're going there.' He reached into his pocket and brought out a small object that he rubbed between his fingers. 'There is an ancient tradition by which a Jewish mother brings a stone from

191

her garden and puts it on her husband's, or son's, gravestone or altar. She does this every year on the anniversary of his burial.' He held out the object and slipped it into my hand. 'This is a very special stone. Notice the shape and the hole in the middle; that denotes good fortune. David carried it in his pocket as a boy as a good luck charm. When his father died, he and his mother put it on the father's gravestone. Against all Jewish law for rabbis, I went to the cemetery, took it from the tomb and brought it with me. I am praying that it may be the religious talisman that brings Jessie back.'

'And how can we help?'

He sat back and laughed. 'You're very astute, Ben Courier.'

'Well, I didn't think you told me all this just for entertainment.'

He nodded. 'You're quite right. I'd like you to help me, particularly your wife, who, again I learned from studying the guide book, was a Lieutenant Nursing Sister on hospital ships. I hoped that I would be able to explain my needs to both of you, but Danielle went before I could introduce myself. Because this is the only time I'll have before we get to France, I've told you and hope you will talk it over with your wife. All I ask is that you stay close to us on the ferry tomorrow and when we go to the cemetery. I have no idea how she will react, if at all. The psychiatrist wouldn't venture a guess. I was encouraged to see that Jessie seemed to accept your wife on the bus. At least there was no tantrum, as sometimes happens when strangers try to help.' His face was pleading and I sure thought the guy had taken on a tough job — so I agreed.

'Thank you. We'll leave France on Thursday night to come back here. She couldn't stand the whole tour, so it's really only tomorrow and Thursday.'

My darling caregiver was fast asleep on the bed when I entered our room, her shoes, kicked off against the wall, were surrounded by packages. My shoes joined hers, I eased myself beside her and slept until dinner. I told her Broden's story as we changed for the one formal meal in England.

'Well, what a coincidence!' she responded. 'How can I refuse, after you so graciously agreed to help Mary Pilgrim?' Her impish smile softened the sarcasm of her words.

The next day was sunny and warm. The air smelled like springtime in England. The ocean was sparkling and smooth and everyone was in a holiday mood. We had a leisurely breakfast, packed, and had time to walk farther along the promenade before boarding the buses. It seemed natural that we took the same seats and Danielle was able to say a cheery hello across the aisle to Herb and give Jessie a sparkling smile of recognition. Jessie turned her head and the eyes seemed to react, but she didn't speak. The ride along the coast to Newhaven was pleasant and the chatter lively, which, to me, seemed rather strange when we were going to cemeteries to honour thousands of dead boys who were barely out of school. But I kept my thoughts to myself and was determined that Danielle should enjoy this vacation in any way she chose. We followed Herb and Jessie directly to the cafeteria on board the Sea Link ferry *Versailles* when the bus unloaded. We sat at a squat table for four. We ordered the full lunch, because we all agreed that we didn't know when we would eat again. I was surprised to see that Jessie ate well, but gave no indication that she enjoyed it or was aware of her surroundings.

We moved into the huge public lounge and found seats so that we were together during a very smooth crossing. Jessie seemed quite content by the window, watching the water and the sea birds that swooped around the vessel. Herb moved over beside me. 'This will be an emotional arrival for you, Ben, returning to Dieppe, I mean. Have you been here before, since the war?'

'No, I've never been back. I really didn't want to come this time, but Danielle talked me into it.' We laughed.

'That raid has produced more emotional discussion, it seems to me, than any other operation during the whole war. What is your assessment?'

I'd avoided getting into that discussion for a quarter of a century and tried to think of some response that wouldn't lead to a lot of rebuttals and arguments. 'It was a success,' I stated bluntly. I figured that would make him think.

He raised his eyebrows in surprise. 'Well, that isn't the answer I expected.'

'It was an exploratory assault in strength to test the defences of the enemy. In that it was highly successful. It proved that the Germans defences were a hell of a lot stronger than our leaders wanted to admit. It was also an exercise in strength to test our methods and equipment for amphibious assaults on defended coasts.' I hoped Danielle didn't hear the bitterness that I knew was creeping into my voice. 'In that it was highly successful also. It proved that our leaders didn't know what the hell they were doing, and that our equipment was no damn good. So I guess the guys died for something.'

Herb's head was low, his chin on his chest,

and he was staring at his feet. 'I can understand your feelings. Your regiment, I believe, was in reserve.'

'Yes, it was called a floating reserve. We were churning around in those damn barges, puking our guts out, and waiting to see what happened and it wasn't hard to tell that things weren't good. We could see the tanks motionless on the beach. We could see the landing craft sideways to the shore, obviously beached. We could hear the guns from the cliffs and see the explosions over the whole beach. We could see that most of our guys didn't get off the beach. So they sent us in. What the hell could we do? The Germans simply watched us approach and wiped us out. And for that, I blame the guys at the top.'

That was my answer. I hadn't said that much in twenty-five years and decided it was too much. I got up, smiled at the ladies and stretched my back by going into the aisle to walk up and down. When we were half an hour from Dieppe, Danielle said she would like to go up on deck and see France for the first time. 'Are you coming?'

I did up my jacket and put on my Legion beret because I knew the wind in the English Channel was always chilly. Danielle pulled a similar beret from her coat pocket and it made her look quite prim. We climbed to an upper deck and stood spread-legged and wind-blown close to the wheelhouse on the starboard side. She wrapped her arm around my waist and drew me close with a quiet smile of reassurance and support. She knew this revisit wouldn't be easy for me. Many times I had vowed never to go back, but here I was. I also realized I couldn't avoid it and hide in the lounge. All these guys were going back to memories of horror and fear and the deaths of buddies, so I guess I could stick it out. I was glad she was beside me and I gave her a hug.

A sailor in a smart blue uniform and a white peaked cap came out of the wheelhouse and uncovered some machinery that looked as if it was controlling the ferry. The coast of France rose out of the sea-mist: first those towering, pale cliffs, to port and starboard, relatives of the ones at Dover, divided millions of years ago. Then we could see the homes and the church, that looked so picturesque, but had been full of guns and Germans in 1942, the lighthouse, pier and breakwater of the ancient port of Dieppe were still indistinct in the deeper haze. The vessel rolled uneasily as channel winds and shore currents churned the water, disrupting the steady rhythm that had started soon after we left the shelter of Newhaven.

'See those cliffs on each side of the harbour?' I said, pointing. 'They were loaded with German guns, all trained and ready for an attack. That church spire on the cliff to the left was an aiming point for the landing craft. When we get closer you will see how the beach slopes up from the water — round pebbles, not sand. The tanks just ground themselves in. You'd have thought somebody in the British Army would know that. There must have been hundreds of snapshots of that beach in Britain taken by English tourists; they came over here on vacation for centuries. Anyway, there are beaches just like that along the coast of England where they could have tested the tanks coming ashore and found out that those round pebbles just grind the tracks off the tanks and they go nowhere, they just get stuck. That was a huge error in preparation.'

'Where were you?' Danielle asked, leaning so close to whisper in my ear that I could smell her hair.

'Way over there to port, bobbing around in circles. We could see and hear that the raid was doomed. The Germans were ready. So they ordered us in, even when some of the early guys were trying to get off.' I felt the old resentment flood over me. 'We were slaughtered. I was lucky, somehow, to get ashore and wait to be captured. There was nowhere to go.'

'Sounds as though you had a really tough go,' a fellow standing close remarked in a precise, clipped, British accent.

I nodded.

'I went ashore at Sword. When I walked up the beach, a little old lady came out of a house and asked me if I'd like a cup of tea.' He turned and marched away.

Danielle gave a little gasp, then kissed me on the cheek. 'Some English boffin what don't like us colonials.' She squeezed my waist and I felt better. 'I think he was having a bit of fun.' Perhaps so, but I decided that was the last time I'd ever talk about Dieppe again.

We were entering the outer harbour, past the concrete and steel jetty that replaced the one destroyed during our raid.

'This is an ancient port at the mouth of the Arques River and the harbour goes in and then curves to the right.' As if to prove me right, the *Versailles* turned starboard into the inner harbour and docked. A large banner proclaimed '*bienvenue les anciennes soldats*' and the speakers, in French and English, directed those passengers who were on the pilgrimage to buses, which were at the far end of the jetty. The immigration checks were made as we boarded. The officials were fast and courteous.

The buses took us to the west end of the Dieppe waterfront, under the high cliff that had once been so menacing, now softened by a walled garden called the Canadian Square, a memorial to those kids who will never grow old. The castle above with its conical turrets and massive masonry looked picturesque, but I remember the flashes of gunfire all around it and the layers of smoke that drifted up and over the highlands. Fortunately, although the welcomes and ceremonies were short, there was no time to visit the Dieppe Cemetery. I was relieved because it was five kilometres south near Hautot-sur-Mer and I really didn't want to recall all those guys I'd trained with long ago. The narrow streets behind the beachfront buildings were colourful with decorations and booths. Shoppers waved and smiled as we moved along until the convoy of buses and official cars headed south and east out of Dieppe for Caen, along the very road where I and hundreds of other Canadian prisoners had straggled in 1942.

The tour map showed it was over 175 kilometres to Caen and it was well after dark when we pulled into the parking area beside L'Otelinn on Avenue du Marechal Montgomery, which proved to be a modern and efficient motel. Mac Boyle and his team helped with the luggage and advised us that a buffet was waiting and we should hurry. We hurried. He also announced that one bus would go to Carpiquet tomorrow with a contingent of veterans from New Brunswick's North Shore Regiment to dedicate a memorial. This Atlantic Canada unit lost a lot of men capturing the landing strip there. Although it was only a short grass strip, Carpiquet airport was an essential part of the consolidation plan for airborne supplies and fighter support for ground troops. I learned afterwards that was the first time they tried the metal netting to lengthen the runway and carry the heavier aircraft. The rest of our group would go to the Canadian cemetery at Beny-sur-Mer. We had already talked with Herb Broden and he told us how we could help him during his ordeal. Friday everyone would join the British, Americans, and French for the anniversary ceremonies on the beaches.

Thursday was a perfect day. We could see for miles across the flat fields of Normandy, reminiscent of our prairies, only here the spires of ancient stone churches dotted the horizon instead of the angular shapes of grain elevators. We drove north toward the invasion beaches. The cemetery was only a few miles inland. As agreed, we stayed in the bus with Herb and Jessie until it emptied and the pilgrims had passed through the squat, white gateposts into the hedge-bordered area where the Cross of Remembrance was the central monument. Beyond the neatly-trimmed shrubbery, white military gravestones stretched in mathematical precision.

'Look at all those graves,' I murmured, really overwhelmed. I'd not expected quite so many. 'And each one was a boy with feelings and a future.'

'And a mother,' Danielle said softly beside me.

We watched as our crowd clustered around the cenotaph and the ceremony of remembrance commenced. Herb nodded and we moved from our seat and out of the bus. I offered to help Jessie down the steps and she accepted my hand without reaction. I could see that our rabbi was nervous as he removed his legion beret to wipe his forehead with his handkerchief. He led us through the entrance and immediately to the right to the second last row. Then we walked slowly along between the stones toward the rear of the burial ground and I could see he was counting. I noticed that one of the nurses and a young man, probably a tour doctor, were keeping pace two rows over and watching closely. Broden stopped by a grave that was marked with a tiny Canadian flag. I looked at the stone, similar to all others in this cemetery and yet so different and personal.

Maple Leaf motif at the top.

Corporal David Caudill.

Royal Canadian Corps of Signals.

Star of David instead of the usual cross.

6 June, 1944.

Rabbi Broden put his arm around the mother's shoulders and said softly.

'We're here, Jessie. At last. This is David's grave.'

She stared.

There may have been a bit of a shudder, a quiver of attention, a slight hunching of the shoulders, but the eyes didn't seem to be telling her brain what they saw. Danielle moved closer to her and took one pudgy, work-worn hand. There was no response although she didn't draw away and Danielle raised her eyebrows at me with a smile of satisfaction. I backed slightly to give them more room between the plots.

'There's his star, *Magem David*, the Star of David,' Broden soothed. 'He was buried with all Jewish ceremony.'

She stood motionless. Her wrinkled face had the greyness of old parchment and her eyes seemed focused on the inscription in total absorption. As she breathed, fast and irregular, there came the faintest and strangest of sounds, a tiny plea or whimper, rising and falling in her throat.

As the seconds passed, I began to think that Rabbi Broden's kind therapy was in vain. Danielle released her hand and came to stand beside me, clutching my arm tensely.

Very slowly and carefully the rabbi took the memory stone from his pocket and held it in front of her.

This time she reacted. Her eyes caressed the icon. She straightened a little and raised a hand.

Slowly and precisely he placed it on top of David's gravestone.

David's altar!

She trembled and gave a shuddering sigh.

Very slowly she shook herself free from his protective embrace. She raised her arms and covered her face with her linked hands. Her shoulders heaved as great sobs began to shake her body. Broden kept his arm across her back as she teetered unsteadily.

Suddenly she flung her arms wide, upward, head back and facing heaven, in the ancient pose of supplication, her bulky purse flying off her shoulder to drop amongst the flowers of another grave. Danielle softly knelt to retrieve it, refastening the metal clasp.

Jessie Caudill, head back and eyes wide, stared skyward as her flabby jowls quivered, and her mouth opened in a contortion of grief and anguish. She screamed and screamed and screamed in torment so that some of the pilgrims around the marble cross turned in alarm. Slowly, as if she had no emotion left, her cries of suffering subsided into gurgling, wordless sobs. Her arms collapsed and she crumpled across the gravesite, her body flattening the Canadian flag.

Her venerable cloth coat rumpled across the grass, the fur collar askew around her neck. A plait of hair came loose from its comb and uncoiled on the grass. The shoe fell from her right foot, revealing a hole in the heel of the rayon stocking that covered her stumpy, writhing legs.

The medical team started to her aid but Broden motioned them back. He knelt beside her as she cried with trembling convulsions. She wriggled forward and wrapped her arms around the base of her son's altar, her cheek against the stone, and hugged. She was breathing rapidly, sucking in air for a long time. We watched tensely. Slowly, gently, pitifully, this devoted mother became quiet, at peace and rested. Danielle's face was taut with concern at being unable to care for someone in obvious distress.

Canada's national anthem, played by some recorded military band, came rolling across the hallowed ground as the remembrance ceremony ended. Voices followed the benediction. Jessie's head slowly rose. She looked up at her rabbi. Her eyes were sharp, alert, with wrinkles of contentment around them. She started to scramble to her feet. Herb Broden supported her by one arm, Danielle at the other. She stood and stared at the stone with a hole in it, sitting black and shiny against the white limestone of her son's earthly altar. She felt around for her purse, saw it on Danielle's arm and motioned for it. She fumbled with the clasp, her stumpy fingers quivering, rummaging inside with years of familiarity and brought out a small, flat object.

She pressed it to her lips for a long time, head bowed, eyes closed, praying.

With trembling fingers Jessie Caudill placed a heart-shaped stone upon her son's gravestone.

David's altar!

She stood, head bowed, eyes closed, shoulders slack, while dozens watched. Her head finally came up, her back straightened and she smiled at her rabbi. He took her arm while I held her shoe and she wiggled her foot into it. They walked slowly and with dignity back to the road. A black official car was waiting with the rear door open and the young medic standing by. Jessie Caudill was helped in, settled back and the door closed.

Herb Broden turned to Danielle and gave her a hug. 'Thank you. *Shalom*.' We shook hands and he hugged me. 'Thank you and *Shalom*. May peace be always within your life.' He started to get in the car, then turned back. 'The day she heard that David was missing, she went into her garden and found that heart-shaped stone. She has carried it in her purse ever since.'

As he climbed in beside her, she wound down her window and smiled at us, a wonderful joyous smile that converted her wrinkles into a madonna. Her hand waved farewell and we heard her call. '*Shalom, dear friends, Shalom.*'

★　★　★

Friday brought an early start and a fast breakfast as traffic on the narrow roads along the Calvados coast would be heavy and slow. I had thought a lot about Jessie before I went to sleep the previous night and intended to contact Herb Broden before they left, but the excitement and haste made me forget. Danielle had all her schedules, maps and programmes neatly arranged in her over-shoulder purse and left me with nothing to do. She wore her nurse's badge on the left lapel of her jacket and miniature medals, which were new to me. I wore my legion blazer and slacks with my medals and wryly admitted that I would have looked out of place without them. But I still had no intention of marching and followed the 'relatives and caregivers' into the bleachers while the majority assembled and awaited order to 'fall in'.

The weather was clear with no rain forecast, but the wind was brisk and chilly, bringing out a variety of parkas and coats. I noticed Danielle was wearing gloves, another indication of how sensible she was. I had my hands stuffed in pockets, most inappropriate for a military man. Somebody, apparently of importance, started the ceremonies. The Queen of England and the President of France welcomed the Canadian and American veterans, thanked them for their help, and remembered their dead. It was relatively brief, after national anthems and much saluting. I admit I didn't know whether to salute or not, which seemed to have been a common cause for confusion amongst the crowds around us. I took off my beret at the start because only Americans salute without headgear and stood as straight as my aching back permitted. We trooped back to the compound, located our bus and returned to L'Otelinn for the only formal dinner of the pilgrimage in France. I looked around the motel unsuccessfully for the Jewish rabbi. When I asked at the desk, I received no satisfactory answer. Once again, the tight schedule made me scramble to catch up, but we arrived in the dining-room on time.

Mac Boyle made the only speech I remember because he was quite emotional: 'I brought you to the battlefields as a collection of strangers who were bonded together by one of the strongest bonds men ever experience, the companionship of battle and the unbelievable privilege of surviving. Now you are comrades in an exclusive club. You shared this great pilgrimage and you are strangers no longer.'

And so this weary veteran, full of salt sea air, assorted French wines, and excellent food, fell into bed. Friday, 8 May, 1970 passed into history and my attentive caregiver crawled in beside me with a groan of weariness and satisfaction.

Saturday saw us covering the invasion beaches going as far west as the flat, swampy reaches of Omaha, where the Americans had had difficulty coming ashore over treacherous, swampy ground and to the cliffs where the rough surf had cost many lives. I gazed in awe at the huge gun emplacements on Pointe du Hoc where US Rangers climbed vertical cliffs to put them out of action. The ground for a mile inshore was pocked with craters from hundreds of bombs that had had little effect on the massive concrete defences. One monster gun installation that had a dome twenty feet thick and thirty in diameter, showed little damage. The bunker that sheltered the gunners appeared to be falling apart from old age more than explosives.

I pointed to it and remarked to Danielle: 'This is part of Hitler's Atlantic wall. Think of the size of the guns it mounted. There was nothing like that at Dieppe.' I recalled for her the Brit on the ferry and his remark about the lady offering a cup of tea.

'I think he was sticking it to you, Ben.'

'And breaking it off.'

'With true British reserve.'

'Teach me to keep my mouth shut.' I felt a little grim. 'I thought we had it rough, but these guys, Germans and Allies, they sure took a pasting.' I shook my head in admiration. I put my arm around her waist and together we hurried back to the bus.

We moved eastward onto Gold Beach where the British landed and moved inland on their D-Day schedule. Remains of Mulberry, the floating harbour that followed, were still dotting the beach and off-shore waters.

We were, of course, most interested in Juno Beach where Canada's Third Infantry Division assaulted. And there in a tiny seaside square near the beach at Courseulles was B for Bold, the Sherman memorial tank of The First Hussars.

'Herb Broden said that David Caudill was recovered in that tank,' I said. 'I guess we'll never know why he was there.' I walked around it with great interest, reading the memorial plaque and the many regimental crests that were attached to the sides. Danielle insisted she take my photograph standing beside it.

I motioned her to come and rest on a bench at the side of the memorial square. 'Danielle, did you hear anything about Jessie Caudill? I looked for Herb several times and I asked at registration, but nobody seems to know. She seemed so much better when she drove off from the cemetery that I half expected to see her on the bus the next day.'

She nodded, rather sadly. 'She was much better, Ben. She went back to her room and one of the nurses stayed with her all night. Jessie talked and talked about David and this trip in quite a normal manner. She asked to see the rabbi and he was with her until almost dawn. Then she went peacefully to sleep, squeezing the nurse's hand. Just as the sun was rising, her hand went limp. The nurse summoned the doctor but she was dead.'

My back was aching from the hard bench, but I ignored it as I felt the cold shock of this news in my guts. I thought about that poor, worried woman. 'That's a bit of a shock. The cemetery bit was too much for her, I guess. How did you find out?'

'Professional secrets between nurses. The one I went shopping with.'

'Where's Herb now?'

'He started proceedings for the body to be flown to Canada immediately. He returned as soon as the details were finished.'

'That is a shocker.' Then I expressed my first reaction. 'What if the same thing happens with Mary Pilgrim? How would we feel then?'

She was shaking her head. 'Jessie Caudill had a bad heart. You saw the difficulty she had getting on to the bus. She was sucking air, that's a bad sign. She was thirty pounds overweight and probably diabetic. She had also been in deep mental depression for a long time. Mary Pilgrim is in good health, mentally and physically. She has no depression unlike Jessie, just a religious-based belief that her son is alive. No, Ben, I don't think we need to worry.'

We had no time to talk any more because we were being called to the bus. The tide was out several thousand yards by the time we reached Bernieres. We walked on the wet sand to look inland at the tall seafront house that was an identifying marker for the photographs of Canadians wading ashore, some with bicycles over their shoulders.

St Aubin-sur-Mer was a neat little town with a seawall and promenade lined with colourful boutiques. This was the eastern end of the Canadian assault area so we drove rapidly to see Pegasus Bridge over the Caen canal. This bridge was a steel structure that lifted to permit water traffic to move up the river to Caen. It was considered a vital link for the ground troops to move across the water barrier and had to be saved from German demolition. British glider troops landed silently within feet of the canal and secured the bridge in the first hour of D-Day before the Germans knew the invasion had started. I was amazed that the glider pilots landed their powerless craft so close to the canal and the defending artillery posts. We learned from our guide that the bridge had been named after the 'flying horse' symbol of the British airborne troops that liberated that area. We went into the bridge-keeper's home, first French home that was liberated, now a tourist focus and souvenir shop.

And everywhere, inland from these battle shores, were cemeteries, thousands upon thousands of graves, each one a boy who went to school, dated girls, worried about exams, and enjoyed his family. I slumped in deep thought as the day faded and rode in silence in the bus back to our motel.

★ ★ ★

Sunday was a day off. Government-chartered buses were going to several churches at various times and lists of the devout and curious were being compiled. French tour operators were selling day-trips to Bayeux to see the Norman tapestry; to Paris for shopping and rubber-necking and to specific military cemeteries where friends or relatives were sleeping in mathematically precise patterns.

The sun was making patterns on the wall as I lay in bed and decided I had to get something off my mind right now before we discussed going anywhere. I rolled on one elbow and my pent-up emotion burst out with more self-pity than I intended.

'Y'know, Danny, I'm a shit. I feel that I should apologize to all those dead kids in those cemeteries for bitching about the tough time I had at Dieppe and in the German camps. I'm alive and they're dead. I should be grateful. And I should apologize to all the vets on this memorial trip for not parading yesterday. I felt particularly ashamed when I was sitting comfortably in the stands and saw John Simundson marching along on his one leg and one false leg and smiling at the crowds as they clapped. And there were a lot of others that displayed a lot of determination to keep up with the pace.' I flopped back on my back, pulled up the covers and waited for Danielle to react.

'Well, that is a surprise. I admit, I would have been proud to see you marching. I would have been prouder if you'd suggested we marched together. It would have been a memorable picture for the boys. But I don't think there's any need to apologize to anyone for anything. Those soldiers didn't choose to be killed. John Simundson didn't choose to get wounded and lose a leg. All of us were on a team, a great big team, and you did what you were told to do, as part of the great big job. You did your bit like everybody else, so you're no different.' She made a chopping motion with her hand to show the subject was closed. I did feel a bit better.

'Well, OK, I suppose that's one way to look

at it, but I want to apologize to you for being such a difficult bastard when this opportunity was dropped in my lap, thanks to you.'

This time she nodded. 'I accept. You were a bit of a problem, but no challenge for a good caregiver.' She smirked.

This time I had nothing to say so I rolled over, wrapped my arms around her and gave her a great big hug. 'I'm a lucky guy.'

Her eyes were smiling. 'OK, so now you feel better and I feel a bit better, let's talk about our travels. The official pilgrimage is over. Now we start our twenty-fifth wedding anniversary vacation. I spoke to Mac Boyle and there's no problem delaying our return. As a matter of fact, he was delighted because several big shots want to get back in a hurry.' Now her whole face was smiling smugly. 'In fact, we're booked on the return flight on Wednesday the 20th.'

My turn to laugh. 'I did the same thing but Mac Boyle didn't say anything about you doing it already. I also reserved a car for tomorrow. I hope you didn't rent one too?'

'No, but I know where we're going.' She was chuckling as she crawled out of bed and reached for her tour folder. She spread a Michelin map on the floor and we kneeled over it. She had a black line drawn along the main route going south. 'I want to go to

Falaise to see where William the Raven was born.'

'Who?'

'*Guilliame Courveau.* William the Norman. William the Conqueror. Now you know? Think of it. The castle where he was born is still there, over nine hundred years.' She was pointing and I knew she had figured this all out long ago. 'That's only thirty-five kilometres. We'll find a nice yummy restaurant and have lunch. Then on south to Argentan, Sees, and Alençon where we'll stay the night at La Petite Maison de L'Orne, which is a cute little hostel, something like a British B&B.'

'How do you know?'

'Charlaine told me.'

'Who's Charlaine?'

'Girl on the desk here. She looked after the reservations for me.'

I slumped back on my haunches and looked at her with renewed respect. While I was worrying about myself, she was making sensible plans.

'You're great. That's all I can say. Just great. What next?'

She was back following her route. 'Tuesday we go to a tiny place called Ste Agathe which isn't on the map but has a guest home called The Seigneury, run by the Catholic Church as a religious retreat, but, because we're

Canadians on the pilgrimage, we can stay there.'

'Charlaine made the reservations?'

She nodded with appreciation.

'Good old Charlaine. And why are we stopping at Ste Agathe ahhh . . . I remember now. I think I remember that Vanderberg said that Pilgrim's pilot . . . so you've been planning this all along?'

'We promised Mary Pilgrim we'd try to find her son,' she shot back, pouting. 'And I intend to keep my promise. So we spend a couple of days asking a few questions in a pleasant little village. Surely you're not going to make a big fuss about that!'

'No, I don't mind, but I really can't see how we can discover anything new. Thousands of professionals searched the combat zones. They studied the records, German, British, American, everybody's. They spent years identifying the dead and plotting those cemeteries. If they didn't find anything about Pilgrim's airplane, how the hell are we going to in a few days — strangers in this country. I haven't a clue where to start.'

'I know, Ben, everything you say is true, but we do have one clue, that note about Hogan, and that's why I thought we should go there.' She looked so plaintive for a second. 'I do want to help her if I can. She really does believe, that's what makes it so hard to brush her off.'

I still thought we were wasting precious time, but I had promised myself not to spoil her holiday and if this was what she wanted to do, we'd do it. 'OK, Danny, let's go!'

We were up early next morning, excited and expectant. I packed away my grey flannels, blue blazer and legion beret and happily donned my old friends, baggy cords, baggy tweed jacket, sport shirt and baggy sweater. I snapped on my Greek sailor hat that I like because it doesn't blow off, although I admit it seems to make my face look chubbier than it is. Danielle looked stylish in beige slacks, green turtle-neck and a string of shell beads, purchased in Brighton.

We were like a couple of kids, squeezing hands as we hurried to the little Peugeot and were soon rolling south through the flat, fenceless farmland. The sun was warm and strong. Danny rolled down her window so that the wind tousled her hair and she sniffed. 'Whether the air smells of sea or vineyards or pastures, it's great.' She had her maps and papers on the seat beside her. 'This is truly historic country, Ben. The ancient Duchy of Normandy. The Normans were great builders in stone so their castles and churches have remained, as they have in Britain. Rouen was the ancient capital. William died there in 1087, twenty-one years after he invaded Britain, but he was born in Falaise and that's right on our way.'

I was trying to listen, because I realized now she must have spent a lot of time researching before we left, but the traffic was building and the huge trucks made our car sway. We navigated the narrow streets of Falaise, saw all the old buildings, had lunch in the garden of a little café which specialized in French breads, green salads and local wines. After a very enjoyable drive, we found our lodgings in Alençon.

The little lady who ran La Petite Maison de L'Orne fussed over us and chatted in such rapid French that I could only smile, nod and keep saying *merci bien*, and I was very grateful to her because I slept better than I had since we left home and was late on Tuesday morning. Danielle was packed and ready to go before I had forced myself awake. I found the driving tiring and the car seat made my back ache. However, I caught up, had breakfast and we were on the road again. The map didn't show Ste Agathe but Danielle had verbal directions. We turned off the autoroute on to secondary roads, heading generally west and a bit back north. I followed her directions and soon became disoriented. The weather was perfect, the scenery was interesting, and my caregiver seemed to be enjoying herself, so I relaxed and drove. She spotted a faded wooden sign, almost covered by bushes and vines that pointed to Ste Agathe and we were cheered on our way. The winding road came alongside a river, rose gradually until we drove through twin hills and there was our valley. Danielle gasped.

'It's beautiful!'

The road curved by a small pond with bushes and spring flowers around the shore. Lily pads floated, ducks and geese scurried little waves at our approach. The stream went under a humped stone bridge and at the head of the valley a waterfall sparkled and sent a mist floating across the far hill. On the right were two stone pillars with a plaque announcing The Seigneury and a curving drive leading to a car park at the side. The building was low and looked modern, although the veranda and white roof columns tried to give the impression of another era.

'This is so lovely,' Danielle sighed. 'Even if we find nothing else, this looks like a nice place for a second honeymoon.' She laughed brazenly and got out of the car. By the time I had hefted the bags out of the boot and carried them up the stone steps into the carpeted lobby, Danielle was in friendly conversation with a buxom woman behind the desk who looked like a retired Mother Superior, except for the jewelled spectacles which perched perilously on her nose with the ear rests disappearing into coiled hair.

'Sister Marie, this is my husband Benoit, and we're on our twenty-fifth wedding anniversary after attending the victory celebration on the coast.' The good sister was nodding and smiling and welcoming so that I found myself smiling and bowing like an Oriental busboy. She showed us to a room that seemed austere. Nothing was provided that wasn't absolutely necessary. There were twin beds with firm mattresses and a cross on the wall above each headboard. Religious pictures were on the other walls above twin dressers. Two upholstered chairs a round table and telephone completed the furnishings. The whole place was hospital clean. Danielle noticed my inspection.

'After all, this is a Catholic retreat, Ben, where the faithful come to denounce all the luxuries of our evil world.' She flopped on to a bed and started reading the promotional literature. 'This, apparently, was the site of the home of the original seigneur who owned and operated all the farms in the area. It was used as a German barracks during the war and was destroyed when an aircraft crashed into the valley. The diocese of Rouen purchased the land and built this retreat, which also will be a rest home for pilgrims to the new Shrine of Ste Agathe.'

I collapsed into one of the chairs and asked: 'Does it say where we can get a bottle of beer and some lunch?'

'Sister Marie said they provide dinners only and they have to be pre-arranged, which I have done. Otherwise, the only café in the valley is Café D'Or in the square.'

'So let's go to Café D'Or.'

We washed travel dirt off our hands and faces, arranged our luggage more neatly, and decided to walk. Gardeners were working in several plots along the drive and paused briefly to nod as we passed. There was a squat little church with a square wooden spire next to The Seigneury with a cottage linked by a cloister, obviously the priest's rectory. We sauntered along the river, past three or four modern houses and crossed on a wide bridge of concrete and steel, which somehow seemed to clash with the rest of the valley. The road turned north and climbed the hill in a graceful curve and disappeared beside the waterfall. The village square was really a park-like area along the river with rows of shops — bakery, grocers, butcher and some variety was provided by a Bureau de poste sign. Several little cottages backed onto the hill. The oldest building had steepled windows, a clock tower, a battered front and broad steps with a sign, Hotel de Ville. An old man was dreaming on a bench under a tree, leaning on his cane. Farther along, closer to the hill, was a squat building with stone walls, a gabled roof and many window boxes of flowers. A creaking sign showed it was, Café D'Or.

We entered a dim, low-ceilinged room with wooden tables and captain's chairs. Three workers were at the bar and several couples at the tables. We sat at one beside a crinkled window and scanned a brief menu. Our choice was simple but good — warm crusty bread, cheese plate, large olives, apple slices and foamy Alençon Sheva ale. We spent as little time as possible over our light lunch and wandered down the path on the opposite side of the river. The stones of the humped-back bridge were scarred, chipped and moss-covered near the water, fitting in with the rest of the village character. We went back to our room and rested until dinner. This was a welcome surprise — fresh fish, curried rice, green beans, more crusty bread, and perfect coffee. When we were finished and looking around at the seven or eight other diners, a thin young man in black with a clerical collar, came smiling toward us with his hand extended.

'Welcome to Ste Agathe, Mr and Mrs Courier. I'm Father Laroque, the parish priest . . . ' He indicated an empty chair, 'May I?'

We were pleased to have company and both smiled approval at the same time.

'How did you know our names?' Danielle purred in her warmest voice.

He smiled and looked quite boyish. 'Sister Marie is our information centre.' He sat and leaned forward. 'I understand you're part of a Canadian pilgrimage to the liberation ceremonies on the coast.' He didn't wait for a response but fixed his eyes on me and asked: 'Where did you come ashore?'

'Dieppe.' I said it without realizing he was referring to the landings, while I thought he meant the ferry.

He looked puzzled for a moment, then showed great interest. 'In 1942? Were you one of the Canadians who came in 1942?'

I took a moment to follow his rapid thinking, then nodded. He grabbed my hand again with unexpected vigour. 'Sir, let me shake your hand again with the deepest of gratitude.' Now I was even more puzzled and he carried on rapidly. 'I was a 10-year-old kid

225

living in one room with my mother just south of Dieppe, my father was killed in the army, and we were thrilled and excited when we heard the shooting and the rumours that the British had landed, but we were so sorry when we saw so many captured soldiers being marched down the road, some of them wounded, and we saw they were Canadians mostly.' He let go my hand but continued his rapid-fire delivery. 'But you gave us hope, my mother said you would come again and the next time you would stay, and we had that glimmer of hope to keep us going.' He leaned back and his face was glowing with enthusiasm.

I had trouble fumbling for a reply. 'Gee, thanks, that's very kind. I must say, Father Laroque, that you've given me a different slant on the raid. I've never thought about it from the French perspective. That's a bit of a plus in what generally has been a negative attitude toward what we did, or failed to do.'

'Why did you come to Ste Agathe?' he pursued, obviously enjoying the conversation. I raised my eyebrows at Danielle and gave a shrug which I hoped would tell her to take over. And she did.

Clearly and concisely she told about Mary Pilgrim's belief that her son was alive. 'We promised to ask around while we were in

France. The only clue was a notation in an American airman's burial records, with the same name as Pilgrim's pilot, that his body had been moved from a temporary grave at Ste Agathe. Now, you may not know it, but there are seven places in France called Ste Agathe. This one is on the path from England to LeMans, which the squadron was bombing that night, so it made sense to try this one first so here we are.'

Father Laroque showed courteous interest, but was looking dubious. 'That's all before my time, and there's hardly anyone in the village from the war years.'

'We were afraid of that.' Danielle admitted, 'but we wanted to try.'

'There's Brittany Paget. She's the only one I know of, although she never comes to mass. She's blind.'

'She might remember something,' Danielle countered hopefully. 'Could we talk to her, do you think?'

He smiled and rubbed his hands together and seemed most anxious to help. 'I'll ride over on my bicycle and ask. She lives just across the river, almost opposite the bridge, in one of the original stone cottages. She has a room with Roger and Emily Martin. He runs the little garage where the blacksmith used to be, so I'm told.' His enthusiasm made him speak so rapidly, I could hardly follow. 'How about tomorrow morning?' He was so enthusiastic that we weren't surprised when Sister Marie gave us a message that Father Laroque had arranged for us to see Brittany Paget at ten the next morning.

'We seem to have recruited an enthusiastic friend,' Danielle observed. 'Perhaps we should show our appreciation by attending his Mass.' We did, in the bright, modern building and afterwards were invited for breakfast. That worked out well because Father Laroque walked with us to the Martin cottage, its grey stonework nearly covered with green creeping vines. The path was lined with early spring flowers and ribbons decorated the iron door knocker.

Emily Martin was a spruce little housewife in a flowered apron. She was obviously flustered by visitors from Canada and the parish priest all at the same time. She bobbed and wiped her hands on her apron and led us down the central hall into a crowded room where Brittany was settled in a wooden rocking chair with a quilt over her knees and a shawl around her shoulders. 'She feels the chill,' Emily whispered after the introductions, backing out of the room with a sliding series of bows. Two chairs were set close to her so we sat.

Danielle spoke slowly and clearly in case she was deaf. 'Thank you for seeing us, Brittany.'

The blue-veined hands on the chairs arms came fluttering up in a gesture of dismissal. 'Not at all. Not at all. I don't have any visitors, not any more, you see, so I'm happy to talk with somebody different, especially Canadians and veterans at that. They tell me you came to France to remember all those poor boys who got killed driving those awful Germans back where they belong. That's very nice, very nice, because we were so grateful when it ended.' She wagged her head sadly. 'But only a few of us left.'

I could see we were not going to have any difficulty getting her to talk. 'Were you here in 1944?' I asked, trying to pin her down to facts.

'I've been here all my life, so I'm sure I was here in 1944. Yes, I certainly was, that was when the big plane crashed into the Grenadine place and killed those poor Boulanger's. I forget their names. Forget a lot of names these days now I'm getting old. Killed a lot of Germans too. Buried them up on the hill, across the river, the Germans I mean. The Boulanger's weren't buried anywhere, burned right up, in their own home, fast asleep, the fuel from the plane, you

229

see, made a big fire. Father Bree gave a wonderful service, the Germans let us open the church, special for that, you see, because they wouldn't let us have regular mass. I went with my dear friend Lilli Longuedoc, ran the post office did Lilli. I went with her because my eyes weren't so good even then. I've been blind a long time, but I still see things in my mind, just as clear as can be.' She finally ran out of breath and settled back.

'Did you ever hear anything about an American or British airman who was buried here?' She was quiet for a long time and the sightless eyes seemed to float around as if trying to find a point of focus.

'They buried Berny, I remember. Father Bree stood in the cemetery with the snow blowing around, it was so cold, but I stayed in the church because I couldn't see anyway, but I heard it was so cold they couldn't shovel the dirt into the grave. It was frozen solid. Those were difficult times.' She sighed.

Danielle leaned forward and patted her hand. 'Who was Berny? Do you remember?'

'Of course I remember. Berny Goineau. Lived in the cottage next door. Died in his sleep, so they said. He was old. What did you say about an airman?'

I asked again if she had heard about an airman being buried here and this time she

230

understood. 'Not in the cemetery. Lilli kept all the records for the church and she'd have told me if a stranger was buried in our cemetery. Maybe up the hill, with the Germans. I don't know. All Lilli's papers were burned in the church. When the church burned down, you know, everything was burned, all those beautiful altar cloths we made.' She ended with a clucking sound of sadness. 'We spent hours and hours making those altar cloths, and now, all gone, all gone, burned in the fire.'

'Did you ever hear the name Joseph Pilgrim?' I thought I may as well get to the nub of our search because we could see Brittany Paget was getting tired. She adjusted the comforter around her legs and then asked alertly, 'Pilgrim. Why that's what you are, pilgrims, they said so on the radio, pilgrims were coming from Canada and America on the anniversary of the end of the war, my, my, twenty-five years since it's been over. I think that's nice, don't you, being called pilgrims.'

We agreed and thanked her repeatedly for being so kind and backed out of the room to see that Father Laroque and Emily were waiting in the little front room and so we ended our first attempt at tracing a missing person. 'Not much help,' I murmured as we left, but Danielle looked satisfied. 'Never

231

mind, I'm enjoying my visit to France,' she remarked. 'Meeting a lot of people we wouldn't otherwise meet.' And again I had to admire her positive attitude. 'Let's go look at this burial place on the hill.'

The priest came with us as far as the walk beside the church, then pointed to the rear of The Seigneury. 'Just go back to where the ground starts to rise and you'll see a path. It's grown over with grass and weeds now, but you can follow it. I don't know what you'll find up there, I've never gone, myself. The official burying parties had been through here years before I came, so I had no reason to go.'

Danielle charmed the little cook in the kitchen at The Seigneury to make cheese sandwiches with pickles and apples. We changed into walking shoes and loose jackets and set out for our climb. It really wasn't that far or high, but we were not in condition for hiking so we took it at a leisurely pace. The route wound back and forth to make the gradient easier and the view was worth the effort. We looked across the green valley with the hills sloping gently to the west and woods stretching to the north. Behind us, the flatlands were beautiful farms so that it was hard to believe that across these fields American tanks by the hundreds had swept in rapid advance after the breakout at Falaise.

We sauntered along the rim of the bank through thick grass and twisty little bushes, not really knowing what we were looking for. However, it was obvious when we saw it. The ground was humped in a series of rectangular hills all in a row, with a second set farther to the north as if segregated from the main burying ground.

'Graves, most certainly,' Danielle commented. 'And no markers. Nothing that would indicate there ever were any, so I guess we must assume that the burial parties did their job and cleaned up after.' I walked back and forth in a widening search, but the only thing I noticed was a single hump, which seemed to be separate from all the others. 'We might also assume that the airman from the British bomber was buried up here first and then the Germans later, so it would seem reasonable that the Germans would separate their dead from the enemy.' I expressed my opinion for something to say because I thought we were spending a lot of time with no results.

Danielle found a fallen tree, sat on the grass with her back against it, and opened our lunch. I sat on the log and we munched in silence, enjoying the quiet and the view.

Then, as if she'd been reading my thoughts, she observed, 'Y'know, Ben, we mustn't be disappointed if we don't find anything. I really didn't expect that we would, but we can honestly tell Mary Pilgrim that we tried, and we can describe Ste Agathe to her.' Then she smiled one of her million-dollar smiles over her cheese sandwich. 'And I'm really enjoying myself. I like exploring like this, learning about the people and the history, rather than being carted about in a bus, on schedule, with professionals giving us their prepared lectures.'

I didn't have anything to add so I just leaned down and kissed her, sandwich crumbs and all, and felt the warmth of her personality that had comforted me so deeply on the hospital ship. We walked back, hand in hand.

★   ★   ★

On Thursday morning we lay in bed and discussed the rest of our anniversary holiday. 'Well, Danny, we've visited the place where Pilgrim's pilot may have been buried and we've talked to the only person who was here during the war; we don't know any more than when we arrived, so I guess we've kept our promise to Mary Pilgrim and can go back without feeling guilty. What would you like to do next?'

She jumped out of bed and retrieved her packet of maps and tourist information. As usual she had everything thought out. 'Let's drive back to Alençon and get on the main autoroute south to LeMans.' She had the route marked in red on the Michelin map. 'Stay there, then southwest to Angers, north to Laval, over to Rouen and Dieppe, on Monday the eighteenth, then back to England for a night in the Gatwick Hotel and ready for our flight on the twentieth.' She smiled with satisfaction,

'Dear lady, how could I do anything but agree with such planning. Let's do it.' So Danielle started to pack while I went along to the office to pay our bill and enquire about the closest petrol station. Father Laroque came along and, realizing our intentions, burst out in his fast, youthful French that left me signalling him to slow down.

'You're not leaving without seeing the shrine?' he gasped. 'I was just coming over to invite you for breakfast and to offer to show you our historic ruins. You can't go before you see them.'

I pondered. 'How long will it take?'

'Just a couple of hours. You can leave after lunch, how's that? I'll even get my house-keeper to make up a picnic lunch which you can eat on the way, there're quite a few beautiful spots on the road to LeMans.'

I could hardly refuse such enthusiastic hospitality so I went back to the room and told Danielle the news.

'That's OK by me. I was wondering where we were going to eat. The Café D'Or isn't the greatest of French restaurants and I guess we should see the ruins.' Mid-morning Father Laroque was leading us along the road to Church Hill at such a pace that I had to call a halt. 'I admire your vitality, good Father, but I have a back that was massaged by German rifle butts and I have to take things easy.' That slowed him down. In fact he became quite concerned. We started up the winding path and I was glad to see benches at almost every turn. When we had climbed past the third one, I accepted its welcoming rest and stretched my legs. Danielle leaned around to read a sign on a post near the bank.

'Father Damion Bree collapsed here during a blizzard in the terrible winter of 1943-44 after visiting Fleury and Allain Boulanger in the village' she read aloud. 'Boulanger? Isn't that the name Brittany Paget mentioned?' I got out my little notebook, having kept fairly detailed records, partially to help my memory, and also to show my official caregiver that she wasn't the only one who was efficient. 'Yes,' I confirmed and added a notation from the inscription about the priest, although I had no idea what it had to do with anything. I stretched the muscles in my back and the ligaments of my legs while I looked across the River. The waterfall was narrow but spectacular because the air currents in the canyon carried the spray into dancing patterns in the sun that were never the same.

We made it to the top on the next effort and stopped, shocked and dismayed. The church ruins looked rather artistic from the bottom of the valley, distance giving them a rhythmic charm. Up close, the devastation was appalling and it didn't require much imagination to tell what kind of an inferno must have created it. We were standing in a flat, flagstoned courtyard, blackened and cracked. Beyond us were the ruins of the church. A stone wall, less than a metre high, ran across the front and along both sides, battered and crumbling, with whole sections missing as if a bulldozer had ripped through it. Splintered stones and blackened timbers, now moss covered, were scattered all over. One part appeared to have been repaired years ago and a small metal plaque attached. I noted the wording 'Roche Joliat died here, 10 June, 1944.'

'Four days after D-Day.' I observed, and

Father Laroque said there were several more memorials like that. 'I think they may have been killed fighting the Germans.'

At the far side of the courtyard was a cairn, obviously fashioned from stones collected from the ruins. In the top was embedded a wooden cross, the type that is seen on the spires of medieval churches across Europe. I took a photograph with my little 35mm Vivitar camera, an anniversary gift from the boys at the shop. This was the first time I had carried it since we left the ceremonies on the coast.

We reverently climbed the steps. The stonework was pitted and broken, with moss and grass poking out of many crevices. The arched entrance was bare of any wooden supports or doors, although rusty iron hinges still clung to pegs in the masonry. We entered and stood beneath the remains of the belltower. Smoke-blackened areas streaked the walls. The smell of burned timber was faint, but still evident the further we moved inside. Danielle peered into a narrow opening that may have been a doorway; worn stone steps ran upwards, disappearing around a curve.

'Probably where the bellringers went up to the belfry,' Father Laroque said. He pointed to the grass and tiny shoots struggled from the holes in the flagstone flooring. 'Where the pews were fastened down.' Farther along the north wall a doorway with blackened frame was barricaded with several cross timbers. 'Would that be the vestry?' Danielle asked and the priest nodded enthusiastically. He seemed to be as curious as we were, so I asked him why it was called a shrine.

'This site,' he explained, 'has been an unofficial shrine for many years, honouring the war-time priest and the resistance fighters who died here. A group of survivors made the memorials and gathered every year on 10 June. They kept the tradition going for many years, so I was told and when they were all dead, the younger villagers kept it going. On the 25th anniversary of Father Bree's death, last 10 June, the diocese proclaimed it an official shrine and that's what's going on now. Ste Agathe was a circuit parish until the shrine was announced. Nine months ago I was appointed as a full-time priest and I've spent all my time attending to those duties and have been up here only once before, so I'm not an informed guide.' I was looking around and taking pictures.

Most of the side walls were piles of stone and rubble. The few window openings had grass growing along the sills. A marble plaque, probably a memorial to some former parishioner, hung by one fastener, the inscription obliterated. The south porch was two piles of stones gathered on each side to clear a path. Straight ahead, where the altar, choir and sacristy should have been, there was nothing.

We moved silently into the cemetery. Dozens of gravestones, moss-covered, partially buried, blackened and cracked were scattered, not in the regular symmetry of burial plots, but in confusion as if from a great wind. Tombs and their covers lay around in a haphazard pattern, covered with brambles, vines and weeds. A headless angel the white marble still remarkably bright, reached for heaven on one wing. The other was stuck, tip down, into the ground with grass bunching around it. The head was a moss-covered ball several metres away. Beyond a massive stone crypt was a crater six metres in diameter and almost as deep. On the far side was one clean stone, upright on a cement base. On the flat face was a metal plaque. We moved around to get closer and Father Laroque, with his younger eyes and athletic legs, was kneeling beside it, reading, 'To the memory of Pierre Bernay, Luc Pepineau, Jacques LaMarr and André Maltais, who died here 10 June, 1944 fighting for France.'

I wrote it all down, observing: 'Same date as the one at the front.'

We stood and looked around in silent respect for those who had died here for their country and received so little recognition. A new-looking steel mesh fence had been erected inside the battered wall that curved around a steep gully, partially filled with debris.

Another cairn, of reclaimed church stones, was close to the fence. A metal crutch was mounted on the top, its tip embedded in cement. A plaque testified that Father Damion Bree was last seen on this spot by Lilli Languedoc, Henri Parent and Jacqueline Maltais, 10 June, 1944. I copied the text and took several photographs.

'Everything seems to have happened on 10 June,' I observed, while Danielle asked: 'Why a crutch?' But our guide just shrugged and kept on moving. I knew we should be on the road if we were going to make Danielle's ambitious schedule. However, I was curious about several things I'd seen and felt I wouldn't be satisfied until I had some answers. As we were walking back, I expressed my feelings to Danielle and was surprised that she felt the same.

'I think we should go back and see Brittany Paget again,' she said. 'Now that we have some names, we can ask more questions.

Surely she will remember something about those memorials. After all, Lilli Longuedoc was her companion.'

Our plans were changed still more after dinner. Father Laroque came hurrying to our table, beaming and excited. 'Monsignor Roney is arriving tomorrow from the diocese. He is in charge of all plans for the shrine and has all the papers. I mentioned that two Canadians were here making enquiries about a missing airman and he said he'd be happy to tell you all he knows.'

Instead of exploring new vistas in the Loire valley the next day, we crossed the humped stone bridge above the millpond and explored the old and new sections of Ste Agathe on the western side of the river. We ended up at the Café D'Or for lunch and returned along the eastern side of the river, arriving at the front door of the rectory exactly at two o'clock as Father Laroque had arranged. His motherly housekeeper was all smiles and curtseys as she showed us into the smart living-room where Laroque introduced us to Monsignor Claude Roney. He greeted us warmly with a cheery welcome, an infectious smile and a brief handshake. Father Laroque immediately excused himself, claiming much work to do before the dedication services and special masses.

Roney was extremely overweight, a fact which his double-breasted black suit did nothing to hide. He had wrinkled bags under his eyes, magnified by large spectacles with black plastic rims and wide earpieces. The tabs of his shirt collar curled up as if strained to the limit by the thick neck. The tie was a narrow strip of nondescript pattern that fell over his stomach from a thin little knot. His French was from a first-class university and was a vibrant baritone that would have thundered through any cathedral. Except that he wasn't a clergyman. He told us that as soon as he had dropped into the most comfortable chair in the room with his short legs spread to accommodate his paunch.

'I must tell you first off, I am not a clergyman. The Monsignor is an honorary title given to me because of my office in the diocese. I'm a lawyer, an ecclesiastical lawyer, a specialist in canonical law of the Roman Catholic Church and the civil laws of France; these often come in conflict. My name is Claude and I think you are Benoit and Danielle. I do prefer unofficial visits.' He settled back and gathered his breath, before sipping a glass of white wine that was handy on a side table. 'Now tell me your mission. You're seeking a missing airman, I understand.' He looked from one to the other and I

243

nodded to my caregiver to take over.

'Thank you for the friendly informality, Claude. We're Canadians and Canadians prefer the use of first names.' Danielle's voice was as smooth as honey and I think she was stroking him just a little bit with her genial approach. 'We are also war veterans: Ben was taken prisoner at Dieppe, I was a nurse on a hospital ship. We met and married. Ben was chosen to come to France for the anniversary celebrations, and I am his caregiver.' Here her throat rippled with a sardonic chuckle that Roney seemed to enjoy. 'A mother named Mary Pilgrim, a most devout Catholic, asked us to seek her son who disappeared on a bombing mission in 1944.'

Roney raised his bushy eyebrows above his enormous glasses and expressed surprise: '1944!'

'Yes, she believed so completely, so devoutly, that he did not die, that she has steadfastly sought help for 25 years. She pleaded with us, when she learned we were coming to France, so that we had to agree to try. So we're trying.'

'And why here?' His voice was a jovial rumble.

She told him about the American. 'The squadron was bombing LeMans and Ste Agathe is *en route*. So here we are, combining a war victory celebration with our twenty-fifth wedding anniversary and answering a widow's plea.'

Claude's chubby face blossomed. 'Well, my congratulations on your anniversary.' He picked up his glass and realized we had nothing to respond with. He apologized and rumbled for the housekeeper. We were soon provided with our own glasses and bottle of local vintage. 'And we must salute those Canadians who helped to liberate France.' Again he drank deeply and put down his glass. 'But I'm afraid I can be of little help on your widow's mission.' He became thoughtful. 'I would think you've tackled a very difficult task. I have read all the evidence that has been gathered over the years from every possible source in this area in the investigation of Father Bree's ministry as priest of the Parish of Ste Agathe, and I don't remember anyone saying anything about a Canadian airman named Pilgrim. I don't have all those documents and testaments here, but I do have the official compilations. They have been approved for the promotion of this shrine, so there is no reason why I can't read them to you. You may learn something helpful.' He sipped his wine again before opening a thick leather dossier and extracting several files.

'This is the official statement of The

Ecclesiastical Court of Rome which, under Canon Law, is charged with assembling the facts on any canonization, beatification, shrine and so on. Many advocates gathered this evidence and these testimonials ⸗ over many years before The Congregation of Rites in Rome sanctified the true writ. I have no first hand knowledge about any statements or witnesses, all before my time, so I read someone else's compilation.' He adjusted his spectacles and read:

' 'Damion Bree was a divinity student in the seminary at Rouen when he lost his left leg above the knee in a motorcycle accident. He completed his studies, was ordained, and charged with the parish of Ste Agathe. Despite his handicap he served his parishioners with heroic and outstanding devotion during the German occupation. His earnest negotiations with the enemy garrison won many reprieves for his parishioners, he was constantly seen throughout the village in all weather, moving rapidly on his crutches, encouraging, visiting and maintaining the Church's presence.

' 'Early in the occupation Father Bree saved the life of Nicole Joyal who had been beaten by German rifles and left for dead. She became his housekeeper and devoted servant. During a blizzard in the winter of 1943–44

Father Bree collapsed while climbing Church Hill, returning from visiting a sick and elderly woman. Nicole Joyal found him, helped him to the rectory and nursed him during his recovery from pneumonia.

"Father Bree's recovery was remarkable, almost a miracle, under most difficult conditions. He resumed his ministry with renewed vigour. On the morning of 10 June, 1944 allied bombers dropped bombs and incendiaries on the North Forest where German armoured regiments were hiding. Several bombs overshot this target and exploded near the church, demolishing Father Bree's rectory and setting the church on fire. Father entered the inferno to save historic church records in the vestry and this was where his body was found. His ashes were buried beneath the flagstone floor of the vestry and form the focus for this place hallowed by memory.

"Three parishioners, Lilli Longuedoc, Henri Parent and Jacqueline Maltais have sworn in separate statements after intense interrogation that they saw Father Bree emerge from the fire and smoke of the church edifice, his habit on fire, hurry along the rearcourt and disappear. One crutch was found on this spot and was preserved as part of an unofficial memorial cairn.

'That's the end of the testament. On the twenty-fifth anniversary of his death, 19 June, 1969, the ruins of The Church of Ste Agathe and its surroundings on Church Hill were recognized as a memorial shrine. They are being preserved unchanged as a stark and dramatic memorial to the bravery of Father Damion Bree and the people of Ste Agathe.'

Claude Roney slowly assembled the papers and returned them to his folder. 'That's the official eulogy, on which I make no comment. However, as I said earlier, I have read all the peripheral material and may be able to answer your questions from memory.' He leaned back, pulled down the tabs of his waistcoat over his ample stomach and finished his wine. He rang for the housekeeper for another bottle. When we were all served, she backed silently from the room and I hastened to thank him.

'Thank you. That's very interesting and it answers several questions for me. I was curious about the plaque on the path up to the church, marking where the priest collapsed in the snow. It has more significance now that I realize he was on crutches. The wording on the plaque doesn't say that. It also explains why a crutch forms part of the memorial cairn, but it makes me ask another one. Why was a French priest using

German army issue crutches?'

Roney jerked forward. 'German crutches! Are you sure?'

'Positive!'

'How can you be so positive?' Here I saw the professional lawyer darting into action.

'Because I used them for several weeks in the POW camp after I was beaten by the Germans for trying to escape. They were made of aluminium, very light, and very well designed. I'll give the bastards credit for that. The one in the cairn has the German cross stamped on it and there is a brass plate soldered on engraved with Bree's name.'

Roney looked concerned. 'I can't answer that, Ben. Do you mind if I use this information? I should like to find an answer.'

'Gosh, no. I would have thought it was common knowledge.'

'Never mentioned in any testimony.' He pulled out a paper from his dossier and made a notation. 'I would appreciate it if you didn't mention it to anyone else. My job is difficult enough. If there is any hint that Bree collaborated with the Germans and received the crutches in gratitude . . . ' he sighed and his droopy cheeks quivered, 'that rumour alone could throw this whole endeavour into chaos. The French are still very touchy about collaborators and France so needs heroes. In fact, our church needs heroes and Father Bree is perfect — young, devoted, a cripple overcoming hardship.' He settled into silence and refilled his wine glass.

'I have a question,' Danielle ended what was becoming a difficult silence. 'What happened to the housekeeper?'

He brightened. 'Ah, that I can answer, dear lady. She's living in a small nursing hostel run by a Chapter of the Grey Sisters on the grounds of the Cathedral Saint-Pierre in Sees.'

'You mean she's alive?' Danielle voice rose with excitement. 'And living just north of here?'

'That's right.'

'What did she say?'

'She refused to talk to anyone. She is a ward of the Order and the Mother Superior supports her privacy totally.'

Danielle looked perplexed. 'Why?'

'I'm guessing, Danielle, but she obviously is very loyal to the memory of Father Bree and doesn't want any doubt to be placed on his devotion to duty. Obviously, if she makes public statements she will be asked for her opinion on the possibility that he, or his spirit, ascended, as three witnesses believe. And the church, you understand, would prefer that a lot of disbelieving journalists don't question the inference of ascension. So she avoids all controversy by saying nothing. Very wise perhaps. And we don't press her, also very wise.' He smiled knowingly.

'Could we see her?' Danielle pursued.

Roney shrugged. 'You can try. You have nothing to lose. You will have no trouble finding the convent. Sees is rather small.' The chair creaked as the great weight shifted and Roney poured more wine. It was obvious he preferred not to pursue that topic, so I asked: 'There's a crater in the churchyard and a memorial to four men. Do you know anything about that?'

'Yes. That witness Lilli Longuedoc, who was quoted, said that they were members of the Resistance and had hidden explosives and weapons in the graves and tombs. When the burning church steeple toppled into the cemetery, the heat made the explosives go off and they were killed on the spot. That has nothing to do with Bree's memorial so was not included in the official documentation.'

I pursued with another question that had been nagging at me ever since we walked around Church Hill. 'Can you explain, if the steeple burned, how did the cross on the top of it end up unburned at the front of the building?'

Roney's jowls jiggled with pleasure. 'Good

question, Ben. You should have been a lawyer. I have no idea. Again it doesn't appear to have any significance to the Father Bree story.'

'And there's nothing in all the documents about an airman being buried here?'

'No, but that's not surprising. The ecclesiastical discovery was to find if the cremated remains of a body in the vestry were the earthly remains of Father Bree and that's been proven with witnesses. And how sound were the witnesses who claimed to have seen him escape the fire. The advocates weren't interested in anything else, and anyway, hundreds of aircraft crashed in France during the war, and thousands of dead airmen were buried, so it wasn't outstanding.'

Father Laroque quietly slipped into the room to announce that dinner was served. Claude Roney continued to be an excellent conversationalist during the rest of the evening, relating interesting stories about his world travels on church business and consuming an amazing amount of food and wine without showing any effect. In fact, I thought he became more convivial as the evening progressed. I found him engaging and entertaining; he also expressed some fundamental views on religion and ethics that I had not considered before. When we were settled back in the lounge and Father Laroque had once again pleaded duties, I ventured to ask when work on the shrine would start.

'Immediately!' Roney responded. 'The plans are complete and approved. The contracts are signed. I thought the workers might have been on the job before now, but you were lucky, because the first job will be to remove the 'crutch cairn' temporarily. That area is being expanded and will have steps built down to a parking lot in the gully. There'll be a life-size statue of Father Bree swinging on his crutches, with his habit flying, on the spot where he was last seen. A glass door will keep visitors out of the vestry but permit them to see the tablet marking Bree's grave. And, of course, a shop against the surviving church wall to sell religious souvenirs, you know, statuettes, medals, rosaries, candles and so on. It's a rather modest shrine. The evidence of any miracle is really quite questionable and all those witnesses are dead. We'll just let it carry on. We know it will never be anything like Our Lady of Guadalupe in Mexico, which attracts millions of pilgrims annually, or even the Shrine of Padre Pio in Italy, which is our Church's most recent Saint, the Pope canonizing him only two years ago, in 1968.'

'You see pilgrims don't have to all believe in a Saint for the same reasons. It's really what they want to believe that becomes the truth in their minds. The church does not create Saints. God creates them in Heaven. The Church, in our case, The Pope, merely recognizes them. It's a form of ecclesiastical recognition, like knighthoods were military recognition or honorary orders for politicians or prominent citizens. Many saints were early Christian leaders, martyrs or heroes. Those who are beatified or canonized are our spiritual celebrities and people love celebrities, whether it's the Queen of England or a Hollywood movie star. Father Bree is a celebrity in this part of France. I'm convinced that he deserves this recognition, and so he will.'

'And what do you believe?' Danielle asked softly.

Roney's watery eyes fixed on her for several seconds. 'You know, dear lady, people have been executed or excommunicated for answering that question. Great crusades and wars have been fought to enforce an answer. I have a stock reply. Faith or religion or belief, is a very personal thing and no one should try to destroy it. But as soon as I, or anyone, express a fundamental religious belief, a dozen voices appear to argue that you are

254

wrong and they are right, they are the only ones who are right. So I say, don't try to change my beliefs and I won't try to change yours.' He smiled benevolently 'It's obvious that the thinking human mind needs some sort of a faith or belief to soften the burden of life and death, that's why thousands of religions and cults have been devised on this planet since creation. So, I say, let them believe what they want to believe and leave it at that.'

Danielle chuckled over her wine glass. 'A worthy and evasive answer, dear sir, and some rather innovative thinking.' She put down her glass and her expression became serious. 'I admit I have often wondered, when I have watched a patient die, whether life has any purpose at all, and if so, what is it. I think that is the reason the human mind creates its own religion. It wants life to have a purpose and so it creates one to suit its own desires.'

Roney was beaming, actually quivering with pleasure. 'This is a most enjoyable discussion. I am so pleased to meet a couple who can discuss religion or philosophy or fundamental beliefs without getting upset if their cherished dogmas or shibboleths are questioned. A purpose for life? A reason for creation? Dear me, I have no answers.' He raised his heavy arms in the air in surrender.

'The defence rests on that one. Did you ever have a glimmer of an answer, as one who faces birth and death in your profession?'

'Only one, which, I suppose, may explain why I always wanted to be a nurse.' Danielle paused and looked at me as if hesitant to speak her inner thoughts. I smiled because I was proud of her creative mind. 'The human race has a multitude of curses settled upon it, sickness, hunger, cold, heat, accidents, depression, madness, on and on and on. It seems to me that mankind's endeavours have always been to eliminate or ameliorate them, whether it's scientists improving our health and reducing suffering, or engineers building better dwellings that keep us warm and comfortable. Maybe that's the purpose.' She stretched and yawned. 'But I really haven't thought it through and I'm too tired to do it now.'

I had to agree. The room had taken on an unreal, hazy appearance that I knew was stupor induced by too much to eat and too much to drink. And I didn't feel like continuing the discussion, even though I had enjoyed it and I was impressed by Danielle's wisdom. I creaked to my feet and thanked him for a most entertaining evening and Danielle flattered Father Laroque with warm words as we left and weaved back to The

Seigneury. If all religious retreats were as enjoyable, I decided as the cool air sobered me, I might consider attending one or two.

I lay in my twin bed in the spartan bedroom and stared at the large print of the massive facade of the Cathedral of Reims and murmured: 'Quite a guy!'

She was a long time responding and then said dreamily: 'He certainly loves life on the church's expense account.'

'Yes, I got the impression he looked on this shrine as a business venture and cared little about the religious honesty. I suppose he leaves that to the clergy. So the church found a suitable local hero and decided to make the site as attractive as possible to as many pilgrims as possible to make money. They preserved the interviews of those who said something to enhance the shrine idea and discarded the others. Surely they would have talked to Brittany Paget, the village teacher and a parishioner but Roney never mentioned her.' I was so tired my brain was slipping into neutral.

With a weary groan, Danielle heaved herself up on one elbow. The glow from the window illuminated part of her face, and she looked dubious. 'Probably they did. She had poor eyesight so wouldn't see them burying anyone on the hill across the river, yet she heard about it, so it would be a secondhand rumour. I think lots of others must have seen, or heard rumours, but since that had nothing to do with Father Bree, it wasn't kept.'

'Anyway Danny, we had a pleasant time, we learned a lot about Father Bree and the Catholic Church, and a lot about Mr Roney, but nothing about Joseph Pilgrim. Tomorrow's Saturday and we leave for home next Wednesday. I suggest we pack up and start on our anniversary tour of France.'

She was a long time responding. 'I think you're wrong, Ben. I think we learned something very important.'

'What's that?'

'About the housekeeper?'

'Yes. I suppose if anybody knew anything about a burial in the village, it would be the priest, and the woman who looked after him.'

'We've got to try to see her, Ben, for our own peace of mind. If we don't we'll be wondering about her for months.'

'But Roney said she refused to talk to anybody. If she won't talk to the big shots from the church, she surely won't talk to us.'

'Maybe so, but we can try, Ben, we can try. All we have to do is ask her if she has ever heard the name Joseph Pilgrim. If she says 'no', then we leave. If she says 'yes', then we have our first solid contact.'

I sighed and had to admit that my wonderful wife was right, as usual. This whole business was nagging around in my head and I wouldn't really relax until we'd followed every possibility. I leaned across, gave her a hug and a kiss and said we'd try tomorrow.

★ ★ ★

So, Saturday morning we were on the road to Sees and had no difficulty finding the church because the spire dominated the skyline. The hostel of the Grey Sisters was a modern addition to a Gothic building that may have been a Chapter House before war damage. It was isolated from the church ground by an orderly pattern of lawns, bushes and postwar reforestation. Benches promised restful moments along curving gravel walks. The shrapnel-pitted stone shell had been converted into an attractive entrance; historic on the outside, but modern inside. We approached the receptionist and Danielle asked if she might see Nicole Joyal. The lady behind the desk, in a modernized version of a Grey Nun's habit, frowned and was a long time replying.

'Nicole Joyal is not a patient here, she's a sister of the order and, for very personal reasons, refuses to see anyone.'

Danielle must have expected a refusal

because she reached in her carryall and took out an envelope. 'We understand. Will you give her this message, please. We'll wait. All she has to do is reply with a yes or no.' Her smile made it almost impossible for the nun to refuse. She nodded and disappeared through a massive wooden door.

Danielle came and sat beside me. 'What did you ask her?'

'I said I was a war-time nursing sister with the Canadian Army looking for information for a Mary Pilgrim about her son Joseph Adam Pilgrim. I thought the woman-to-woman touch might be better. Hope you don't mind.' She was the experienced nurse again.

I shrugged and we waited. The receptionist returned, nodded at Danielle, which, I assumed, indicated she had delivered the envelope, and went back to work. I used the time to make a few notes in my travel diary. Danielle perused the publications that were on a side table. And we waited. Finally a girl in working habit came with a paper for Danielle.

'If you will answer those questions, I will return it to Sister Joyal.' She made a slight 'bob' like a well-trained servant and waited for our reply.

Danielle glanced at the writing, her face lit

up with excitement and her voice was loud as she exclaimed: 'She wants to know where I live in Canada, why am I in France, who gave me her name, and who is Mary Pilgrim? At least she didn't say no.' Danielle thought carefully as she answered the questions in her neat, professional way. She reviewed them again before returning the paper and the girl hurried away.

The messenger returned in twenty minutes. 'Sister Joyal will see you tomorrow morning at ten.' We left, excited at our success and returned precisely on time. Being Sunday, there were more people around the church and in the grounds. There was a different receptionist but she knew our names and escorted us through a side door into a gracious lounge that was obviously part of the original building. Heavy, floor-length drapes covered the one window and cut out all the light. Sombre tapestries were on the walls. The furniture was dark wood and cloth so that the whole space was dim. A small, shaded light illuminated papers on the table top, leaving the figure seated beyond in deep shadow.

We sat in the two chairs that our guide indicated. I blinked repeatedly while my eyes adjusted to the dimness. Finally I could make out a head covered with a black wimple, and shawl-draped shoulders. The light reflected on large, opaque glasses so that the chin was the only facial feature visible. Her hands were clasped and resting on the table.

'Thank you for seeing us,' Danielle breathed after we had been seated and the silence seemed to get uncomfortable.

'You have been in Ste Agathe talking to Father Laroque and Monsignor Roney.' The words were a harsh monotone that made me feel I was looking at a manikin and the sound was coming from a tiny electronic speaker. 'Under no circumstances will you tell them that you have seen me or spoken with me. Promise that or this discussion is ended.' The hands that picked up the papers were trembling but the voice was rock firm. 'Do you promise?'

I looked at Danielle and she looked at me, rather startled by the abruptness of the opening. I licked my lips and had to clear my throat before I said: 'I see no reason why we should talk to either of them again, but yes, I promise not to mention anything about this visit.'

'So do I,' Danielle added. 'We're not interested in the memorial to Father Bree. The only reason we went to Ste Agathe was because we promised Mary Pilgrim we would ask about her son. She is a very religious woman and believes completely that he is alive.'

'I accept your solemn oath of silence. Why Ste Agathe?'

'Because a burial record for an airman with the same name as Pilgrim's pilot was originally buried there. However, Brittany Paget was the only person who vaguely remembered the incident but thought it might have been a rumour.'

'You saw Brittany Paget?' the voice asked, showing a slight warming of the monotone. 'How is she?'

'Blind, very vague and very frail.' Danielle responded. 'Rooming with Lilli Longuedoc's daughter.' There was a long silence.

'What does Mary Pilgrim teach?'

I was shocked by the sudden change and was groping for the answer but Danielle responded right away. 'Religious history. It's a Catholic girl's school. Joseph Pilgrim received a very religious-oriented education.'

The dim figure of Nicole Joyal seemed to relax and the hands disappeared from the tabletop. 'It's obvious that I recognized the name Pilgrim, or I wouldn't have responded. I am doing so only because of his mother. I will need another promise from you if I tell you about him. You must promise never to write any details about this, and to tell only

Mary Pilgrim. Nobody else in France or Canada, only Joseph's mother, so that she may find the mental tranquility she has been seeking. I have very strong reasons for demanding this. Do you promise?'

We did, and for the next hour that hard, lifeless voice told us a story that left me in a world of disbelief. I was staring sightlessly at the carpet pattern, my mind trying to grasp all that I had heard, to grapple with the million questions, to . . .

The light on the table snapped off. When my eyes adjusted to the darkness, I looked up. Nicole Joyal's chair was empty.

I stumbled out of the room in a daze and I think I might have fallen if I hadn't been holding Danielle's hand and the receptionist took my other arm as we walked to the door. Certainly I was far from steady as I started the car and drove out of the property and turned on to the highway. I was having so much difficulty concentrating that I pulled off the road a few kilometres south of Sees. I got out of the car to straighten and stretch my legs and back muscles after sitting for over an hour in an over-stuffed chair. We had to talk before we got back to Ste Agathe. We had to agree what we were going to do and what we were going to say if we were asked. Danielle strolled across the grassy verge and sat on a little knoll, knees pulled up to her chin and arms wrapped around her legs. I think she was as disturbed as I was. I joined her, not knowing how to begin. She stared at me with huge eyes.

'We did it Ben!' she whispered. 'After all these years, we found somebody who knew Joseph Pilgrim.'

I shook my head in disbelief. 'Amazing! Absolutely amazing.'

'And she was right!' Danielle persisted. 'Mary Pilgrim was right! Her son was badly wounded, and he did survive, just like she's been claiming.'

I nodded agreement as I looked into the distance over those beautiful French fields but I was seeing that grotesque apparition behind the table, trying to convince myself that she had been a happy village teenager once.

'She must have been through hell several times.' My voice sounded strange in my ears. 'Nicole Joyal, I mean, I can't get her out of my mind, how she suffered. Imagine, being buried in the rectory root cellar for three days, with only a tiny grill to let in light and air. I think I would have gone mad. Solitary in POW camp wasn't as horrible as that.'

Danny grabbed my hand and squeezed, just like on the hospital ship. 'I suppose it could go down as another miracle that one American soldier happened to go poking through the rubble and heard her shout.'

We let silence and the beautiful spring day in rural France slowly calm our reactions. After many minutes Danielle's voice floated toward me as if coming directly from her thoughts. 'I can understand . . . now . . . why she refuses to talk about her time in Ste Agathe . . . she loved Joseph Pilgrim, loved him like any girl loves a man . . . and she loved Damion Bree . . . but like a brother . . . she lost them both and she's devoted to preserving their memories . . . but she can't talk about either one without revealing the impersonation so . . . nothing must blemish Bree's heroic ministry . . . if there was any hint . . . any insinuation that questions his integrity . . . that would destroy everything . . . so Pilgrim must never appear . . . and the only way she can be sure is to remain silent.' She shifted on the grass, her face twisted in concentration for several minutes while I gradually regained my focus.

'Ben!' her voice was suddenly sharp. 'What if Roney's suspicious legal mind wants some answers about the German crutch? That would destroy all her efforts.' She didn't finish that thought because she was off on another. 'I just realized something else.

Nicole Joyal thinks that Pilgrim escaped
. . . remember . . . she says she saw him going
down the gully . . . the night before the
bombing . . . she couldn't see him come
back. She was trapped in the cellar . . . She
thinks that maybe he's still alive . . . that
would be another reason for her silence . . . '
Again Danielle paused. 'Maybe Mary Pilgrim
is right . . . about that too . . . that's he's still
alive . . . that a miracle . . . '

I wasn't thinking about any miracle. I was
thinking about something that blind school-
teacher had said the first day we were in Ste
Agathe. I also thought it was time to change
the subject. 'What do we do, Danny, when we
get back to Ste Agathe?'

Now she was back with me again. 'Pack
and head out as fast as we can. No
good-byes. No nothing.' I agreed enthusiastically.

We stopped at a beautiful garden teashop
just before we had to turn off the N138 for
the side road to Ste Agathe and lingered a
long time over our food and drinks. We were
enjoying the restful quiet and fresh smells of
spring in rural France. We were also trying to
rationalize our encounter with Nicole Joyal
and how we were going to handle her story.
Several nagging questions made it impossible
for me to be completely satisfied but I didn't

know where to find the answers. The sun was low on the horizon by the time we reached the hill above Vesle Falls and looked into the valley.

We were a little startled! A lot had happened since this morning, even though it was Sunday. Tubular steel scaffolding was stacked beside the church ruins. Trucks, shovels, cement mixers and graders were parked in the forecourt. In the gully, another cluster of diggers, trucks and loaders were assembled ready to start the parking area. The carpark beside The Seigneury was almost full of cars and panels trucks.

'Looks as if Roney's contractors for the shrine have started,' Danielle commented. 'Time for us to go anyway.' As soon as we were parked she headed for our room to start packing ready for an early departure Monday morning. I excused myself. 'I want to have one last look around the church ruins and at that crater in the cemetery, now that I knew what happened.' That wasn't entirely true, but it stopped Danielle from asking questions as I hurried away.

I walked to the rear of the hostel along a new, concrete pathway, past the modern kitchens and employees' quarters where it ended. I continued toward the hill and after a bit of searching found the trail, now overgrown with fresh grass and vines, that ran northward. I came to a stretch of wild bracken that almost hid the fork. The one that led up the bank to the former burial plots was little more than an indistinct variation in the green undergrowth. I moved to my left and trudged toward the gully, the walking rough and the weeds clinging to my trousers so that I had to stop several times and pull vines from my shoes. I eventually was able to follow the original road of the stonecutters because it had survived as a series of open patches of rock and ruts in the soil. The shadows became deeper and deeper as the sun went behind the trees on the west bank and I ventured farther into the depression. Up ahead, the debris from the demolished rectory provided direction for me because it was a cascade of lighter shadows down the slope. The corner of the stone foundation and root cellar, which had saved Nicole, were a memorial battlement on the crest of the hill.

When I calculated I was in the right area, I left the relatively open space along the walk and climbed toward the east cliff. The going got more and more difficult until I was forcing my way between thickets and bushes and tangled vines. Finally I was driven down onto hands and knees and clawed my way upward. At first I tried to save my clothes and shoes but had to give up as the ground became rockier and rough. My sweat attracted hundreds of tiny midges that didn't seem to bite but clustered around my ears and eyes and forced me to stop, get out my handkerchief and wipe. I realized I was a damn fool to start on this venture in the light clothes I had worn for our visit to the hostel.

One of my fingers was bleeding from scrabbling with a sharp rock and I could feel the knees of my trousers getting damp from the moist ground. I reached the granular face of the cliff and peered into several small openings where stonecutters had tested for the quality of the quarry.

I moved gradually to my left, up toward the steeper rise and found only brambles and moss-covered stone. I rested on my belly, my head on my arm, and decided to give up. I cursed with closed eyes and gritted teeth and asked how the hell I ever got involved in this bloody affair. I looked down the slope but going back appeared as hard as moving along the face of the cliff so I carried on. I was trembling with fatigue, my back was hurting so that a couple of times I couldn't help crying out. I wiggled and scrabbled and crawled until I was panting.

Finally I found it!

The opening was a lot smaller than I had

envisaged, only about two metres wide and a metre high. Now I was on my belly and easing myself forward on my elbows, but once inside the floor became smooth. I eased my back against the wall and straightened my legs with a sigh of satisfaction. I was able to see further and further into the cave as my eyes adjusted to the dim light. My heart was beating fast from all the unaccustomed exertion and my brain was on fire with the excitement of my discovery. I folded my arms and stared . . . I couldn't believe my eyes!

I rolled on to my knees and wiggled a little closer.

I blinked, but it was still there!

Nobody will believe me!

I relaxed for a while, then decided.

I started edging out as fast as my weary muscles would move me. Again I cursed myself for not thinking before acting. But if I hurried . . .

I was a scratched, dirty, weary mess when I sneaked in the back door of The Seigneury and ran smack into Danielle.

'Where the hell have you been?' she burst out. 'And look at your clothes! I've been looking all over for you.' I didn't have time to think up any explanation before she went on: 'Ben, the most amazing news!' she started, as we made our way to our room. 'This nurse

271

. . . Therese, she's from Caen . . . sent down here to set up a small clinic, four beds in the hostel here, like a nursing station . . . for workmen who may get hurt . . . or old folk who will be staying here . . . we got to talking . . . being nurses, you know . . . and all of sudden . . . out of the blue . . . I never said anything, Ben, I swear . . . out of the blue she says . . . isn't it funny, they're building a shrine to a one-legged priest who was burned in his church and in the palliative care ward we have a one-legged priest who was badly burned and nobody knows who he is . . . isn't that amazing Ben . . . it's got to be Joseph Pilgrim, remember, Nicole Joyal said she saw him going away the night before the bombing, she knew he was escaping and she never saw him again . . . I think he did escape . . . and that's him in Caen and we've got to go and make sure.' She stopped because she was panting so much she could hardly keep breath in her body. She sat on her bed.

I stared at her and collapsed in a chair. It was amazing! After all the unbelievable revelations that had shown themselves to me on this one day, another didn't excite me as it had Danielle. In fact, I felt a twinge of irritation. I had my own solution worked out in my head. I knew what I was going to do tomorrow morning before we left. And now some unknown person had made a casual remark and everything was upset again.

I tried to slow her down with a little timetable logic. 'Tomorrow is Monday, 18 May. We leave Gatwick Airport on Wednesday, 20 May. We have to be there tomorrow night. How can we go to Caen . . . '

'I thought of that,' Danielle countered. 'Therese says we can get a plane from Caen direct to Gatwick airport. She's offered to drive back tomorrow, we can follow her car and she can be there to show us the way and get us in fast. We leave the car in Caen instead of Dieppe, simple as that.' She sensed my reluctance. 'Ben, we can't possibly go home and not be sure. We would be wondering for the rest of our lives.'

I sat back and let my eyes wander out of the window, up to Church Hill, where I could see the ruins of the church and almost make out the silhouette of the crutch on the top of the cairn. Danielle was right, as usual, absolute common sense, we had to make sure, one way or the other. But why did she have to run into this nurse, just when we were agreed to leave. I grasped one last possibility.

'She offered to drive to Caen and back tomorrow?'

'Yes, she's going to be here for most of next week.'

'So we could go there and back with her?'

'Yes, but why would we want to come back here? I thought we'd decided we were leaving.'

'We had, but I have one thing I must do here before we leave. I must come back. Don't ask me why, please, I'll tell you later.' I was pleading for her understanding.

'But why? I don't understand. Why won't you tell me?'

'I'd rather not. I may be wrong. If I am wrong, it doesn't matter.'

'But it does matter, Ben. You're not levelling with me. That matters a lot and I don't like it.' Her lips were compressed and her face was flushed. 'Can't you do it now?'

I looked at the window and shook my head. 'Too dark. Tomorrow morning. Then I'll tell you while we're on our way.'

She sighed and relaxed. 'Well, all right.'

'So tomorrow we go to Caen and then drive back with Therese. On Tuesday we leave here as soon as I'm finished and drive to Caen and fly to Gatwick for Tuesday night, and home on Wednesday. Agreed?'

'Agreed, but I still don't understand.'

Therese was a tall, slim, bundle of decisive energy inside a person who looked in her mid fifties but had the vitality of one thirty years younger. She had the big Citroën at the front steps, gunning the motor, five minutes before our agreed departure so that we had to hurry and Danielle completed her make-up while *en route*. I collapsed in the back seat and soon admitted that it was rather pleasant, being driven at 120 kilometres an hour and decided to enjoy the luxury. I also appreciated her commentary on the history of the land we were seeing.

'This land has been fought over so many times that it's a wonder anything grows. But nature is marvellous. Huge tank battles were fought across many of these farms in 1944 as the allies moved south and east, but now . . .' she swept a hand at the spring farms. 'By the way, the hospital where we are going is also very ancient, originally the Hospice Templar but now part of La Companie du Saint-Sacrement. And it's in the restored and modernized Chapter House of L'Abbaye de la Trinity. Don't try to remember all that,' she swept on, 'but just so you recognize that Caen is a very old city. They've done a marvellous job of restoring many buildings, because they were sure pounded to hell by both the Germans and the Americans.'

We were approaching the city and Therese started on a traffic commentary. 'We're going round this huge traffic circle which was built in an area flattened by bombs and shellfire.

Up there on the hill you'll see the ancient fortress with the red lion flag above the turret. On one of the battlements there's a plaque to the memory of the Canadians who fought for the liberation of Normandy.'

She had to stop acting as a tour guide because we were almost in a collision. It seemed to me that cars were coming from every direction and all blowing their horns. I shouted from the back seat: 'French drivers use their horns more in one day than a Canadian driver in one year.'

Therese laughed. 'They sure like their horns.' She resumed her explanations. 'This is Rue D'Auge and the traffic's not bad. Avenue du 6 Juin is wide and relatively peaceful until we hit the old section near L'Eglise de St Pierre which was heavily damaged but has been restored almost unchanged, even the carriage entrance to the chapel house, which is where we are going to stop.' She swung the big car confidently through the narrow opening and parked behind a stone structure where there were a few car spaces. 'I can park here for a few hours because the verger knows my car and I can't take it up the hill.' We got out, she locked the car, and we headed for the street. 'We walk from here.' She smiled. 'It's not far.' But she didn't tell us that it was all up hill. We followed a paved walk that curved into a narrow street. Then it got very steep. We rested on one of the stone benches and carried on until we reached the remains of L'Abbaye aux Dames.

'Matilda, wife of William the Norman who conquered Britain in the eleventh century, founded this abbey for women. It was battered by bombs and shells in 1944 and reconstruction is far from complete even now.' Therese led us through a narrow port in a wall that blocked the end of the medieval avenue. We were in a beautiful garden with walks and flower beds and surrounded by modern structures. At the end, partially hidden by trees and vines was a sombre building of time-darkened stone. 'That's the hospice,' Therese pointed. 'A restored part of the original monastery. You can see how you would never find your way in here without a guide.'

She led us along the path with neatly trimmed grass edging and into the building. The entrance was lofty and echoing. Semi-circular arches supported a ceiling decorated with religious murals. A lump of rusty iron sat on a block of charred timbers with a plaque that said it was the prayer bell, dated 1250 AD and melted in the fires of June 1944. Within minutes they were welcomed by an elderly cleric in white habit, with a rosy, unwrinkled completion, wisps of white hair roaming across his skull and small round spectacles perched on a rather bulbous nose. Therese introduced him as Father Infiniti. His voice was very faint.

'I understand from Sister Therese that you are interested in Father Orator. His records have been read to me and there is nothing recorded except the medical treatment that he has received here.' I realized, as he felt for a railing to guide him, that he was blind. 'If you can give us any information about his identity, we would be most grateful.'

'Then Father Orator is not his real name?'

'That is his church name, called that because when he arrived he was quoting Scriptures and rituals and whole Masses in a most irrational manner but it was obvious he must have been well-educated in religious matters. France was chaotic after the war and this hospice was damaged and flooded with homeless, injured, lost, sick and dying, all needing care for soul and body. There are still several here who have no memories, but many, many have gone to their reward.'

'Does Father Orator ever talk about his home, his family, his boyhood, anything like that?' Danielle asked.

The padre shook his head sadly. 'Father Orator no longer speaks at all. He has been silent for many years. He seems to have lost all memory and his brain is dormant, which is so sad, because it must have been a remarkable brain, reciting liturgy, the breviary, many masses.'

They were following him along a dark corridor. 'Can we see him?'

'Oh yes, we are ready.' From the dimness of the old construction we emerged into a modern bright room with large windows looking into the gardens. 'We have moved him in here so he and you may have privacy.'

The bed, with the head raised, was by one window. The sheets were crisp and blue, the light blanket a golden brown. The man, propped up by pillows, was staring outside with eyes that never flickered or moved. His skull was bare, the face was blotches of red and grey skin, puckered as if seared by flame, horribly disfigured. His neck was thin with folds of flesh drooping over the pyjama collar. He was breathing in whistling gasps, shallow and rapid, through holes that his nose normally covered, his chest rising and falling. Fingers, like bony claws, plucked at the edge of the blanket. Slowly his head moved until the eyes were directed at us but there was no indication of focus or question.

Danielle moved beside the bed, bending close like the compassionate nurse of old.

'Hello!' she whispered warmly. There was no reaction. She turned to the priest. 'Can you get his attention?'

'No,' the old man sighed. 'He's fed and bathed, kept comfortable, but there is no indication he knows. The doctors agree there is no hope of improvement. The psychological wounds are deep and permanent. We pray for him every day.'

Danielle whispered, slowly, watching for a flicker of recognition with each word. 'Pilgrim . . . Joseph Pilgrim . . . Mary Pilgrim . . . St Jean-sur-Richelieu . . . Nicole Joyal . . . Father Bree . . . Ste Agathe . . . '

She reached for the scarred hand and studied it briefly. Then her fingers slid gently to the wrist as she counted his pulse. All the time she was murmuring familiar phrases in French and English. She turned to the priest.

'Are there any patients who were here when he talked?'

'I doubt it.' Father Infiniti responded, his head quivering. 'If there are, I doubt they would remember anything.'

'When he was reciting the liturgies and masses, was he speaking French or English?'

'I don't know. I would suppose French, because if he was speaking English it's doubtful that this brotherhood would have taken him in. He would have gone somewhere else.

This is a French-speaking hospice.'

Danielle moved back beside the bed, again talking softly but there was no reaction. She came back to where Therese and I were standing. She was crying, silent, caring tears. 'The poor, poor man!' she softly sobbed. 'Therese, would the hospital have any medical records, diagnoses, X-rays, clinical reports that would show something about the amputation?'

The nurse shook her head. 'The medical staff has no records on any of these patients. They are all hopeless cases and the doctors are quite content to turn them over to the palliative care that the good brothers provide. They receive everything they need here, food, washing, comfort and prayer. This order of hospitallers has been caring for the dying for eight hundred years.'

We left Father Infiniti with many thanks and murmured comments and walked into the garden. Without any words we simultaneously sought the restful solace of the stone benches. The delightful smell of spring, the hum of insects and the cheerful colour of the flowers were such a traumatic contrast to the reality of the palliative care hostel that we rested in silent gratitude. I could understand why convents, abbeys and monasteries of medieval Europe were surrounded by such beauty. They were sanctuaries of peace and quiet in a world that must have been full of violence and hatred and clamour. After letting my brain slow down for twenty minutes I looked at Danielle beside me. 'What are you thinking?'

Her face was set in the calm composure that, to me, was her great strength and the quality I loved so dearly. But she was still a little cool from last night. The toe of her shoe was making little circles in the gravel. 'At the moment, I can't answer that. I need time, Ben, time, to adjust.' She raised her head and smiled at me. 'Let's just let everything rest for a while.'

I nodded and squeezed her hand. 'OK. I feel the same way.' I looked at my watch and realized that noon was near.

'Therese,' I moved over to sit beside her because it seemed sacrilegious to shout from one bench to another. 'Thanks for everything. We'd never have found Father Orator without you.'

'Any help?'

'Don't know yet. We have to think about it. In the meantime, the Courier's would like to take you to lunch, if you'll guide us to a restaurant.'

She jumped up, with her typical decisive energy: 'I accept. Thank you. Café William le

Roi is just across Rue St Pierre from the cathedral. We can walk and I won't have to move my car.'

We found a quaint alcove on the second floor in a building that might have been hundreds of years old except that Therese showed us pictures on the wall when it was a pile of rubble in the street, with Canadian soldiers trying to clear a route. We sipped Calvados frappé and ate the best steaks we'd enjoyed since coming to France, while Therese's amazing memory allowed her to pour out interesting stories about this ancient Norman town. Never once did she refer to our visit to the hospice or the tragic patient we had seen. I respected her professionalism even more.

We were a lot quieter on the way back to Ste Agathe. When we arrived, I felt mentally and physically pooped and just wanted to have a hot shower and fall into bed. I knew we had to talk about our discovery, or neither of us would sleep. So I propped myself up in bed with an extra pillow while Danielle did her final pre-sleep rituals of creams and lotions and things.

I ventured: 'Do you want to hear my thoughts, Danielle, or do you want to wait?'

She kept applying her creams at the mirror, and without looking around said quite eagerly: 'Go ahead, Ben, I'm listening.'

'We have to consider two possibilities,' I began, 'Father Orator is Joseph Pilgrim or Father Orator is not Joseph Pilgrim. So let's take the first possibility first. We have found Joseph Pilgrim. We decide on that. What do we do? We can keep quiet and nothing will change, except that we will always be wondering. We can loudly proclaim our discovery. That would create confusion in the Roney's complacent establishment that is creating the shrine to Father Bree because we would have to explain how Joseph Pilgrim survived the plane crash. That would also violate our oath to Nicole Joyal. We could say nothing in France but go back to Canada and tell Mary Pilgrim her son is alive in a religious retreat in Caen.' Danielle was quietly going about her grooming but I knew she was listening and would have her say when I was finished. 'What will Mary Pilgrim do? Will it make her happy or will she have a relapse like the Jewish mother? I'm sure she wouldn't quietly hear the news and go on living unchanged. She would want to come to Caen and see for herself, thereby proving the belief she has voiced for a quarter of a century that her son was alive. If she did that, the story would make headlines on two continents and the religious pundits would have a field day. And would this really be the best for Mary Pilgrim?' I paused. 'If we decide that Father Orator is not Joseph Pilgrim, then we carry on as before.' I waited for Danielle to respond but when she didn't, I finished my assumptions: 'Whatever we do, Danielle, we are going to be cursed for the rest of our lives with the uncertain spectre of Joseph Pilgrim . . . alive or dead?' I was finished, tired, confused, and just wanted to go to sleep, but I added one embedded feeling: 'I wish to hell Mary Pilgrim had stayed in her cloister and never entered our lives.'

Danielle slipped off her gown and climbed into bed, propping herself up and leaning to face me. 'Well said Ben. My thoughts entirely. Whatever we do, we're jinxed, at least while we're here in France. So let's take the easy way out and say nothing to anyone, at least until we get home. Agreed?'

'Agreed.'

'Now are you going to tell me why we had to come back here today?'

Smart, smart Danielle, never forgets anything. I snuggled down and pulled the covers over my shoulders. 'Tomorrow.'

I could hear her breathing and knew she was angry but she didn't respond. She rolled away in her bed and turned off her light.

★ ★ ★

The little alarm bell in my wrist-watch tinkled in my ear and I opened my eyes to a dark room, although my conscience was already prompting me that it was time for me to go. I dragged on my old cords and heavy sweater, wool socks and rubber soled shoes and felt for my Vivitar, with its new flash battery, where I had carefully positioned it before going to bed. My plan was to finish my chore and be back in bed before Danielle knew I was gone. That plan went up in smoke as I was creeping out the door and her sleepy voice murmured, 'No more secrets, Ben.'

Night lights illuminated the corridors enough for me to avoid the odd piece of furniture but the front door stopped me. It was bolted and on a time release system. I went towards the back of the building where windows were casting bright rectangles across the lawn. In the kitchen, three cooks in white aprons and caps were busy at the stoves and looked surprised as I kept on going out of the back door. The air was chilly and the grass was wet but the smell of a spring dawn was almost worth the lost sleep. The sun burst above the eastern cliffs as I left the smooth cement path and followed my trail through the long grass until I was oriented on the

286

narrow track. I headed steadily up the shallow basin, now spoiled by a clutter of construction vehicles. The light rapidly crept up Church Hill, making a black jagged silhouette of the ruins. I waited for dawn to reach the stonecutters' road before going the rest of the way.

As the shadows rapidly disappeared at the highest point, I stopped and stared in disbelief.

The realization came crashing down on me!

There was no sense in going on.

I turned and walked back, slumping with disappointment.

PART FOUR

I'm sitting in my favourite chair looking out at the familiar neighbourhood scene and grateful to be home. Our Quebec spring is just starting and the trees have the first hint of returning life although there is no green yet. Syd Lamonte across the street is carefully washing the winter's grime off the Dodge I sold him two years ago and Mrs Pomfret next door is raking dead leaves and brambles from her flower bed. I'm glad I bought this property on the Richelieu because the scene at the back is always changing and, when the trees are bare, I can almost see Mount Johnson.

Danielle is swishing about the room in green satin slacks and blouse that she bought in France, although I really don't know when she found the time. I like it. I also noticed that she's wearing green nail polish, and for the first time, as far as I can remember. The emerald necklace and earrings were my anniversary gift before we left on the veterans' pilgrimage to France. They match her outfit perfectly. She is a beautiful and colourful splash to counter my grey mood. I suddenly realized she had carefully chosen everything to brighten our encounter with Gil Vanderberg, who is due in a couple of hours. She knows that I am nervous and prepared for an ordeal, although it isn't his fault that it's a tough encounter for me, but still, he was the one who talked us in to listening to Mary Pilgrim.

The last hours of our 'so called' pilgrimage to France were rushed and hectic. Danielle was very cool when I returned from my morning walk up the gully. The departure from The Seigneury was almost furtive as we tried to avoid any conversation and particularly any encounter with Father Laroque. I drove to Caen in a dark mood . . . We waited for the plane to Gatwick in a tiny room with uncomfortable chairs and a lot of tobacco smoke. My Canadian pride perked a bit when I realized that a DeHavilland Twin-Otter, made in Toronto, was going to whisk us across the English Channel. The Gatwick Hotel was close to the London airport and was astonishingly expensive. Clients could use the free shuttle bus service, which, we learned at the last moment, didn't go to the military terminal, so we took a taxi. The RCAF transport left on time and the crew made our flight as pleasant as possible, although no cheery smile could soften those utility seats. Then train to Montreal and bus to St Jean and finally home on Friday night, my back sparking with pain from humping the luggage and sitting in cramped seats. Saturday and Sunday we did nothing except order in our main meals and let two sons know we were safely home. They are competent managers of our Chrysler dealership and reported 'no problems'. Monday was May holiday. We did go out for a walk along the beautiful Richelieu, past the yacht club and the eel traps. The spire of Saint Athanase Church across the river in Iberville was an old friend. Somewhere, in the girls' school close by, Mary Pilgrim was waiting. The twin humps of Mount Johnson and Mount Yamaska seemed like old friends on the eastern horizon. Their trees produce the sweetest maple syrup this side of heaven. In the hazy distance we could see the hills of Vermont.

I was enjoying the return to familiar scenes although my mind kept flicking back to my discoveries in France and how I was going to control my stories. Most of all, I felt depressed that I had to deceive Danielle, something I'd never done before. Gil Vanderberg had telephoned on Saturday afternoon, anxious to hear our news because we were a week later than the rest in getting back. I stalled him to Tuesday and this was it. The doorbell rang, Danielle answered and ushered him in with hostess grace.

'Welcome back,' he boomed 'How was the trip? Must have been good or you wouldn't have stayed longer.' He settled easily into the chair Danielle indicated and accepted her offer of coffee. He looked harassed; as if he had more worrying patients than he had time to doctor, but his voice and interest were obviously strong.

'It was our twenty-fifth anniversary splurge.' Danielle explained, pouring the coffee. 'Help yourself to cream and sugar.' She indicated the tray. 'That was the original reason we arranged the extension.'

'Thanks. Well, I didn't realise that was why you stayed longer. My congratulations.' He tipped his cup in a salute to us both.

'And the VE Day celebrations were terrific.' I started, anxious to get rid of my guilty feelings as soon as possible. 'The Canadian Legion did a super job and I was sure proud when those guys marched past, but I felt guilty, a lot were on crutches, or needed a cane to help them along, and some were in wheelchairs and there I was sitting in the stands, watching and complaining about an aching back.' He looked at me over his coffee cup with raised eyebrows and a frown, so I hurried to add: 'but I did wear my legion jacket and beret.'

We all laughed and that got rid of my guilt and his questioning eyes.

'But the cemeteries,' I pressed on. 'My God, Gil, acres and acres of gravestones, absolutely numbing when you think, each one represented a Canadian kid. I'll never complain again about being a POW or being forgotten. And I'll never think that the Canadian Legion isn't the greatest. I don't think the government would do anything to remember the war effort if it wasn't for the legion needling them along.' I ended my confession and cleared that out of the way.

'No question,' Gil confirmed. 'The legion, right across Canada, has done a lot for the veterans, and remembering those in the cemeteries.'

'I might even join your branch so I can have more of Janette Voiseau's hot toddies.' Another laugh all round but I could see Vanderberg couldn't wait much longer to ask: 'Did you find out anything about Joseph Pilgrim?'

Danielle's lustrous eyes told me the time had come for us to carry on as we had agreed. She would do her bit first.

'Yes, Gil, we did, and you won't believe how much. We went to Ste Agathe to follow the only firm clue, the one that you unearthed about the airman buried there temporarily. It's a beautiful little valley. We drove in from the south, between two lovely green hills and there's a waterfall at the far end, sparkling and foaming in the sunlight. The Vesle River runs down the middle and there's a cute hump bridge at the south end, made of local stone and very old. Further up, closer to the falls, they've built a new one to carry the traffic. There are cliffs on the right and very little room to build, but the west bank is gradual incline and they've built cottages almost up to the top.'

'On the right there's a Catholic retreat called The Seigneury. That's where we stayed. Apparently there was a big house built by the seigneur years and years ago. The Germans used it as barracks until it was destroyed when an aeroplane crashed into it. The German soldiers who were killed were buried on the top of the cliff right behind the barracks. I guess that's why the airman, who came down by parachute, was buried there. We went up to look. You were right. All the bodies had been removed to military cemeteries and nothing was left except the humps in the ground.'

'Next to the hospice was a new little church and rectory and a few modern homes, and up on the hill were the ruins of the original church and rectory. The village square and stores and more houses were on the west side, up by the falls, where there was more flat space. This is kind of a round about way to get to Joseph Pilgrim, but Ben and I have talked about it so often and we have to give this background. The priest during the war was named Father Bree. He lost his left leg in a motorcycle accident when he was going to seminary in Rouen. The Germans let him continue to live in the rectory although the church was closed, apparently. Anyway, Father Bree did a good job of looking after the people of Ste Agathe, even though he had only one leg. There's a plaque on the path up to Church Hill that marks the spot where he fell and almost died during a blizzard. He had given last rites to an elderly woman and was on his way home. The girl who was his housekeeper found him and saved his life, nursing him over pneumonia, which was pretty remarkable because they had no medicines.'

She paused long enough to re-fill our cups and pass the cookies. 'Shortly after the invasion in June 1944, the Americans bombed a forest just north of Ste Agathe and several bombs overshot and hit the church. Apparently the rectory was destroyed and the church set on fire. Afterwards they found the priest's body in the vestry. They think he had gone into the church to save the historic records and was overcome by smoke.' Here Danielle paused and took a deep breath. 'There's an interesting addition to the story, Gil, particularly from the church's view. Apparently several villagers were in the cemetery at the time of the bombing. We were told the French Resistance members hid weapons and explosives in the graves, waiting for the liberation. They claim they saw Father Bree come out of the fire and smoke of the church with his hair and habit on fire and disappear. And so he became a heroic legend and several parishioners built a cairn to his memory and the ruins of the church gradually assumed the aura of a holy place, a shrine. When we were there, the church was officially recognizing it as a shrine and, I think, promoting the impression that a miracle may have occurred there.'

She swished her green legs off the chesterfield and stood, serene and smiling, having done her part with her usual calm confidence. She tossed the conversation to me by saying; 'I'll get more coffee,' and flowing out of the room carrying the tray.

'How interesting,' the good doctor observed from the depths of his easy chair, 'but nothing about Joseph Pilgrim.'

I had made some notes from my travel diary when organizing my thoughts, and I suddenly wished I had them before me, but they were tucked away in the folder with all the other material we had brought back.

'We found only one person who was in the village during the war, a teacher who was blind. We talked to her but she knew very little. Her conversation wandered on a lot about her marvellous priest, how brave he had been and what a shame he died in the fire and maybe his spirit was still alive and it was all a miracle but she couldn't remember anything about any airman being buried there although she did remember about the plane hitting the German barracks because it also killed a friend of hers.' I realized I was rambling on but I didn't want to give Vanderberg too much time to ask questions, but he did.

'Weren't there any records?'

I shrugged. 'Lost in the fire, I suppose. We didn't see any.'

'And there was nobody from wartime? What about the priest's housekeeper? She would know what was going on, wouldn't she?'

The soft June evening had ended and the light on the pole across the street came on while I was staring out the window. Danielle came gliding back and turned on the floor lamp and the one on the side table. She swished around behind my chair, patted me on the head, and curled up in the big, overstuffed chair in the corner. This was the tough part coming up.

'Strange you should ask that, Gil, because we did locate the priest's housekeeper. She was a teenager in the village when the Germans arrived and took her parents to work in a garment factory. I understand her father was a tailor and her mother was a dressmaker. Anyway, she fought the Germans to keep them from taking her parents and a rifle butt hit her in the face. It crushed her skull above the right eye and tore her cheek. She was horribly disfigured.'

'You saw her then!' Vanderberg exclaimed, jerking forward in his chair. I raised my hand for a little patience and carried on with the story I had prepared.

'She was taken to Father Bree for last confession but he bound up her wounds and nursed her in the rectory and saved her life. She stayed and looked after him. When the bombing started that morning just after the invasion, she went into the root cellar and was trapped there when the house collapsed. I'm not sure how she was rescued but she ended up in a hospice in Sees, which is a few miles north of Ste Agathe, a sort of a crossroads community with a church that's a lot bigger than you'd expect for the size of the community. She had not been out in twenty-five years. It's sort of a cloistered order of nurses who respect each others privacy. She also refused to speak to any of the church people who were gathering evidence about the Father Bree shrine. The Mother Superior supported her vow of silence and so there was little chance that she would speak to strangers from Canada. Anyway, Danielle and I decided we would try. We'd promised Mary Pilgrim we would and we decided if we didn't try to see Nicole Joyal, that was her name, Nicole Joyal, we'd never be sure that we had done our best.' I realized once again that I was rambling on but I had to get this over as fast as possible and I didn't care how it sounded.

'The Sister on reception told us that Sister Joyal saw nobody so Danielle simply asked if she would give her a message which she had already written. It said; 'We are friends of Joseph Pilgrim's mother who misses him very much.' The nun said she would pass it on and we waited. We waited for a long time and finally another novitiate brought out a questionnaire that Nicole Joyal had written.

Danielle answered the questions and after another wait we were told to come back at a certain time the next day, which we did, although it meant delaying our vacation trip to the south of France.'

My back muscles were starting to twitch with the tension so I got up and walked back and forth across the room. 'Backache,' I explained and the good doctor nodded while I twisted my hips, swung my arms and this time sat on one of the dining-room chairs with a hard back.

'The next day we were ushered into a dimly-lit room that was furnished in a style current a hundred and fifty years ago. There was a long table with a shiny top of dark wood and behind it the strangest looking figure I've ever seen. She wore huge, dark glasses that covered a lot of her face, she had a dark wimple that covered her hair and cheeks and fell right down to her neck. She was in some dark habit that made it impossible to figure out how big she was. Her hands, which were on the table clasping, I presume, a rosary were starkly white even in the dim light.'

I paused and automatically reached for a drink of coffee, but I realized Danielle had deftly whipped the cup away and replaced it with a glass of whiskey with lots of ice. Bless her forever. I drank and plodded on.

'Nicole Joyal knew all about Joseph Pilgrim but before she said anything, she made us promise that we would tell the story to nobody, in France or Canada, that's the way she said it, very definite and precise, in France or Canada, except Mary Pilgrim. We were not to make any notes or repeat it later. That was the condition she demanded before she would even admit to knowing anything so we had to agree and we are going to keep our promise to her so we can't tell you anything from here on.'

Gil Vanderberg sagged in his chair and, with a nod of gratitude to Danielle, raised his glass of whiskey. 'Why would she do that?' he finally asked.

'Here I'm guessing, expressing an opinion, I have no other way to answer that, but she was devoted to Father Bree and she didn't want anything to detract from his perfection as the courageous, wartime parish priest. She had no knowledge about him being seen coming out of the fire and she would certainly be asked about that.'

Here Danielle helped me out. 'I think she might have been afraid of what some today might think about a young girl staying in the same house with a young priest. You know how a few insinuations can get the rumours going, and, of course, few people nowadays really know the terrible conditions the French people endured during the occupation.'

I carried on with my proposal, 'So, Gil, here's what I want you to do. Danielle and I will tell Mary Pilgrim about her son, but we want it at her place, where she lives, or some quiet room close by. And we want you there ready to look after her when we leave, because after we have told the story, we want to leave and never see her again or think again of Joseph Pilgrim. We want medical help right there because we don't want a repeat of Jessie Caudill.'

'Who's Jessie Caudill?'

We told him about the Jewish mother we had met on the pilgrimage.

'She went into a deep depression?' Dr Vanderberg was frowning his lack of understanding. 'For fifteen years? And she didn't come out of it when her son's body was discovered?'

'Not until the rabbi took her to the grave in France and performed that little ceremony with the stone. Apparently her very religious approach to death and bereavement depended on the presence of a body and when that was denied her, she went into a mental cloister.'

'And you think the sudden release from that mental restraint contributed to her death?'

'No, I don't know. All I know are the facts of what happened, not why they happened. That's why I want you to be responsible for Mary Pilgrim after we tell her our story. I have no idea how she will react and I'm not hazarding any guesses.'

He seemed to accept my position after several minutes of silent concentration. 'Right, Ben. So I will arrange for you and Danielle to talk with Mary under those circumstances. I must say I'm disappointed that I won't be permitted to hear the story.'

'Not from us,' I responded. 'But if she wants to tell you or broadcast it to the whole community, so be it. We will have kept our vow to Nicole Joyal and we will have kept our promise to Mary Pilgrim. And thank God it's all over.'

★ ★ ★

Gil Vanderberg wasted no time in making arrangements. I was in the middle of my breakfast on Friday morning when the postman came and slammed down the lid of my box. I smiled at Danielle as she quietly nodded and said: 'I'll get it.' I was no longer irritated by that noise every morning. In fact, the first morning home I rather looked forward to it. The telephone rang while she was at the front door. Vanderberg's voice was professional and his information clear. I had the impression that he wanted to finish this business with Mary Pilgrim as rapidly as I did.

'I've done as you requested, Ben,' he began. 'Can you and Danielle meet Mary Pilgrim on Monday evening? That's the first of June, at seven o'clock?' I said yes. I knew Danielle would cancel anything to go with me on this final encounter. 'She is very anxious to see you again and very, very grateful.' He paused and I mumbled some acknowledgement. 'I have spoken to Mother Superior in confidence and she understands the situation and wisely didn't demand any explanation. She has made preparations for an emergency, both physical and emotional and for a celebration among the sisters of the order, if that seems appropriate.'

'And you'll be there, Gil?'

'Yes, I'll be there but you won't see me. I've arranged for the receptionist to show you directly into the Mother Superior's office, which is more like an attractive lounge in any home. We decided this was the best atmosphere, quiet and comfortable. You can take as much time as you want and when you've finished, simply get up and walk out and go home. You'll have done your job.'

Again he paused and I waited. 'You've got that? Monday at seven. Saint Athanese School.'

'We'll be there.' I added, then, as a sudden thought. 'And thank you Dr Vanderberg.'

He chuckled and I could sense his relaxation. 'On second thought, Mr Courier, and as medical advice, I think, rather than going home, you should take your beautiful wife to the legion and buy her one of Janette Voiseau's hot toddies.'

★ ★ ★

The Ursuline School of Saint Athanase in Iberville was a contrast of ancient and modern construction. The main building was of rectangular stone with the Quebec peaked roof to reduce the snow load and huge chimneys at each end for fireplaces which would burn complete tree trunks. The three rows of ten windows were each identical and geometrically perfect. Above them, ten dormer windows broke the monotony of the utility roof. A squat five-sided steeple attempted to soften the starkness of the architecture and form a sort of welcoming gesture for the massive double doors. The steps were shallow and semi-circular with no railing to reduce their hazard during the ice and snow of winter. All in all, I thought, not a school whose appearance would encourage creative thinking. However, we continued along the curved gravel drive and parked in front of an attractive brick residence, all on one floor, with picture windows and flower boxes just starting to colour. There were white wooden pillars on each side of the door and more flowers. This was the residence for the teaching sisters and here Mary Pilgrim waited to hear our story. Danielle and I had lived just across the Richelieu River for twenty-five years but we had never ventured this far east in Iberville. I was surprised at the extent of the church property. There were more buildings amongst the trees. We could see the wire of a tennis court and open sports fields.

We entered at exactly seven o'clock and the receptionist had obviously been briefed and was ready for us. She was a smiling young lady in the modern version of the Ursuline habit. Without a pause she led us through into a warm, pleasant room, furnished with flowered curtains, green broadloom carpeting and sensible, comfortable chairs upholstered in greens and browns. A desk, filing cabinet and bookshelves occupied the part to our left, obviously the working area, but the remainder was for relaxing.

Mary Pilgrim was in a chair at the far end.

She rose as we entered and came forward to greet us. I had only a vague memory of her from that one meeting at the legion. Then she had been wearing drab outer garments damp from the rain, and her head had been covered with some depressing mantle. I had retained that first impression that she was an old-fashioned frump. Now I saw a rather statuesque woman, large-boned and taller than I had thought, in a long-sleeved tailored dress. Her hair, still dark, was drawn back with combs into a large, glossy bun that seemed to be exactly right. Her face was broad and surprisingly free of wrinkles, because I knew she must be seventy or over. Her pale blue eyes were bright and alert although they still gave that impression of great sorrow. I remembered those eyes.

'Mr and Mrs Courier, thank you for coming. I am so extremely grateful.' Her voice retained that rich, mellow quality that I could recall from the first meeting. She indicated the chairs, already positioned on each side of her. There was a round, glass-topped table in the centre with three settings for coffee with individual carafes. She resumed her seat and her hands, now resting on the upholstered arms, were shaped liked those of a professional pianist. A plain, dull ring was biting into the flesh of her wedding finger. 'Particularly since I understand my rather brazen request interrupted your wedding anniversary vacation. Please accept my apology for that.' She was being courteous and gracious but I could see she was quivering with restrained emotion. 'I understand you did have some success?' Her voice was marvellous, deep and refined. Her French pronunciation was of a lifetime academic. She settled back and crossed rather trim ankles over black low-heeled shoes. 'Please help yourselves to coffee as you wish.'

'Thank you for the warm welcome,' Danielle responded. 'Please, no formality. My name is Danielle and this is Ben.' She paused, and I could see she was waiting to see if Mary Pilgrim wanted any 'get acquainted chit-chat' but the pleading in her face gave us the answer. Danielle and I had decided that the direct approach would probably be the best, so she smiled and began very softly. 'Yes, Mary, we were able to learn what happened to your son on the night his bomber was shot down, but there are a few things we must explain first. The information we obtained came from a French woman who had been the housekeeper for the priest in the village of Ste Agathe during the war. All those years, she has refused to talk with anyone about her experiences. She agreed to speak with us only if we promised that we would not write anything down and that we would tell no one in France or Canada anything that she told us about Joseph Pilgrim, except to Joseph's mother. She was very strict about that and you must understand that we must keep that promise. So we were unable to tell Dr Vanderberg, or anyone else. You understand?'

She nodded. 'Dr Vanderberg indicated something like that and I didn't ask any questions. I am quite content to do anything you ask.'

Danielle relaxed and I could see she was relieved that was over. She finished: 'However, you may do as you wish with the information. We will have fulfilled our pledge.' Danielle unscrewed the top of her carafe, saw the steaming coffee and poured some into her cup. I indicated that I wasn't ready. It was my turn to carry on with the story.

'I'll tell you the story as close as I can remember it.' I took over with an encouraging smile from Danielle. 'The woman, whose name was Nicole Joyal, told it only once, and then only as a rambling collection of memories.' I settled back and found the chair remarkably easy for my cranky muscles. 'Joseph Pilgrim's bomber was on a mission to bomb LeMans when it was shot down. German cannon shells struck him in the left knee and almost severed that leg. So you were right, Mary, when you said you knew that he was severely hurt. He jumped and his parachute was caught on the cross on top of the steeple of L'Eglise de Ste Agathe, which is on the Vesle River. The priest, whose name was Father Bree, a local woodman and Nicole Joyal, rescued him and hid him in the church tower while he recovered from his injuries. So you were right again, when you maintained with such conviction that your son had survived the plane crash.'

She showed no reaction to this confirmation of her belief, no smile of satisfaction, although I thought those pale blue eyes may have lost a little of their suffering.

'They placed the body of Joseph's pilot, which had come to earth in a nearby forest, in your son's parachute harness so that the Germans wouldn't know he'd been rescued. The Germans buried the pilot in an area where some of their own men had been buried. That was very fortunate because it was the only solid clue that led us to Ste Agathe. Nicole Joyal and the priest, who had also lost his leg before the war, looked after him in the church tower and saved Joseph's life. Eventually they taught him to walk on crutches. In the winter of 1944, the priest got pneumonia and died. This is the amazing part, Mary. Because your son had lived in this religious community, and you had raised him in the Catholic faith, he knew the masses and prayers and was able to impersonate the priest and take over his duties and deceive the Germans that Father Bree was still alive. This was very dangerous and he was brave to do it. He was very kind to the villagers so that they loved him. He even conducted a memorial service for a village woman. Shortly after the allies landed in France, American bombers bombed German tanks nearby and several bombs hit the church. The rectory was destroyed and the church burned down. They found the charred remains of Father Bree in the vestry and concluded that he had gone into the church to save the historic records and was overcome by smoke. This was, of course, your son. Bree's remains were buried beneath the flagstone floor in the vestry with a bronze plaque to commemorate his bravery.'

Mary Pilgrim was motionless in her chair. Her hands were cupped in her lap. Her eyes were closed and tears were running down her cheeks. Her lips were moving and I realized she was praying. I glanced at Danielle who simply raised her eyebrows in uncertainty. I waited until I thought she was listening again.

'There is a plastic shield covering the

doorway to the vestry so that pilgrims may see this hallowed site without entering. That is the focal point of the shrine, Mary. Your son's grave really is the Shrine of Ste Agathe. The church ruins have been left as they were except the debris has been cleared for safety.'

Without opening her eyes, Mary Pilgrim began speaking.

'God bless you both. I am so very, very relieved. I have just said a prayer for you in gratitude for your devotion. This has all been ordained. The hand of God guided Charles Pilgrim to our convent in France when he was wounded and without friends. It was Divine destiny that I nursed him, fell in love with him, bore his son, and came to Canada. It was His guidance that led me to this hospice where I raised him in the full glory of Holy Orders to fulfil his destiny. The Lord saved Joseph from death in the aircraft when all his friends perished and guided him to the church where he fulfilled his final destiny, his final sacrifice. Those who trust in the Lord now sleep in the Lord. You have completed the prophecy and my burden is laid down. Praise God from whom all blessings flow.'

She opened her eyes and I saw the warmth of her happiness radiating from her smile. She reached out and clasped my hands, then

314

Danielle's, and I had to blink and swallow before I finished.

'Yes, it may be that miracles still happen. Three villagers who were hiding from the bombs near the church claim that they saw Father Bree come out of the flames and the smoke and then disappear, leaving one of his crutches. They claim it was his spirit, his soul, ascending into heaven. I certainly know nothing about such things, but that's what we were told. There are those, in that tiny congregation, who talk about a miracle happening that morning. There are those who pray that Father Bree will be declared a saint. Whether that is true or not, I can't guess, but I do know, Mary, that the spirit of Father Bree is very much alive in that village. And that spirit is mostly due to the kindnesses that your son administered under terribly difficult and cruel circumstance. He was a brave warrior and a dedicated servant of Christ.'

Her eyes were still closed, as if she was following my story in her mind. She was sitting proudly upright, her massive head high on her shoulders, the jewels in the combs winking in the light. Those cultured fingers were passing the beads of the Rosary, recanting the decades of Christianity.

We were finished. We had nothing more to say. We sat and watched that strong, motherly figure until I felt we were intruding on her private grief. I reached out and grasped Danielle's hand, and she squeezed her understanding. Although I felt that our departure might appear to be rather abrupt, I was relieved that her reaction had been so calm and only wanted very much to leave. I preferred not to answer questions, which I'm sure would come rushing into her mind as soon as the numbness of closure wore off. Slowly we rose and crept to the door. As I was leaving I glanced back.

Mary Pilgrim, mother of Joseph, was smiling at us, a Madonna smile that released us from her pleading.

★ ★ ★

June is a busy month in the car business. The boys had organized a weeklong promotion at Courier Motors to sell the 1970 Chryslers and Dodges that were on display in our showroom. The exciting Dodge Challenger was being introduced, a racy little pony car that came as a coupé or convertible with leather upholstery and for the really avid fans, a shaker hood scoop. Danielle and I had a memorable day driving a Challenger convertible down to Vermont with the top down. We felt like young lovers again, and I guess that's the idea of these novel designs for the young and the 'young at heart'. Even though the boys were putting on a special promotion for this new generation of young car buyers, they asked us old folk to help. We had been rapidly reading about the good features that made these the best cars ever built. Danielle, with her good looks and friendly personality was a natural on the showroom floor. Middle-aged men looked longingly at the convertible Challenger, although they knew they had to buy a family sedan. They loved to sit in the cars with her and chat about the automobiles they owned when they were young. It was Danielle, when I was just starting the dealership, who suggested having a raffle for a set of snow tyres, free and installed. 'Then you'll have the names and addresses of all the curious who just dropped in, and the salesmen can follow these leads during slack times.' This week we were raffling a week for two at Club Med. That's the way the week had gone after our session with Mary Pilgrim, and I was glad to be busy. I didn't want ever again to think of her or her problems.

So, after that tiring week, we took Saturday off. It was the kind of a beautiful day that makes you feel life is pretty good after all, particularly if the Quebec winter has been a real freezer. Danielle and I were lounging on the patio, soaking in the sun and enjoying our first gin-and-tonic. I had dug out a pair of shorts, hoping to get a bit of tan on my legs. Danielle had on yellow, floppy slacks and a loose T-shirt and a ridiculously large-brimmed hat, which, on anyone else, would have looked silly, but on Danielle, was perfect. We were dreamily looking toward the river, where the masts of some sailboats were beginning to move, when the telephone rang. Danielle went in to answer and was gone for several minutes.

'That was Gil Vanderberg,' she announced, resuming her lounger and her drink. 'He said Mrs Pilgrim has said nothing about her talk with us. She came out of the lounge and carried on as if nothing had changed, except that she was obviously a much happier person. But, and this he emphasized, at a special church service on Thursday night, she sang like an angel, absolutely thrilling, he said, as if her soul was flowing out with the music.' She leaned back and crossed her legs. 'Interesting, eh, Ben? He said she seemed totally at peace.'

I looked into the distance for a long time without answering. I was relieved that she hadn't gone into hysterics or a coma or whatever, and I was glad she was happy, but I really wanted out. I didn't want to think about her or Ste Agathe or Roney or anything, but I knew I had to. I couldn't put it off any longer. This was the time.

I picked up the Saturday paper to see what our competitors were advertising and glanced at the date. And, as if it was an omen, I suddenly realized that this was the sixth of June, twenty-five years since D-Day. The paper had a front-page story about the Canadian pilgrimage of veterans who were in Normandy doing exactly what we had done last May to celebrate their victory. I didn't want to think about that either, but twenty-five years ago I was one very miserable young prisoner because the Germans had herded everyone out of the camp and were driving us eastward away from the advancing allies who would liberate us. They later called this a 'death march'. It sure as hell was death. Guys who had hung on in captivity for months and years just didn't have the endurance to walk ten or twenty miles a day without food. But it certainly wasn't a march. It was a pitiful, foot-dragging, slope-shoulder, head-hanging shuffle. I wish I could meet again that valiant British airman who dragged his sick buddy along in a kid's wagon with no tyres and saved his life. Finally, the American mobile troops were so close the Germans left us to save their own skins.

I tossed down the paper and tried to get cheered up by looking at Danielle. She had that huge hat flopped over her face to keep the sun out of her eyes, and I thought she was dreamily resting. However she suddenly said: 'Yes, and almost twenty-five years since Joseph Pilgrim burned to death in the church.' She whipped off the hat and sat up, suddenly intense.

'Ben, Mary Pilgrim may finally be at peace and you may be satisfied with the job we did for her. You may also be able to put it all aside and cheerfully go on selling cars, but I shall never forget that poor man in the hospice at Caen. And I shall never convince myself that we were right not to tell her. I know there was nothing to show that he was Joseph Pilgrim except that he was a priest and had lost his left leg and was burned and had the same washed blue eyes that Mary Pilgrim has. Those eyes are what still bother me, Ben. They were her eyes, that same sad, pleading look that she had the night in the legion and she had last Monday night. I think you were wrong, Ben. I went along with you because I knew this whole thing was getting you down and I was the one that said we would try, but it bothers me. I've been thinking about it all week.' She flopped back on her lounge and pulled her hat over her face.

I sat squinting into the distance wondering how I was going to tackle this final mile. I knew, ever since we left Ste Agathe for the last time, that I would have to tell Danielle the rest of the story, or I would never have peace of mind again, but I wanted to get Mary Pilgrim out of the way first. We did that, and Vanderberg's report seemed to be the closure for which I was waiting. This was it! As good a time as any, right here in our quiet garden. I procrastinated by going into the house and mixing both of us tall drinks. I carried them out. Danielle was still stretched out on the lounge with the hat over her face so I went into the study and found my travel diary. I had been keeping very complete notes of all my thoughts since I got home and I sure needed them now.

'OK, Danielle, let's talk about it.' I started out rather loudly and rapidly softened my voice. 'You may think I have dismissed the whole business since we talked with Mary Pilgrim, but I've been doing a lot of reading and a lot of thinking. I haven't forgotten about that poor guy in Caen, so let's agree, for discussion, that Father Orator is Joseph Pilgrim. So Monday night we walk into that lounge, sit down beside her and say: 'Mrs Pilgrim. We found your son. He is alive. He is in a palliative care unit in a monastery in

Caen. He has one leg. He is burned so badly that you wouldn't recognize him. He doesn't know who he is. He hasn't spoken for twenty-five years. The people at the hospital don't know who he is, but he has blue eyes like you so we know he's your son.'

I paused and took a long swig of my gin because I felt I needed some false courage to get everything off my chest.

'What would be her reaction? Would she calmly sit there and say her beads, then walk out, carry on as if nothing had changed and continue to sing like an angel in the church? Or would she go into hysterics and a wailing spell when she heard such terrible news about the boy she raised and loved? Or would she immediately demand that we take her to him, that she was going to bring him back here and nurse him for the rest of his life? And what if she went to Caen and saw Father Orator and realized that he wasn't Joseph at all? Do you think, Danny, that any of those possibilities would be better than what has happened?'

I settled back and dropped more ice into my drink from the cooler. I didn't want too much alcohol. This was not the time for tongue or mind to be lubricated. This was a time for sombre discussion. And I waited.

Finally Danielle said, very softly: 'But

you're not telling the truth, Ben. That's really what's bothering me. You told one version to Vanderberg and another version to Mary Pilgrim, neither of which was the truth. You told her a story that you knew might satisfy her and get her off our backs, and I'm having a lot of difficulty accepting that. And I'm very upset that you're not being truthful to me.'

I took a long time to think before I answered. 'I know how you feel. I had to wrestle with myself before I decided what to say, but Claude Roney helped me.'

'Oh? How's that?'

'I figured if the Catholic Church could fudge a little on the truth just to embellish a shrine, I could bend it a little to satisfy a distraught mother.' I finished my drink and sat back with a sigh of satisfaction. Danielle slid her hat on to her lap and sat up to face me. I could see the determination in the way her mouth was set.

'That's just an excuse for not facing the fact that Father Orator could be Joseph Pilgrim. Now that Mary Pilgrim appears to have been satisfied, there's no reason why we can't tell Gil Vanderberg about Orator.'

'What good would that do?'

'It might solve the mystery.'

'How?'

'He could investigate quietly through

medical circles, without making any great uproar.'

'Investigate what?'

'Medical evidence.'

'Of what?'

Danielle was irritated by my scepticism and her words became very precise. 'Joseph Pilgrim's leg was blasted off by a high calibre bullet. The bone was shattered. The amputation certainly wasn't medically done. We could write to Nicole Joyal and ask her for details. Was the knee intact? Was the severance in the tibia below the knee or in the femur above the knee. Dr Vanderberg could request the hospital in Caen to send details of Father Orator's amputation, X-rays maybe. Then they could be compared. If they are identical, we have the answer. Hard medical evidence.' She plopped back on her lounge. 'Anyway, Ben, I just can't sit back quietly in our smug comfort without trying to do something about that poor man. After all, I was the one who found him. For the sake of human kindness, we should make every effort to find out, one way or the other.' She stared with narrowed eyes into the distance, her features taut with determination. 'And if I am right, Ben. If we prove that the man in Caen is Joseph Pilgrim, think of the achievement, the revelation of a really unique war hero. He would be decorated and the nation would recognize him. Think what effect that would have on Mary Pilgrim. Wouldn't she be the proud mother!' She seemed to run out of verve and settled back, pulling her hat over her face again.

She was right, of course. There was absolutely no reason, in her mind, why she shouldn't tell Dr Vanderberg about the Caen patient. And her suggestion for medical research was very sound. Except that it was unnecessary. It was time I told her the truth.

'Danielle, you are right. You discovered Father Orator. You can tell Vanderberg about him if you like, but I can tell you, positively, without any doubt, that Father Orator is not Joseph Pilgrim.'

Now the hat went flying across the patio and she was tense and feisty, her dark brown eyes blazing at me with most unusual intensity.

'How can you say that, Ben? How can you be that sure? You've assumed a very superior, pious attitude since we left France, demanding that you tell the story the way you see it, ignoring my opinions entirely.' She flopped back and her pout told me I had to be very careful or this could become a serious quarrel. I took a long time to respond because I needed so desperately to tell it properly so that Danielle would be satisfied and I could get on with selling cars and enjoying life.

'Danielle,' I began softly, 'I have tried to present this unusual story in the best way for the person concerned. I admit I twisted the facts here and there, but now I will tell you what happened on 10 June, 1944 based upon fact, not opinions or wishful thinking.'

'Do that!' she shot at me.

'OK, let's think about Joseph Adam Pilgrim for a moment as a person. He was raised without a father by a kindly mother who was a religious zealot, swamped by a religious atmosphere throughout his youth and grew up in a girl's school. Did he ever have any chums? Did he play baseball or hockey or have a fight with another kid? He must have hated it.'

'That's an opinion!' Danielle interjected from under her hat, which she had angrily recovered.

'Yes, it is, although I'd rather call it a conclusion based upon evidence. As soon as he could, he joined the air force. We know that. He escaped the female, religious world that had smothered him all his life. And he was very successful in the male world of the military. He was a good navigator because they made him an instructor. And when they wanted an experienced navigator on a squadron in England they sent him over rapidly. He went on his first mission, his first great adventure, when he was shot down. He was wounded and survived initially by hanging on a cross. Then he was saved by a priest, the church influence again, and by the priest's housekeeper, the female dominance again. This again is an opinion, but I'm sure he wanted to escape as soon as he was physically able, even though he'd lost a leg. He showed a lot of courage and determination to recover. He walked as much as he could to get in shape, disguised as a priest. I know from my own imprisonment, that the easiest route was to give up and lie in your bunk. Those in my camp who were determined to escape, kept walking and exercising as much as they could so that they would be physically capable when the opportunity came.'

The sun was getting strong. I could feel it on my legs and I was dry. Abandoning my earlier decision not to mix gin and talk, I drank it all and sucked the ice cube.

'I think Joseph Pilgrim was ready to head out as soon as his opportunity came, and that happened when the allies landed. On the night of 9 June, he left the rectory, wearing Father Bree's religious habit, and went over that low wall beside the church, slid down the slope, as Nicole Joyal told us he had done many times and he headed down the gully and spent the night somewhere in the south end of the valley. We know that because Joyal told us. She saw him leave. She knew he was intent on joining his comrades, and she watched him out the rectory window.'

'The next morning, at dawn, the Americans started to bomb German tanks in the forest just north and west of the valley. Joseph heard and saw the bombardment. He also saw the bombs hit the church and destroy the rectory. He knew Nicole Joyal was in that house. He remembered how kind she had been to him. She had saved his life. He forgot all about escaping to meet the advancing allies. He ran back up the road on the east side of the river. The old school teacher saw him. What was her name?'

'Brittany Paget. She was blind.'

'When we met her, yes, but in 1944, her eyesight was failing, but she told us someone with her pointed out the priest hurrying up the road, returning to his church. He was a unique and familiar figure in the village, with his black habit flying as he swung along on his crutches. Joseph Pilgrim went up Church Hill and tried to rescue the girl from the rubble of the rectory. Then the burning steeple toppled and probably the wall of the church, his clothes were set on fire so he ran out of the fire and smoke along the side of the church. It was Joseph Pilgrim those three witnesses saw come out of the smoke. He jumped over the low wall, losing one crutch at that spot. That's how the apparition disappeared, in the eyes of those three villagers. He slid down the hill and crawled to the one haven he knew that was safe from fire and bombs and the retreating Germans.'

'The girl's cave!' Danielle whispered from under her hat.

'Right. Her 'all alone' spot as she called it. She'd taken him there. They spent happy times there away from the horrors that surrounded them. It was natural that he would go there. Hoping that Nicole would be sheltering there too. Joseph Pilgrim crawled into that cave, across the stone and dirt floor, using one leg and one crutch, and lay on the remains of the palliasse and died.'

There was a long silence from under the hat. I watched the birds fighting for their turn in the bird bath that I had re-filled that morning. The masts of the sailboats were moving in and out of the marina as crews took advantage of the warm day for an early sail. The clouds were floating across the sky to give me a most happy picture so that a dark, damp cave in the brush-choked ravine in the valley of Ste Agathe seemed far away, in another world, another life, a dream best forgotten. Danielle slowly slid her hat on to her lap, swung her legs onto the patio, and sat, looking at me with demanding eyes.

'How do you know that?'

'Because I walked around on Church Hill. I figured out where the rectory had been, even though grass and bushes covered most of the foundation. I could trace the stone paths that led to the church. And I could follow the remains of the wall that stopped anyone from falling down the slope. I studied the spot where the villagers had built the cairn because that's where they'd seen the priest for the last time and found his crutch, creating the myth that he had ascended into heaven from that spot. There were still depressions in the earth on the other side of the wall where I figured Joseph and Nicole and probably others, slid down. Then I walked down to the bottom of the hill and back up the gully. The narrow roadway that the stonecutters built was surprisingly even until almost the top. Then the under-growth was thick and I had to push my way through vines and brambles. I wasn't dressed for that kind of exploration but I did find Joyal's cave. I lay on my stomach and wiggled part way in, far enough to see a rotting doll's chair with a mouldy stuffed doll in it and a skeleton in the far corner.'

Now Danielle's mouth was sagging open with amazement and she had difficulty speaking. She cleared her throat, sipped the ice water left in her glass and exclaimed: 'A skeleton? Bones you mean?'

I nodded.

She stared at me for a long time, then flipped her hand in dismissal. 'Could be anything, an animal, a soldier wounded in the battle, a deserter hiding . . . '

I kept nodding and now I was smiling. 'That's right. I knew that would be everyone's reaction, so I didn't say anything to anyone even though I was bursting with excitement. I knew nobody would believe me because they wouldn't want to believe me, and I couldn't prove it, so I knew I had to get solid evidence. I hurried back to our room at The Seigneury to get my camera with the flash. I knew that pictures would be hard to argue against. But when I got back, you were all excited about the story you had been told about the priest in Caen who you thought was Joseph Pilgrim for sure.'

'And I still do!'

'I realized that wasn't the time to tell you about my discovery in the cave so I kept quiet, even though I was bursting to tell everyone. I went along to Caen and saw that unfortunate man and hoped to get back in time to go back to the cave but we were too late. So the next morning, if you remember, I went out early, before you were up. I wanted to get back to that cave and take a roll of pictures that would prove my story beyond all doubt.'

'Why didn't you then?'

'Because when I was half way up the gully I could see I would never get into that cave. Nobody would ever get into that cave again. While we were in Caen, the workmen started moving earth for the improved shrine. The cairn with the metal crutch had already been carted away and trucks had dumped tons of rubble and earth into the gully, covering the entrance to the cave. Joseph Pilgrim is entombed in the cliff at Ste Agathe forever.'

'And you still maintain that was Joseph Pilgrim?'

'I know beyond all doubt that was the skeleton of Joseph Pilgrim.'

'How?'

'The bony fingers of the right hand were still gripping the handle of a German Army metal crutch!'

We do hope that you have enjoyed reading this large print book.

Did you know that all of our titles are available for purchase?

We publish a wide range of high quality large print books including:
Romances, Mysteries, Classics
General Fiction
Non Fiction and Westerns

Special interest titles available in large print are:
The Little Oxford Dictionary
Music Book
Song Book
Hymn Book
Service Book

Also available from us courtesy of Oxford University Press:
Young Readers' Dictionary
(large print edition)
Young Readers' Thesaurus
(large print edition)

For further information or a free brochure, please contact us at:
Ulverscroft Large Print Books Ltd.,
The Green, Bradgate Road, Anstey,
Leicester, LE7 7FU, England.
Tel: **(00 44) 0116 236 4325**
Fax: **(00 44) 0116 234 0205**

Other titles published by
The House of Ulverscroft:

THE BODY IN THE MARSH

Katherine Hall Page

Faith Fairchild's husband, the Reverend Thomas Fairchild, learns that nursery school teacher Lora Deane has received threatening phone calls. And she's not the only resident of Aleford, Massachusetts, who is being terrorized. Some local environmentalists, protesting about the proposed housing development that will destroy Beecher's Bog, have become targets of a vicious campaign of intimidation — reason enough for Faith to launch into some clandestine sleuthing. But when a body turns up in the charred ruins of a suspicious house fire, Faith is suddenly investigating a murder — and in serious danger of getting bogged down in a very lethal mess indeed!

A DEAD MAN IN TANGIER

Michael Pearce

Pig-sticking is a dangerous sport . . . for the pigs and the huntsman. While pursuing that recreation Monsieur Bossu gets stuck himself. A police matter? Perhaps, but in the Tangier of 1912 who are they answerable to? The new international committee to which Monsieur Bossu was Clerk? It is decided that Seymour of Scotland Yard will investigate. He can be safely disowned if things go wrong in a country caught between the ancient and the modern, where traditions are harsh. Soon Seymour realizes that getting to the truth of Monsieur Bossu's demise will bring him in danger of getting stuck too . . .

THE FINAL CURTAIN

Ken Holdsworth

With shoulder-length blond hair and cornflower-blue eyes, Ronnie Simmons is quite irresistible to his fellow actors — of both sexes — and in the jaundiced opinion of his boyhood friend, TV soap actor Nick Carter, he loses his heart with regularity. So it is surprising when Ronnie's sister, Susan, begs him to talk her brother out of his latest relationship. Being between jobs, Nick sets out for the rural backwater where Ronnie is appearing with an Arts Council sponsored touring company — but behind the idyllic pastoral facade lies a disturbing mystery, and Nick is soon involved in violence and murder . . .

CONFESSIONS OF A MAP DEALER

Paul Micou

'My first mistake was to be heterosexual.' Such is one of several complaints in the first of four conversations between Henry Hart, a married father of two young girls — and his childhood friend, Darius Saddler, who is gay. Crippled by debt, Hart — a dealer in antique maps — has managed to ruin his marriage, commit an undeniable act of theft, and become, in France, a suspect of a serious crime. With a lover on the side, a stolen map, a French detective on his trail, and a wife who is unusually cold, Hart enlists the help of his oldest friend.

FOOTFALL

Christine Poulson

Snow is falling. An old woman reads alone in bed . . . there is the sound of breaking glass and footsteps on the stairs . . . When Cambridge academic Cassandra James learns that her friend, Una, has been found dead, she is shocked, then suspicious. Was it a bungled burglary? Una had tried to ring Cass just before she died, and she'd changed her will, depriving the Cambridge Literary and Philosophical Institute of her library of Victorian literature. Why? And it seems that there is another Cassandra James running around Cambridge getting her in trouble! The line between appearance and reality is blurring . . .